BLACK TABLE

ANTTIMATTI PENNANEN

ISBN 978-952-94-3804-4 (paperback)
ISBN 978-952-94-3805-1 (PDF)
ISBN 978-952-94-3806-8 (EPUB)
ISBN 978-952-94-3807-5 (MOBI)

This is work of fiction and facts. References to size of our universe are based on current understanding within the science community. Names, places and events are mixed products of the author's imagination and real-life experiences. Any resemblance to actual persons, living or dead, is entirely coincidental. No aliens were harmed during the writing this novel.

Edit by Kim's Net Solutions
Front cover by 100Covers.com
Interior design by FormattedBooks.com

https://anttimattipennanen.editorx.io/author

MAP OF NEW THATHO

Author's note

The main characters in this story are from Finland. When Finns speak English, they use a mix of American and British English idioms, so gas not petrol, mobile phone not cell, jello not jelly. As the Finnish language does not have articles ('the', 'a', etc.), Finns do occasionally drop these when speaking English. To reflect this, in certain circumstances the characters do not use the definitive article. This is a style choice and not an error.

For Krisztina and for fans of Science Fiction
"With our thoughts, we are already there."

CONTENTS

CHAPTER 1

COMIC CON

"C'mon Jon, let's go!" shouted Gus, holding their heavy hotel room door open. He twisted the door handle back and forth, unable to hide his excitement. His stomach growled for the food they'd missed when arriving the day before.

This was the best hotel Gus had been able to find near Portland's event hall, and today was the second day of the three-day Rose City Comic Convention. They'd waited six months for this, not so much for the annual event itself, but because today's honoured guest speaker was someone both of them had idolised since they were kids: Dr Kevin Wells.

His novels had given birth to the best sci-fi movies and TV-series of all time and gained millions of adoring fans. He'd also authored several books on space and interstellar travel that had made him a respected member of the scientific community. His legions of devotees rarely got the chance to see him speak live, but today would be one of those occasions.

Those six months ago, Gus had stayed awake until midnight, lying on the bed in his Helsinki seaside apartment and holding a computer tablet above his head. He kept refreshing the browser every few seconds to be first in line to access ticket sales. Finally, as the clock hit twelve, a new link appeared on the screen, a purchase button. Hands shaking, Gus clicked for two tickets, full weekend, pay! As the payment went through and confirmation appeared on the screen, Gus realised he had held his breath throughout the entire process. It had felt like an hour, but it couldn't have lasted more than a minute or his body would have taken over and forced him to draw breath. Fingers shaking slightly, he messaged Jon: "I got the tickets! Portland Comic Con, here we come." Then he settled back on his pillow and smiled at the ceiling. It would be a long while before he could come down to anywhere near sleep.

And finally, the day had arrived. Jon and Gus headed for the à la carte breakfast buffet, talking about today's programme even as the more basic parts of them homed in on the smell of food. As they entered the breakfast hall, they were aware of several heads turning towards them for a better view.

At Comic Con events most fans dress up as their favourite characters. For Jon and Gus, as huge Star Trek fans, it was an easy choice of uniform: Next Generation original black designs with partly coloured tops, Jon's blue and Gus's yellow. Gus also had pointy extensions to his ears, completing the costume of a Vulcan officer. Gus liked Vulcans. Mainly because, like him, they based their life on logic, but also for their well-known greeting style.

Jon had an appearance of a modern Viking, with an athletic body, sky-blue eyes, blond short hair with a man bun on the top, and a shaved face with a few day's stubble, while

Gus had slightly longer, curly hair and a short beard, both yellowish with more than a hint of red. He claimed this came from his Irish ancestry, to which Jon always joked back that his features were pure Scandinavian heritage. They'd become best friends in school almost twenty years ago and, perhaps helped by none of the girlfriends they'd ever had becoming a permanent fixture in their lives, they were still as close as ever. More eyes began to follow them as they walked past the tables. They'd both been told they were handsome, but neither sought the attention.

Fortunately, the focus of the room now moved to Azog, a goblin character from *Lord of The Rings* who had just entered the hall. Azog had a perfect self-made mask, but his eyes looked terrified by the kind of attention he was receiving. Waving awkwardly at Jon and Gus, the goblin looked relieved to spot someone else wearing character costumes. Jon and Gus waved back in response, and the goblin relaxed visibly.

Gus gave a despairing shake of his head. "I feel bad for any alien coming to visit Earth. It will be a brutal welcome. How would we treat those from other worlds if we can barely stand each other?"

After collecting their coffees, both descended on the buffet bar and brought back plates covered in bacon, scrambled eggs, tomato and cheddar. They sat down at a free table near a family of four. The smallest family member, a girl, peeked sideways at them and Jon waved back with a smile.

"I can't wait to see Dr Wells in the flesh," Jon said. "If you could ask him one question, what would it be?" He watched, one eyebrow raised, as Gus cut his tomatoes into mush and mixed them with eggs and cheddar.

"Et voilà! Scrambled eggs, a la Gus," he declared proudly. "I have some thoughts, but I haven't decided yet. Maybe his speech will shed light on some things I've been wondering about."

Gus had two primary hobbies, space theories and science fiction collectables. Where young single males usually decorate their homes with basic furniture, Gus's resembled more a museum of science fiction. And why not? Jon shared the same passions, having read most science fiction novels available and amassing an extensive movie collection, but kept his home more what people would term normal.

"Today, Dr Wells will talk about universe and how we comprehend it. I am super excited about that," Jon said, sipping his coffee with milk.

By the time they were finishing their breakfast, the buffet hall had filled with various characters from different movies and comics. Harry Potter was waving his wand at a coffee machine and, as if by magic, coffee appeared into a cup in front of him. His friends from Hogwarts liked it. At the warm food buffet, someone dressed up as a Superman kept having to pull up his fake arm muscles to reach deeper into the food tray. Now normal people seemed weird and out of place.

"Shall we?" Gus announced, and got up. "I don't want to get stuck at the security check line."

"Engage." Jon replied with Captain Picard's hand gesture, pointing out with index and middle finger together. And they were off.

The event shuttle buses left every fifteen minutes from outside the hotel main doors. Jon and Gus were ahead of the day's herd and only one other passenger travelled with them, the same nervous goblin from the breakfast buffet, but now with a more confident appearance.

The event was taking place in Oregon Convention centre, which is the largest venue of its type in the Pacific Northwest, offering floor space for over a hundred stands, a stage for speeches, and designated areas for celebrity guest signings.

After a short ride, the hotel shuttle arrived at the exhibition entrance driveway and came to a stop near tall doors made of glass. Before going in, they asked their fierce-looking travel companion, Azog, to take a picture of them. Jon handed over his tablet, and the two of them stood shoulder to shoulder in front of a massive Portland Comic Con sign while Azog snapped away. Jon thanked the goblin, and they joined the small queue already forming at the bag checks and metal detectors.

Jon took a deep breath. "Scary world we live in. You need a metal detector to go to a freaking Comic Con. When we were kids, I thought cars would fly by now, and everyone would be super happy."

Soon the hall was bustling with convention goers in an incredible array of costumes. By one stand the Hulk seemed to be chatting up Black Widow but was interrupted as a gaggle of Ewoks pushed past. There were a few people in casual clothes – jeans and tees – but they stood out like Batman at a Marvel convention. Everyone was picking up things from the stands: merchandise, books, magazines, or figures and miniature models. It was now mandatory for event organisers to reduce plastic waste by providing fabric event bags for purchases.

Two hours and a dozen Vulcan greetings later, Jon and Gus had found new Star Trek novels and limited-edition Marvel comics. At the small food court, Jon selected two drinks from the smoothie bar, one bright green and one dark red.

"Which one? This one is called Super Monkey" – Jon held the green one in front of Gus before switching hands and offering the red one – "and this one is called Angry Flamingo."

"I guess the Monkey?" Gus hesitated, his head tilted back and eyes wide open with suspicion that wasn't entirely for comic effect. As Jon handed him the green smoothie, hall speakers crackled and there was the familiar whine of feedback, causing people to scowl as if they'd just bitten into the sourest lemon ever.

"Let's go, I want us to be as close to Dr Wells as possible."

When they got closer to the speaker area faithful fans had already filled the first two rows nearest the stage and were lifting handheld mobile devices, ready for taking photos of their idol.

"I don't get it, why are people still busy queuing for smoothies when one of the great minds of our era is about to speak?" Gus wondered, checking the time on his mobile.

"I have no idea," Jon replied, looking almost nervous. "It's been a long six months of waiting."

As Jon and Gus positioned themselves as close to podium as possible, the number of people behind them grew rapidly, filling every empty space.

"Just in time, I suppose?" Jon smiled and fist bumped with Gus.

There was another shriek of feedback. "Sorry about that! One-Two, One-Two ..." Sound filled the hall. Someone tapped the microphone, completing the soundcheck.

"Ladies and gentlemen, may I have your attention?" declared a short man wearing blue jeans and a black suit jacket with a white T-shirt under it. "I hope you are all enjoying yourselves?"

"Great, great, good, good," he said happily when some people cheered and lifted their reusable event bags.

Short man raised his voice, "I know you have all been waiting for this, so without further delay, let me introduce you to our special guest, Dr Kevin Wells." His left arm shot out to welcome the main speaker onto the stage.

Applause erupted from the crowd as a tall man who looked to be in his seventies strolled towards the centre of the podium. He had a shock of pure white hair like Albert Einstein, but his face resembled more that of Abraham Lincoln, elongated with a strong, thin jaw and a long nose. He wore sandals, beige cargo shorts, and an old T-shirt with a Van Halen logo on it. Over his T-shirt he wore a slightly too small blue suit jacket, which drew a few grins and whispered comments from the crowd. Dr Wells stepped up to the podium and looked around the audience with a gentle smile on his face.

"Hi everyone! I am so happy to see you all in such a wonderful mood." He nodded, and it seemed as though he wanted to meet every pair of eyes in the audience. Then he inspected himself. "Did you expect me in a lab coat, or perhaps a suit and tie?" He smiled again softly. "I have never been comfortable in expected forms. And, honestly, my luggage got lost during the flight and I expected to have shelter behind this podium. The jacket I borrowed here from one of the security guards."

This was met with smiles and random cheers from the audience.

"So, I am here to talk about time and life in the cosmos, and how these two ideas intrigue and control us. Especially this crowd. I bet every one of you would like to know whether there is more life out there somewhere. And if so, are they like us, are they friendly, are they able to travel through space, and do they know about us?"

As people nodded in agreement, the wall-sized screen behind him lit up showing a picture of the cosmos timeline squeezed into one calendar year, starting with January 1st, when the cosmos was allegedly born, and reaching to 9:25pm on December 31st, the time when humans appeared on Earth.

"They call this a Cosmic Calendar. Not my work, to be clear. When looking at this calendar one cannot but realise that, even with the high probability of other intelligent life existing out there, those beings finding us have the same chance as locating a certain grain from all the sand in the Sahara. Also, this specific sand grain would be visible for only two seconds ..."

A contemplative silence ran through the audience.

"The probability someone finds it is astronomically small."

Some nodded their heads, and some smiled in confusion, as if the speech had been in Greek.

"So you see, you would not only need to be in the correct place but also there at the correct time. And as if that weren't hard enough, do not forget that we are not in the same place all the time. As we speak, we are hurtling through space at a speed of 31 km per second. Not only do we go around our sun once each year, we also spiral through space with the rest of the Milky Way galaxy. That little trip takes from 225 to 250 million years, and it keeps our position in constant movement."

The presentation continued for an hour of mind-blowing details that made clear just how small we on the Earth are.

"And for the first fourteen billion years we were not even around," explained Dr Wells. "Who knows how many times civilisations like ours have been born, grown old and then died, erased one after another into a vast timeline. Our last 100 years of technical advancement feels like less than the blink of an eye compared to the time before us." He paused and let his gaze sweep through the audience. "There is also something I would like to ask all of you. If we could travel through space to other galaxies, how would you do it?"

He pointed to someone near the stage. "Yes, you. A pilot from *Battlestar Galactica*."

Laughs all around.

"I would use hibernation to cross the space," Pilot said.

"Not bad, sleep through the long trip," Dr Wells responded. "This is one way to do it, if we do not come up with a faster way to travel." He nodded to the audience and then continued. "But have you ever thought about waiting, instead of setting off on your journey the minute it becomes possible? Until a point when technological advances mean higher speeds become available? Let's say you start your trip with the fastest speed available today, sleeping all the way to the finish line. No problem, you get there when you get there. But if you waited just another 200 years, we might come up with technology that takes us there much, much faster, easily arriving ahead of the sleepers who started out 200 years ago."

Again he waited as people looked at each other, their faces showing their changing thoughts. "Or is that exactly what makes us, us? We just cannot wait if we have the means. Even imperfect ones. The same way brave people who once crossed the oceans using the simplest of methods. We must know what's out there. Is it in our nature?" Dr Wells let his words sink in with his audience, and the whole hall was now silent.

"Let that brew in our minds for now. Meanwhile, what do you think about gravity and how to overcome it?" He gazed fondly at his audience his eyes filled with curiosity.

He led the discussion for another hour, from gravity to black holes and on to warp drive.

"If anyone could come up with a means of faster space travel it would be you, with your imagination and your drive for exploration. I hope you all had a great time, and I hope my musings have given you something to think about. I wish you all the best. Live long and prosper." He finished the sentence with the Vulcan hand gesture for farewell, and the audience exploded into full applause.

As he walked offstage, he searched the audience once more with his eyes, then muttered something to himself.

"Did you see that?" Gus poked Jon with his elbow. "Something is off."

Short man appeared back on the stage and shook hands with Dr Wells as he exited.

"Dr Wells everyone," he declared, and the crowd applauded again. "And don't forget you can meet Dr Wells in person by the exit where we have a stand set up for his latest book signing."

"I will buy his latest book and have it signed by the man himself. How about you?" Gus asked.

"For sure." Jon replied in agreement by lifting his now empty smoothie mug.

At the exit, a stand for book signing had erected near the two massive glass doors. Behind the stand were tall posters with illustrations of space. In front of it, behind a table, sat Dr Wells. To either side of him stood piles of his books, and behind him a young assistant kept loading more to replace the ones Dr Wells handed over after signing them.

Even though Jon and Gus had skipped several interesting stands on their way to exit, several people had managed to get there ahead of them.

"What? How?" Gus cried out after seeing the line in front of them.

"Don't worry," Jon calmed his friend. "We have plenty of time."

Twenty long minutes later they were next in line. The girl in front of them exchanged a few words with the doctor and giggled when she received her copy of the book.

"Thank you, Doctor. I'm a big fan of yours," she spoke adoringly and leant in closer, thanking him again and again. Her movements were clumsy and erratic causing the line to react, moving back and forward like an old steam train taking off from the station. As it did Jon and Gus found themselves bumping into Dr Wells's table, and his gaze swung round to the source of the disturbance.

"I do apologise, Dr Wells. We really loved your presentation. Fantastic work! I'm Gus and this is my friend Jon," Gus said nervously in English, and out of habit started to lift his hand into the Vulcan greeting even though Jon was pulling on his sleeve to stop him.

Dr Wells let the book he'd been about to sign drop. He looked like he had seen the magic trick of a lifetime, amazement mixed with confusion and curiosity. Then he smiled, gently, just as he had at the podium, and his eyes became glassy with tears.

Jon hadn't noticed it earlier, but Dr Wells had a long, thin scar reaching from between his hairline and left eye, down to his chin, like an old battle wound. He opened his mouth to say something, but then his smile dropped and now his eyes were taut with fear. He grasped his left shoulder with his right hand and grunted in pain.

"Not now," he rasped in agony.

"Oh, shit, I think he's having a heart attack," Jon said to the assistant who gaped at him for a second then started dialling 911.

Dr Wells fell off his chair. On the way down, he pulled a pile of books with him. Jon pulled the table out of the way and told people to stay back and leave some space. On the floor Dr Wells was lying on his side, doubled over with pain. Even so, he reached for one of the fallen books and started writing in it.

"Holy crap. Is he *really* signing that book ...?" Gus stared wide eyed at Jon, who gave the same reaction in response. Jon knelt next to Dr Wells, his hands cradling the man's head to stop it from hitting the floor. The pen fell from the doctor's hand and suddenly the book was being pushed into Jon's hands.

"Here Jon, find the ..." Then he seemed to be hit by a wave of pain so strong that he could not get the final words out. He closed his eyes and stopped breathing.

"Move!" Two paramedics burst in from the tall glass doors, one of them shouting orders. They always had a unit close by when bigger events were happening. Telling everyone to make space, Jon and Gus joined the others in a large half circle of people around the exit doors. The hall had become silent, apart from paramedics who performed their routine on Dr Wells.

"He is in a cardiac arrest," declared one kneeling next to unconscious Dr Wells, holding a stethoscope on his chest while the second paramedic began pulling out electric pads from a portable defibrillator. The one with the stethoscope raised his body up and used his whole upper body weight to press Dr Wells's chest with both hands. After thirty rapid presses on his chest, he used a manual pump placed on Dr Wells's face to squeeze air into his mouth. The second paramedic cut open Dr Wells's T-shirt with medical scissors and placed two pads from a portable defibrillator on his body.

"Clear!" the paramedic operating the defibrillator shouted.

Both lifted their hands into air. Dr Wells's back arched upwards and dropped back against the floor. Reading the defibrillator screen, he called out once more, "Again! Clear!"

Both lifted their hands, Dr Wells's body arched again, nothing. Jon and Gus looked at each other in disbelief. The entire scene seemed unreal. The person they had been idolising their entire life was slipping away right in front of them, and there was nothing they could do. Jon could feel how the urge to help slowly changed to helplessness. Gus instead kept thinking it was all part of some nightmare he could wake up from any time now. He did not. The paramedic operating the defibrillator opened his small red medical bag with a white cross embedded on the top and pulled out a long injection needle and a tiny bottle.

"Adrenaline?" he asked his colleague, who confirmed it with a firm nod. He placed the needle firmly against the disinfected area of Dr Wells's skin until the needle sunk in and watched the liquid disappear into Dr Wells's arm. When done, he quickly pulled out the needle and wiped the arm again with a disinfecting pad.

"Again!" he shouted.

"Clear!" the other paramedic shouted, and all hands were off the body. Dr Wells's back arched again. They performed the shock three more times. Jon and Gus stood motionless, watching their hero lying inert on the cold event hall floor. They waited for a miracle to come, but it never came.

"He's gone," said the one with the needle still in his hand.

The show was over. When the paramedics opened a white sheet to cover their lost patient, people continued whispering to each other and lowered their upheld mobile phones.

"I think we can call it a day," Jon said in shock.

Gus agreed and both walked out through the exit next to them, catching the shuttle already waiting for returning passengers. During their short ride to the hotel, they agreed to fly back home. After all, their hero was dead. There was no reason for them to return and live through the horrific memories next day.

Once back at the hotel they passed reception and took an elevator to third floor. Their room was the second on the left. Gus slid a white credit card sized key into the key slot and pulled it out. A red light appeared on top of the lock. Gus took a deep breath and repeated the key routine, only slower this time. This time a green light went on, and the lock made a mechanical sliding sound. Gus pressed down the handle and opened the door.

"If we leave in half an hour, we could still catch a taxi and get an earlier flight back to Europe," Gus said and threw his cabin-sized luggage from the floor onto his bed. "Did he really sign the book?" he said in disbelief. "Or did he write, *Nice meeting you, gotta go and get a heart attack*?" he finished with sarcasm in his voice from the anger and sadness he felt throughout his body.

Jon poured the contents of his fabric event bag out onto his bed and pushed aside brochures and collectables to reveal his signed treasure in a form of a black book with planets and galaxies printed on the front cover, and Dr Wells's picture with a short book description in the back.

"Smart, it looks like space, being black and all. Look." Jon turned the book in his hand towards Gus.

"And the signature?" Gus asked.

The book was a hardback and Jon opened it, on the first page was a handwritten line.

"Just gibberish," Jon said, confused and feeling sorry for Dr Wells. "I guess he had no idea what he was doing?" He closed the book and handed it to Gus, who opened it to the same first page and examined the text.

"Well, it's not his signature, that's for sure," Gus said frowning and read out loud what Dr Wells had written down, "*minus lampshade dreamer.*" He gave Jon a puzzled look and then returned his gaze to words to the book. "*Minus lampshade dreamer. Minus lampshade dreamer,*" he repeated the words at a different pace, as if they would then make more sense. "I suppose he was delirious and thought he is still writing his name?"

"There's one thing though ..." Jon held out his hand towards Gus, who handed the book back to him. "When he pushed the book into my hands, he said; 'Jon, find the ...'"

"Find what? And how did he know your name?" Gus wondered with a dramatic pause. "Although I did introduce us when we met him. But even so, lucky guess." They stared at each other, unable to accept the words being just gibberish.

Gus sat on his bed dug into his satchel and pulled out a tablet which he activated with his thumbprint. As the display switched on, he opened a browser.

"Maybe it's a password of some kind? He typed *Dr Wells* in his search engine with the word *minus* and hit the search button.

Several links to mathematical signs appeared on his screen.

"Well that's not it," said Gus disappointed, and then removed *Dr Wells* and added words *lampshade* and *dreamer* in the search bar, just like Dr Wells had written them during his last seconds.

After pressing the search button, his browser window filled with links to studies what dreaming of lampshades could mean. Gus could feel frustration grow inside him, raising tension in his body and making him sweat. He searched again, this time with words *Dr Wells* and *dreams*, only to get another list of meaningless links. He tossed his tablet back on the bed close to his pillow and stood up.

"I'm taking a shower," he said, kicking off his shoes and pulling off his shirt on his way to bathroom.

Jon picked up his own tablet and opened a browser. He used the words Dr Wells wrote down and crosschecked them with various keywords like: *studies, space, Portland, home, missing, planet, person,* but all searches came up empty, or with links that made no sense whatsoever. Even so, Jon clicked the links and checked if they would lead somewhere. They did not. He leaned back and lay his back against the bed with his legs bent over the edge and his feet touching the floor. He pulled the pillow closer and placed it under his head. He took a deep breath and glanced at his tablet display once more before switching it off and placing it on his stomach.

Gus came out from the shower, a towel wrapped around his waist. He had another, smaller towel, which he used to run over his reddish hair.

"Any luck?" he asked, seeing Jon staring at the ceiling with his tablet in his belly.

"Find the ..." Jon kept repeating quietly, his eyes searching the air in front of him. He sat up, catching his tablet with his left hand and holding up his right-hand index finger in front of his face. Gus knew from their past this meant Jon was having an idea, or at least thinking he had an idea.

"Just say it," Gus blurted out as Jon waved his index finger about.

"Show it to me again." Jon stretched his right arm. "Yes, of course," he said once the book was open on his lap. "Search this with your tablet ..." He waited for Gus to find it. "Type; *minus.lampshade.dreamer.*"

"Been there, done that." Gus raised his eyebrows as he felt slightly annoyed by Jon's request.

"I know, but this time write them all together, separated with dots."

A massive lightbulb lit up in Gus's processing mind.

"How come I didn't see that?" he cried out, blaming himself for not realising it first.

He typed the words with dots on his search engine. Nothing. Another lamp lit up in Gus's head. "It won't work on search engine," he said. Now Jon looked confused. "I remember! It's a tool or an application called *what3words.*"

"Exactly! That's the one!" Jon remembered he had read an article about it on the plane prior to their arrival. The article was about a global mapping tool which would pinpoint an exact location with just three words. He found the article interesting as it turned out that rescue personnel and law enforcement are already using it to find lost people.

Gus opened a home page made for the application and typed the three mysterious words into the search window.

Before hitting 'search' he looked at Jon, who nodded approval for proceeding. Gus pressed the search button. A map grid appeared and indicated instantly the location with a black dot surrounded by a white circle. Gus felt his pulse rate going up and his breathing accelerating when he zoomed out from the spot, revealing the location from a higher point of view. Several location names appeared on the screen: Cameron Lake, Cathedral Grove, and MacMillan Provincial Park. Gus kept zooming out.

"MacMillan Provincial Park, on Vancouver Island, in Canada!" Gus shouted excitedly, then paused, not realising why he was so excited. "MacMillan Provincial Park on Vancouver Island, in Canada?" his voice inflecting upwards.

"Canada? Why there? What does he want us to find?" Jon wondered, standing now next to Gus and leaning in to see the map. "Maybe coordinates to his pacemaker?" he said sarcastically. "Too early?" He stopped smiling, realising Gus might still be in shock from today's tragedy. "Sorry," Jon apologised and placed his arm over his friend's still wet shoulders. "Whatever it is, I think it's our duty to find it out." He looked straight at Gus's eyes with determination. "These were his last words after all, kinda. Or technically also my name was in his last word, but you know what I mean?"

"I do," Gus finally responded. "And seems like it's about nine hours' drive with the ferry crossing." He paused. "What if we do not check out today, but stay tonight here as planned, and leave early tomorrow morning, driving towards Vancouver, Canada?"

"I'm all in. I will go to reception and ask if we can get a car rental directly from hotel." Joh picked the hotel key from Gus's night table, gave a fist bump to Gus and hurried out.

CHAPTER 2

ROAD TRIP

Early next morning, Jon and Gus were the very first ones at breakfast. They walked in as soon as the door to buffet area opened. They collected their white porcelain plates and filled them with various breakfast foods. After taking their plates to the same table they sat at the day before, they picked up several juices and coffee.

As they dug into their breakfast, Gus pulled out a tablet from his black fabric satchel. It was one of those tablets, where the cover had a full keyboard while the display still worked as a touchscreen. While eating and sipping drinks, he typed words into his keyboard and then moved the tablet screen with his fingers.

"Here." Gus turned it towards Jon. "I have my own application for navigation. This is one of our company's products. Not only is it free for users, but it also knows the traffic jams, speed traps, and the best of all, scenic routes. But what makes it different from other navigators, this one has an augmented reality."

"Augmented what?" Jon asked before taking a bite of his perfect breakfast creation.

"When you hold your tablet or phone in front of you, like this," Gus held his tablet display towards Jon, "the app will show the way on the screen as you see it in front of you, through your camera," Gus explained, full of excitement.

Jon took the tablet from Gus and moved it in front of himself. The display had the vast breakfast room in view, with a three-dimensional arrow pointing the way where to go.

"Now," Gus said, "if we take this route that the app recommends, we can make the drive almost an hour faster."

Jon stared at the screen and gave his approval by nodding as he had mouthful of croissant filled with fresh tomatoes and overcooked ham.

"This is so good," he mumbled, croissant pieces dropping down to his plate.

Gus was always the tech guy. Wherever he went, he always took with him not only his phone, but at least two tablets and two backup power banks, one equipped with small solar panels. One of the zippered compartments in his satchel was filled with cables. Whatever cable ending was needed, he had them all.

While Gus was the tech guy, Jon was the survival one. He also had a fabric satchel, but in military dark green, including an outside pocket with a military issued metallic water bottle peeking out from it. He did not leave the house without his satchel, always equipped with water, first aid kit, some protein bars, compact flashlight, his tablet, fire starter flint, and a red Swiss Army knife, just like the one MacGyver had. He had begged his parents for it on their road trip across Europe when he was ten years old. They were visiting a small village called Zermatt in the south of Switzerland. This was also the first time he had tried cheese fondue and Swiss chocolate. Only twenty years later he learned that the 4500-metre-high mountain to the side of Zermatt, called the Matterhorn, is the mountain on his favourite chocolate bar, Toblerone. When life gives you; *aha* moments, this had become his favourite by far.

When they finished with their breakfast, they headed for reception. Behind the counter, a hotel employee, named Philip according to his name tag, handled their check out.

"And how was your stay?" he asked while typing on the computer. "Anything from the minibar?" Still typing. "And would it be cash or credit?" he said, all in a rehearsed dialogue.

"Credit, and no, nothing from minibar," Gus said, still without getting any eye contact from Philip.

"That would be $275 with city tax," Philip declared.

"Great. Where do I ...?" Gus wondered and flipped his credit card.

"Here." Philip stretched out a credit card reader with cables attached to his terminal. Gus finished the payment and received the receipt. "Here you go sir, have a beautiful day. Next!" Philip called in a firm and loud voice.

Gus turned around.

"There's no-one else here," he said and put away his receipt, still not getting eye contact from Philip. "Freaking robot," Gus said quietly.

"What's that, sir?" Philip asked, looking finally at Gus.

"I said, I forgot my yogurt ..." Gus made up a lie and turned around with a flat grin.

Both Gus and Jon now had their satchels and cabin-sized hard black flight bags with them. One after the other, they went out through a rotating exit door and turned left towards the rental car parking area as indicated by a small sign attached to the exterior wall.

"Nice!" Gus shouted happily when he saw a massive new white SUV that seemed to be the only car in front of them. "You *really* did it this time," he said and gave a fist bump for Jon.

"I'm glad you like it," Jon said, and fist bumped with Gus, "because our car is the one behind it." Jon stretched his arm with the car keys and remotely opened the doors to a little red hatchback Toyota. The car honked twice when the doors unlocked. The Toyota had hidden easily in the shadow of the massive white SUV next to it.

"Like I said," Gus added and laughed, "you really did it this time."

Even though Gus would have easily afforded the massive new SUV, he had no problem enjoying the simple and small things in life, which this time was a trip with his friend in a tiny vehicle.

They put their cabin bags into the Toyota's tiny back trunk and their satchels on the backseat.

"I can take the first drive," Jon said, and they hopped in.

Jon started the car with a traditional ignition system by turning the key. He reversed and then pulled them out from the hotel parking area.

"Road trip!" both shouted in unison and fist bumped again.

◆————— ◆ ◆ ◆ ————— ◆

The weather turned out to be perfect for a road trip, not too hot, random clouds, and the sun shone most of the time on their right side and later behind them. After an hour or so, they switched drivers on a stop with a scenic view. The trip went fast listening to music on the radio. The driver always picked the channel, and Gus had found one that played rock ballads. With the more popular songs, they both knew the lyrics and tried to sing along. Between songs, they were trying to guess what Dr Wells's mysterious location could be.

"Best beaver and raccoon spotting in Vancouver Island?" Jon guessed, googling from his phone what Vancouver is known for. "A personal bear encounter?"

"There are bears?" Gus said horrified, imagining what they would do if they ran into a bear. "What do you do, if you encounter a bear?" he finally asked. "They're dangerous, aren't they?"

"If we run into a bear," Jon said, knowing Gus was not too familiar with animals and nature in general, "you have to stand absolutely still, while I go and run for help." Jon let it sink in before his friend realised Jon was messing with him.

"Very funny," said Gus. "You stay, and I run for help."

They both laughed.

"What else is in Vancouver? What does he want us to find?" asked Gus.

Jon looked at his phone again.

"There are massive trees, and a strong indigenous heritage called First Nation." Jon paused. "I know, he wants us to find a house built on old burial site which is haunted with angry souls and is a portal to beyond this realm." Gus moved his hands and made a spooky howl while referring to the movie *Poltergeist.*

"Noooo, I think it's a secret laboratory," Gus said in return. "Or his man cave with all kinds of alien conspiracy theories on the wall."

Both laughed.

"Oh, you remember this song?" Gus shouted excitedly when Aerosmith's 'Don't Want to Miss a Thing' came on the radio.

"Sure, from the movie *Armageddon*," Jon said and turned up the volume.

"Oh yes, that's right, *Armageddon*." Gus clearly remembered something else, which was right away caught by Jon.

"Aaa, Jenni?" he asked and poked Gus with his elbow.

"What? Don't be absurd." Gus waved his hand like he didn't care.

"Absurd? You don't use words like absurd," Jon pressed the subject and got more exited. "I remember now. It was one of the songs at the sport camp a long time ago."

"I remember." Gus looked smiling at his friend. "It was a very special time. Anyway, I don't know where I would be today if we hadn't had met back then."

Gus was in the fourth grade and outside on recess with all other students. He had been an outcast since he had moved from Ireland to live with his uncle and aunt in Finland. When he was five years old, a police officer and a social worker had picked him up from day care. He was told his parents had been in a car accident. A drunk driver had ploughed into them at full speed, running a STOP sign. Both of his parent had died instantly. Gus's only option was to move to Finland and live with his father's brother, who had married a Finnish woman. In time, he had learned Finnish, but was unable to disguise his Irish accent. For him, every recess included a routine of trying to fit in, while being invisible. Even among his classmates, he was constantly watching for bullies. Boys are boys, they say. You only need to wait till you get older and it gets easier, they said. They, being the teachers and parents of bullies. Nevertheless, for kids in school, what was fun for some, was hell for someone else, someone else like Gus.

During class, everything seemed fine. Bullying was not visual, only whispers and flying pieces of paper, but it affected Gus so much he didn't want to raise his hand or answer any teacher's questions. That would attract the bullies' attention, and there were many questions he knew the answers for. It was a silent but violent oppression.

Once the recess bell rang, he became completely aware of his bullies. He always tried to find an exit through dark corners where his tormentors didn't pay attention. He used the same routine when going back to class, trying to blend into crowds, sneak ahead, pretend as if being in teacher's shadow would give some kind of invisible shielding. The shielding was faint and narrow, and worked only when the teacher looked directly at you. Bullies knew this very well.

It wasn't the constant pushing in aisles and stairs, nor the random nicknames being shouted, it was the group consciousness that got to him. The common echo when other kids joined the chanting and humiliation. That made Gus feel like he didn't have any friends. It was him against the whole world. And what did he do to deserve it? He was guilty of having reddish hair, which was not common in Finland. He was also guilty of being a new student, transferred from another country, Ireland. He spoke with a different accent, and that seemed to be enough for the bullies. The most active ones had come up with different nicknames to call him. They called him *a carrot, Irish loser*, and what he hated the most; *red riding orphan*. Also, the way he spoke gave the bullies more fuel to come at him. Once they had heard Gus compliment someone during the class by saying 'nice'. But he had said with Irish accent; *noice*. Since then, people passing him in the hallways just chanted; *noice, noice, noice ...* over and over again. Gus could have fought back, but he didn't have a violent bone in his body, and because he didn't want to become like them, he got stuck with his situation.

Without friends, he spent his time with puzzle solving games and learning programming algorithms with a Commodore-64 and early PCs. The programs he made weren't anything fancy, but it gave him early access and insight on how software worked. As anyone who has done programming knows, you either have it or you don't, similar to a musical talent. Having a piano standing in the house does not mean you are able to play it. Either you need lessons, or you have so great a passion for it, you'll learn it all on your own. Gus had the latter for computers and programming. He and algorithms spoke the same language.

But right now, he stood in the hallway, surrounded by five thugs holding his maths book.

"You want it orphan? Ha? Do you?" said one of the thugs with a brown messy undercut hairstyle, holding Gus's maths book above his head.

Others around him kept chanting, *noice, noice, noice*. Gus didn't go for it, knowing from experience the book would be tossed to the next guy and then the next, keeping him just an inch away from its reach.

"C'mon, you may as well give it back," Gus said, "it's not like you understand any of it."

This made other thugs go, "Uuuuuuu ..." while holding their fists in front of their mouths.

The one with the book became red with anger.

"I'm gonna—" he said but was interrupted by another voice coming from behind him.

"You're gonna *what*? Tommi?"

The sound made Tommi turn around to see who interrupted his malicious routine, and once he did, he tossed the book on the floor in front of Gus. The red anger had vanished from his face and been replaced with ghostly white.

"Do that again, and I'll break your nose and fingers, and while we are at it, I'll break your legs just as a bonus ..." the voice continued.

Gus was pushed on to the ground along and, with revengeful looks, Tommi and his compliant minions fled. Jon rushed to Gus's aid, helping him up. Gus couldn't help but notice that Jon stood a full head taller than himself.

"My name is Johannes Peterson. But everyone calls me Jon." A kid with a short blond hair and a broad smile said, offering his hand. "Nice to meet you."

"You too." Gus shook Jon's hand. "My name is Brian. Brian O'Brien."

"Ouch! Perhaps your parents didn't like you very much either?" Jon asked, leaning backwards, trying to avoid catching the name like a flu.

"I know," Gus answered. "That's why I like to be called Gus, from my middle name, Fergus."

"Fergus, nice. Gus it is then."

Both laughed while exchanging their very first fist bump.

They were both in the same year level but different classes. Gus recognised Jon as one of the popular kids in school. He was athletic, and Gus never saw him tormenting other kids. Jon was known to be in few fights, which he never started, but always ended. A year back, some fifth-graders tried to push him around when he was just in the third grade. To the bullies' surprise, Jon jumped on them and gave a bloody nose to the two main bullies. The others ran away after realising they had taken too big a bite to swallow. Since then he'd been left alone, and by now, the legend says he fought against ten kids and won. Jon never corrected this error.

After the sudden rescue, Gus and Jon stayed friends. Jon got Gus to try some sports, and Gus got Jon interested in computer games and computers in general. In common sport lessons, Jon made sure Gus was picked first into soccer and basketball teams, not last, as Jon was always the one choosing the teams. And once they were in the same class together from grade five, Gus covered Jon in maths by blurting out the answer if Jon hesitated on his turn on the blackboard. The teachers never made the connection. The chanting and bulling continued all the way to high school. But with Jon, Gus pushed it through.

At the beginning of the summer when they were fifteen years old, Jon planned on going to a sport camp, but not without his best friend. One evening in Gus's room, as they lay prone upon the carpeted floor supporting their heads with their arms watching *Total Recall*, Jon popped his question.

"Are you crazy?" was Gus's reaction. "You know I suck at sports."

"But they are not like real sports." Jon defended his plan. "More like games and stuff, and I know Jenni is going ..." Jon poked Gus in the ribs a few times. "I saw the signup list at coach Aalto's office."

"Really? Jenni is going?" Gus looked surprised. "I mean ... why would I care?"

"Oh c'mon ..." Jon pushed the topic. "I know you have had a crush on her since you came to this school."

"I doubt she's even aware I exist," Gus said, looking disappointed.

"Then this camp will help to change that injustice," Jon encouraged. "So, shall I sign you up?"

"Fine" – Gus gave Jon a serious look – "but she better be there."

"She will be. And now shut up, Arnold is about to tell himself to go to Mars ..."

"Get your ass to Mars!" they both shouted at the scene on the small TV screen on the floor in front of them.

Camp started in two weeks, and Jenni was also there. But no matter how much Gus wanted to talk to Jenni, he couldn't bring himself to do it. With the games requiring light physical, as well as strategic and thinking tasks, Jon and Gus were an unbeatable team. They won every competition, every day. Jenni also noticed this and finally came over to Jon and Gus with her friends. There was a lot of blushing by Jon and Gus, and a lot of giggling by the girls. In the closing days of the camp, they all spent more time together, but Gus could not get over his fear to get to know her better. Gus felt like the last days just slipped through his fingers.

On the final evening, the camp had a party with dancing and games. For the very last song, Gus collected all his courage and asked Jenni for a slow dance. It was the very same song by Aerosmith. They had their moment, but with fear of being rejected, Gus never asked her out. Maybe because he didn't know what they would do on a date.

For much of their free time when growing up, Jon and Gus went to the movies and spent their summer holidays at Jon's parent's cabin at the lake reading comics together. Only after they both turned eighteen, and when girls became interested in Jon, his time became more divided. And that was okay, they stayed friends living only a few blocks from each other in Helsinki.

Gus graduated from Helsinki University of Technology top of his class and was now running one of the most innovative start-up companies in Scandinavia. He had his own office space rented near the university and currently had over fifty employees. He was referred to as the brains of the company, but without ambition for leadership, he hired someone else to do it for him. The company specialised in software development, hired by companies to rewrite their core software to become more efficient and user-friendly.

For Jon, school was never his thing. His grades were not bad, and good enough to get him into the university he was interested in, majoring in biology, with extra language courses on the side. After a few years, Jon decided to drop out and escape from all the pressure of what to do in the future. To his own and Gus's surprise, Jon enlisted in the army and was instantly recognised to be fit for more demanding training. Right after enlisting, he was approached by Army Special Forces for commando training. Altogether, Jon spent three years in the army. Gus didn't hear from Jon until he had returned to civilian life.

After his return, Gus noticed how it seemed like Jon had lost his smile. They didn't talk about it much, but now and then Jon hinted about war-game stories like how he once lived in the forest for six months and engaging in secret operations like you only see in movies. One time, according to Jon, he and his team were travelling by foot at night through hostile territory when enemy learnt of a possible incursion and started searching for them. All Jon could tell Gus was that the enemy used heat sensor technology to chase them down. The enemy surrounded Jon and his team, who had dug themselves under the snow to avoid detection. Massive enemy armoured vehicles rolled up just two metres from their heads, before coming to a full stop. Jon and his team could hear the vehicle crews talking, but after a few minutes they drove away, believing Jon's team was somewhere else. Still, to this day Gus got chills every time he thought about it.

Without any diploma, Jon settled on working as a barista in a coffee shop he opened between the local university and Gus's office, earning enough money to go to the gym and hang out with Gus almost every day. He enjoyed being around people, and most of all, he loved coffee.

Then, out of the blue, Gus and Jenni met again after all those years at Jon's cafe, which Gus still thinks was orchestrated by Jon. He vaguely remembers Jon smirking behind the espresso machine. Something was off, but the meeting with Jenni was worth it. They were together for a year. Jenni even moved in with Gus, but eventually they realised they wanted different things from life – a clash of Gus's boyish sci-fi decorations, and Jenni's dreams of having kids. They parted as friends. Jenni now had two kids and Gus worked with his company, and his collectable toys.

On the road after crossing the border into Canada, hunger took over and they decided to take a little detour to get some food. Based on reviews, the best local Mexican restaurant was located just on the edge of downtown Vancouver, before their ferry ride to Vancouver Island.

"Burrito a day, keeps the doctor away," Gus said.

Another Gus's weird sayings, Jon thought.

"I'm so hungry I will go full zombie and start chewing your arm off if I don't get some food, and fast," Gus cried.

"Ten more minutes and we are there. Keep your zombie fixations to yourself till then ..." Jon pulled away his hand and laughed. "We can just pick up food and eat it during the ferry crossing."

After a refreshing ocean windy ferry ride from mainland to Vancouver Island, they were back in their car with their bellies so full they didn't need words to keep going. As they drove the surrounding trees were massive.

"Just follow the map," Gus said, and waved to his tablet displaying the remaining trip ahead of them, showing an arrival time in twenty minutes.

"Have you seen anything like that?" Jon asked, looking at the trees.

"Only in pictures," Gus said. "Our destination is not near any road, so we need to do a little hike."

The closer they got, the bigger the trees grew. They travelled in the midst of giant western red cedar and Douglas fir trees. Gus googled the trees while Jon was driving.

"Douglas-fir trees are also known as Oregon pine and Colombian pine," he read out loud. "And what makes them so special, is that they grow up to 100 metres tall, and their trunk at ground level can become so thick, you could make a tunnel through it for cars. Both tree types can be found from California to British Columbia, Canada."

The surrounding nature was awe-inspiring as they arrived at the parking area reserved for hikers.

"This seems to be the closest parking area to our destination," Gus read from his tablet while Jon looked for an empty place amongst the other cars. Jon accelerated and pulled on the handbrake, causing their car to slide directly into a parking space.

"Like a glove!" he shouted with his best Jim Carrey Pet Detective impersonation, and they fist bumped.

They exited the car and picked up their satchels and jackets from the back seat. Jon locked the car and threw his satchel over his head, landing it perfectly at his waist with the strap across his back and chest over his left shoulder. On his head, he put on a dark green baseball cap from his work, with a brown coffee bean embroidered on front above the visor.

Gus wrapped his grey hoodie around his waist and hung his black fabric satchel on his right shoulder. In his left hand, he held his tablet with a map to their destination.

"Looks like we have a one-hour hike ahead of us," Gus said, pointing to a barely discernible path leading away from the official trail routes. "We keep Cameron Lake on our right and then cross through the forest. We should easily get back before it gets dark."

The terrain turned out to be relatively easy to walk on, young saplings were growing here and there, but there was no thick understory or rocks – groomed in every shade of green imaginable. Above and around them, leaves and needles turned sunlight into green beams. On the ground, branches and stones were covered with soft mosses and widespread ferns. Compared to their surroundings and massive trees, Gus and Jon felt tiny.

"So, this is what ants feel like," Gus said, looking up and around after a few minutes' walk into the forest.

"Impressive, right?" Jon said and touched one of the massive trees. "Gives you a new perspective on things. No distractions, only raw nature. Some people cannot take it. They go crazy or feel anxiety. Too much to be simply with yourself. I, on the other hand, find this peaceful and comforting." He handed the water bottle to Gus. "Drink some, before you start feeling dizzy."

"Thanks. I can see that you are more in your element than I am," Gus said and took a sip from the bottle before handing it back to Jon. He turned his tablet screen on again. "That way," he pointed a direction away from the lake. "Only two kilometres left."

After an estimated five-kilometre hike, they were close to the location indicated on Gus's screen.

"What are we looking for?" Jon asked, already breathing heavier. "All I can see is trees and rocks."

"Twenty metres ahead," Gus replied and pointed the way between two man-high rock formations. "Funny ... there are similar rock pillars over there." He pointed to their left.

"Also over there," Jon said, pointing to their right.

They were surrounded by rock pillars of different heights. Next to them, where the black dot and exact target was located, grew a massive red cedar.

"Would you look at the size of that thing," Gus said. "It's standing precisely where the coordinates are pointing."

"Is this what he wanted us to find?" Jon asked. "Some stones and a tree?" He sounded disappointed.

To make sure they were in correct place, Gus turned several times 360 degrees, pointing his tablet to all directions.

"It is kind of a bummer," he said and took another spin. "I must say, that those rocks do seem very similar to Stonehenge." Gus turned to Jon after a pause. "You know, the rock formation in Wiltshire, England?"

"I know what Stonehenge is, just not where ..." Jon replied with a fake smile and head shake.

"Anyway, I think Dr Wells owes us some gas money. This was a trip for nothing."

"I agree, those stones have been here for a long time and seen by anyone walking by, nothing extraordinary about them. But the coordinates do point to the middle, one area we can't access due to that massive tree in the way." Gus pointed at the tree, which grew larger than anything they had seen so far, with a diameter at least of six metres. "Whatever he wanted us to 'find'," Gus made air quotes with his hands, "it must be either under it, up there, or in it." He pointed up towards the treetop.

"In it!" both shouted at the same time.

"You saw some of those trees on the way here?" Jon asked. "One had a hole to fit a car through it," he explained excitedly. "You go around that way and I'll go this way," he told Gus, who started walking and studying the tree trunk on his way.

After a while they came both around and met on the other side, where the trunk forked out with a large gap between them, filled with rock rubble and covered in a thick layer of moss.

"Does that look natural to you?" Jon asked. "Have you ever seen trees dropping stones and rocks?"

Jon began removing the moss and pulling rocks away. Gus joined the discovery, both now pulling out rocks of all sizes.

Twenty minutes of hard work later, they had managed to pull out all the rocks except for one. The one remaining against the tree was thin, but as wide and tall as a washing machine, and it did not budge no matter how hard they pulled at the same time.

"This is a stubborn one!" Jon shouted and let go. "We will need a different approach."

"Maybe there is something we could use to pry the last stone away from the tree?" Gus asked while looking around.

"Here's a sturdy looking piece of wood, but it's very long!" Jon yelled from further away.

"How long exactly?"

"About from the closest Stonehenge rock to the tree," Jon said while pulling a sturdy tree trunk with him.

"Maybe we could use the momentum of that Stonehenge rock to break the rock in our way?" He pointed at an already leaning pillar that was closest to them and then laid his hand on the last stone in their way against the tree. "We place the long trunk you found between the leaning stone and the blocking stone. If we topple the leaning stone, it should give enough force to break our rock against the tree. The Stonehenge is our hammer, and the long wood trunk you found is our nail."

When they'd finished with the setup, they dug out as much ground away around the Stonehenge stone as possible. Then, while Jon held the long tree trunk between two stones, Gus pushed the standing stone towards the tree.

"You think we might get into trouble because of this?" Jon asked while aiming the long trunk to middle of the thin stone on their way. "That stone setup seems quite old."

"Maybe," Gus replied, while jumping against the leaning stone. "We'll put it back as it was."

"Right," Jon mumbled back, knowing that would never happen, not with the muscles they had.

The earth lifted under Gus's feet when the Stonehenge stone fell with its full force. The tree trunk Jon held plunged into the blocking stone, breaking it into several pieces.

"Wahoo!" Jon celebrated and kicked the long wood trunk aside.

Excitedly, they pulled the remaining stone pieces away from the massive tree, revealing an opening. Both leaned in towards it. Jon pulled his small army flashlight from his satchel and switched it on.

CHAPTER 3

DISCOVERY

"Ladies first," Jon said, and offered the way for Gus. "Just kidding, no way you would go first." He laughed and pushed himself through the opening.

Pushing his satchel ahead of him, he crawled forward using only his toes and forearms. After only a metre or so, he came to an opening inside the tree. Jon stayed on his knees and used his flashlight to investigate his surroundings. The sheer size of the tree struck him even harder now. The opening was as big as a small tool shed. He stood up and had still plenty of headroom from the natural wood ceiling.

"What do you see?" Gus called impatiently.

Jon couldn't resist. "There is a treasure!"

"What? Wait for me!" Gus yelled and rushed into the narrow hole.

Jon turned the light towards the opening and saw Gus's hands pushing a satchel through inch by inch. Gus crawled forward like a caterpillar, grunting his way through.

"Here," Jon said, and offered his hand for Gus, who accepted the help and pulled himself upright with a small jump.

"Thanks man," he said, and his eyes followed the light beam coming out from Jon's small but bright flashlight.

"Amazing," he was able to say. "So, where's the treasure?" He kept looking around, touching the natural wooden wall around them with Jon smirking behind him. "There's no treasure, is there?" Gus turned to look at Jon with narrowed eyes.

"Of course not, but it doesn't mean we can't look for one. Maybe something above us?"

Jon turned the light upwards, only to observe the same solid wood above as around them. On the ground lay a long dry vine-like rope, as if tossed aside after usage.

"There's nothing. Except the rest of that piece of root hanging in the middle of the ceiling." Jon tried to reach it by stretching his right arm as far as he could, but the root was just too high. "Hold this, I will try to jump for it." He gave his flashlight to Gus.

Jon waved his arms down past his knees as he bent them, and then swung them up again and pushed with his legs as hard as he could, propelling himself upwards like Michael Jordan dunking a basketball into a hoop. He managed to get a grip on the root and stayed mid-air.

"I think it's just a dried-out root or something," Jon said, yanking the root as hard as he could, his legs waving around.

The root did not give way. Then, with a loud crack, almost like a whip, the root snapped off from the tree, sending Jon into free fall towards the ground, his arms still raised and his legs forward, as if he were sitting in mid-air. Gus made a heroic attempt to catch his friend by holding his arms out.

Jon crashed straight into Gus's arms and, for a fraction of a second, they looked like a bride and groom crossing the threshold for the first time as a married couple. However, instead of going through a door, Gus fell backwards with Jon in his arms. On hitting the ground, Gus realised the earth did not cause him any pain but welcomed them with a soft embrace instead. The ground had given way, allowing them to sink through the soft forest floor. They dropped straight down for a few seconds before landing on something hard, something leaning downwards. After sliding down the hard surface for several seconds, they landed on the ground, both rolling forward from the momentum from the slide. While coughing out dust caused by the fall, they called out to for each other. Jon pulled out his mobile phone from the pocket of his tactical pants and enabled his phone's torch mode with his thumb.

"What just happened?" Gus asked, sitting up coughing and dusting off his clothes.

"No idea, but a nice catch," Jon replied and turned his light around, creating a foggy view before the dust started to settle around them. "I think we found whatever he meant us to find." He laughed coughing and turned the light into Gus's face, making him lift his hand between the beam of light and his eyes.

"Not into my eyes, man," he whispered.

"Why are you whispering? And where is my flashlight?"

"I don't know, and I don't know," Gus answered, and then raised his voice back to normal. "I dropped it in the fall. I feel like we are breaking and entering to a place we have no right to be in."

Jon turned the mobile phone's torch light away from Gus's face and inspected their surroundings. A curving wall in front of them reached higher than their beam of light could reach. Several metres away on their other side was a low wall made of stones and earth. He turned the light back to the curving wall they slid down from.

"Looks like some kind of a dome," Jon said, and placed his palm against the wall.

The surface was cold like metal, but it did not feel like metal. The surface was patterned like a tree or plants but was not organic.

"Have you seen anything like this?" he also whispered now, while moving his hand along the wall. "Reminds me of floor tiles, with some random pattern printed on them."

"Pretty much," Gus answered and placed his both hands against the smooth wall. "What is this place?"

"I have no idea" – Jon dug into his satchel – "but let's find out. Wherever we dropped down from, it seems we cannot get back from here." He pulled out the small MacGyver knife from his satchel. "Maybe we can climb out?" He pulled out the largest knife blade from the Swiss Army knife's selection.

He poked the wall with the knife in few places without any effect. He then picked up a sharp stone from the ground and hit the wall with it several times.

"Nothing," he said. "The wall is strong as metal, but I can't make even a scratch. I guess climbing out of here is out of the question. How about mobile reception?" He looked at Gus, who pulled out his phone and turned on the display.

"Nope, nothing."

"Let's go this way." Jon pointed his light to the left side of the wall. They started walking along the wall, and after a while the wall started to shift from dome-like into straight up vertical. They arrived to an edge that seemed like an entrance to the other side of this strange wall. The entrance was formed from two large black rectangular pillars, about four metres apart. On the ground in front of them was a large part of one to the pillars, lying on the ground. Gus knelt down next to it.

"Look at this. Seems like the top of second pillar had broken off and fallen down," Gus said, while studying the broken surface. "Seems like it's grown."

Jon squatted next to Gus.

"Look ..." Gus continued excitedly. "There are similar layers like on tree trunks."

"This piece must weight a tonne," said Jon, leaning against the large broken piece, which bounced away like Styrofoam, landing him on his side on the ground.

"What the ..." Gus stood up. He carefully approached the broken piece of pillar and placed his hands on both sides of it. Expecting to use all his power, the piece lifted up like an empty carton box instead. "Awesome!" he shouted and tossed the piece towards Jon, who was still squatting on the ground.

"Are you crazy!" Jon shrieked and reflexively raised his hands in front of him to protect his face from being crushed from the weight of the broken pillar piece, which bounced off from him like an air balloon.

"Sick, no?" Gus shouted with excitement like he was a kid again. A kid who just came out from an amazing new ride at an amusement park. "Do you know what this means?" he asked Jon while studying the piece again. Jon looked at the piece and then directly into Gus's eyes.

"That I just shat my pants?" Jon shouted back sarcastically.

"It's not from this world." Gus looked back into Jon's eyes.

Jon lifted the piece without an effort and then nodded to confirm Gus's suspicion with the same words, only slower, "It's, not from this world."

They had a silent moment. After a long pause, they fist bumped and shout in uniform, "Awesome!"

"What else is there?" Jon asked. He stood up and turned his mobile torch towards the entrance.

There was no door to open, only an opening into a dome of some sort. Inside, the ground was covered with the same gravel as on the outside. They were now both beaming their lights towards the middle of the room, revealing something, a table, that would easily seat six people, made of the same black material as the outside pillars and walls. The table was higher than a dining table and it had only one large leg, almost as wide as the table itself, making it look like a rectangular mushroom.

"Maybe it's some kind of an altar?" Gus guessed.

"Maybe," Jon replied, sliding his hand over the dusty surface. "Maybe it's as light as the piece outside?" He placed his phone on the table and took a firm hold with both hands of the table edges. He pulled up as hard as he could, but the table didn't budge. To pick up his phone from the table, he moved his hand over the table again, feeling the surface.

"I don't feel any markings or signs of wear," he said. His sliding hand had almost reached his phone when he stopped. "Wait, here is something," he said, and he leaned over and blew the dust away. "Looks like here is some kind of a hole, a triangular hole," he corrected and kept blowing and cleaning the area where the hole was discovered.

"Here's another one," Gus called out, "and another one. Only these are round and square." Gus was thinking for a second. "I know! Maybe this, hmm, maybe *Black Table* is an intergalactic baby intelligence test, where you put different shaped pieces into correct shaped holes."

Jon looked at Gus.

"You've named it already? And yes, that must be it, all the extraterrestrial babies come here to play and find out if they are worthy." Jon said, and they laughed.

"Maybe there is more," he continued and untied the black sweater from around his waist. He rolled one end a few times around his free hand a few times and created small fan, which he started to swing around vigorously above the table. The dust moved aside like magic, revealing two more patterns. These were not holes though, but more like embedded print markings. They were deeper in the surface and not just any markings. One was a half a sphere the size of a grapefruit. But the last marking was something else.

"Is that?" Gus asked.

"Yep, a palm print," Jon replied with eyes wide open.

"Look at the size of that thing." Gus tried to wrap his mind around what he was seeing. "And why are there only three fingers?"

The palm print was the size of car steering wheel, with three fingers instead of five, all the same length, with the middle one being twice as wide as than other two.

"Last time I saw something like that was in the first *Jurassic Park* movie. Remember, when the water trembles on tyrannosaurus' footprint when they realise T-Rex is coming towards them?" He looked up at Gus with at eyes wide open.

Gus nodded. "I remember!" he shouted back. "And in the movie *Total Recall*, in the end, when Arnold is releasing the oxygen to Mars' atmosphere."

Jon smiled back. This is one of the reasons they were best friends, they both had an undying respect and unbeatable memory for science fiction movies.

"Good one," Jon said, and put his phone back into his pocket while tying his sweater back around his waist.

Something glimmered on the edge of the room and caught the corner of his eye. "Put your phone away," he urged Gus. "I can see something."

After Gus turned off the light and secured his phone in his pocket, they could spot something with turquoise light glowing under the dust near the dome wall. They walked hesitantly closer, like approaching a snake, or an active land mine.

When they were close enough, they knelt down and moved the sand and dust aside above the glow. Under the sand, a triangular glass-looking object revealed itself. Jon first poked it with his phone, and when not getting any reaction, he poked again, this time with his index finger.

"Seems safe," Jon said, and picked the object up. The glowing object was a size of a TV remote control, long and triangular, not hot or cold.

"Are you thinking what I'm thinking?" He looked at Gus. "Let's see if the glove fits."

They stood up and returned to Black Table at the centre of the room.

"I'm taking a wild guess here, and think it goes to the hole number one," Jon said as he lowered the object into the triangular hole. When almost halfway in, the object pulled itself further into the hole as if by some magnetic force, and locked into place, making both Jon and Gus jump.

"We need to find the rest," Gus said. "Let's turn off the lights and see if we can find more."

After both had hidden their lights, Jon removed his sweater for a second time and placed it over the glowing object on the table, making the dome pitch black. They saw nothing.

"Wait for a while. Let our eyes take some time to adjust," said Jon, who had used to do work in the dark during his time in the military.

After about five minutes, Gus poked Jon's shoulder gently. "Over there," he whispered and turned Jon's shoulder to the direction where he'd spotted something.

"I see it," Jon whispered back as if the light would escape if they were heard. They approached the turquoise glow slowly when a soft thump sound echoed inside the dome.

"Ouch!" Gus cried out loud. "I think we are at the wall again. The dome is about fifteen metres in diameter." He stroked his head. "And we are at the door, or whatever where we came in from. The opening is this way." He walked slowly towards the exit, his hand sliding against the dome's interior wall. "I see one more!" This time he shouted.

Jon picked up the second glowing object from the edge of the wall and went after Gus for the third object. Gus knelt down and picked it up.

"I guess you have the round one, because this one is square," Gus said, holding the last object in his palm. Both turned their mobile torches back on, making glowing objects looked like sticks of glass.

"They look like crystals. Like ones hanging from chandeliers at some fancy restaurants and hotels." Jon said, turning and studying crystals closer.

"What is this?" Gus asked, still on his knees on the ground. His light focused now on a round stone next to the place where he picked up the third object. "Look ..." he said. "This is something bigger and round, like a sphere."

Jon joined Gus, kneeling closer.

They pulled away the sand surrounding the sphere with their fingers. Once the sphere was out in the open,

Gus studied it with his phone torch before pulling it fully out from the sand.

"Wow. This one is much heavier than it looks, but clearly not made of iron or lead. I can also feel some heat coming from it," Gus said in surprise, and handed it to Jon. "Here."

Jon took the sphere and hopped it on his palm the way baseball players do before their pitch.

"Maybe it's radioactive?" He realised what he had just said and dropped the ball back on the ground while lifting his arms in surrender position.

"Nuclear?" asked Gus. "I don't think so. I think whatever that is, it would not be in the open like this and have a place on the table if it was hazardous. But let's use caution, just in case."

Gus picked sphere back up, using his scarf stuffed into his satchel pocket. With the rest of the objects now in their hands, they approached the table once more. At the table, they placed crystal pieces into matching holes. The last two crystals clicked into their places, just like the first one did, but nothing extraordinary happened.

"We didn't pass the baby test?" Jon asked, disappointed. "Maybe they are just fancy alien decorations?" He laughed.

"I have a guess why the sphere is warm," said Gus, his hand above the dipped round shape on the table. "I think it might be a power source of some kind."

Gus revealed the sphere from his scarf and then carefully placed it on the round dip just under the glass sticks. The sphere made a slight vibration sound and turquoise light glowed from within, making it look like a cracked egg with light inside. The sphere spun around several directions on its own, positioning itself how it was meant to be. The table came into life and they both took a step back.

It was no longer a table, but looked like a large interface, displaying planets and constellations above the table with a three-dimensional map filled with stars, planets and moons. The map was so bright it filled the dome with light.

"Holy cow," Gus said quietly, and walked back to the table, Jon following his example. He placed his hand above the stars and planets, they moved. "You remember the *CSI* TV-series, where they have those screens to study something in detail? Look." Gus moved his hands above the hologram, and the constellations moved on his command.

Jon watched in awe as Gus spun the galaxy in front of them. Then with both of his hands, Gus pushed them into the middle, and then opened his arms as wide as he could. This movement worked like a zoom feature into stars. He did it again and again, until they had a clear constellation displaying in front of them. It was clearly a sun with four planets around it. From those four planets, two of them had alien looking symbols next to them. Each symbol had three parts, pieces of circles expanding over each other. The first part was the smallest and looked like a letter C. The second part was bigger than the first, surrounding the first one and looked also like a letter C, but in mirror image. The third part was bigger again, surrounding both the first and second parts, looking like a small cut from the letter C. The positions and lengths of each part kept changing.

"Okay, definitely not the Google maps," Gus said, and looked at Jon.

"Check another one," Jon said, and Gus worked his magic.

First Gus opened his arms as wide as possible and then pulled his palms towards the centre, having the same effect as before, but in reverse. More planets and stars filled the map. He swiped his hand from right to left, moving planets on the screen all at once to the left.

"There, that one," said Jon, leaning closer and pointing to a small solar system, which instantly zoomed in and now filled the screen. "Whoa!" both shouted out in stereo.

Again, they had a sun in the middle, and as many as fifteen planets surrounding it. From those, eight had similar alien symbols changing shape next to them. One of them seemed like a single symbol, changing its form a few times before coming to a full stop.

"Look," Gus pointed out, "that symbol just stopped." The planet next to it started pulsing with the same turquoise light as the crystals in the table. After no more than ten second, the pulsing stopped, the light dimmed, and a long string of alien symbols appeared next to it, changing their form just like before.

"I know what those symbols are!" Gus shouted to Jon's surprise.

"You can read that?" Jon asked in disbelief, part of him actually believing it.

"Of course not. They represent counters. See, the number of characters gets shorter with time. There, and there." He pointed out a few for Jon. "And as we just saw, when the symbols run out, they start again. It's part of basic coding principles. You have a counter and input value for it. We just don't know the input values, but I am pretty sure that's a counter."

"You rock!" Jon shouted.

Jon was always impressed about Gus's IT skills and his ability to think outside of the box. "But nothing else happened. What was supposed to happen?" Jon said and looked at Gus, who looked like a kid who just got the best Christmas present ever.

"I don't know, yet." Gus made an arm movement that zoomed out the stars and planets.

"Why didn't those dots move when you zoomed out?" Jon asked, standing at the edge of the table where the crystals were placed. "Here is a single turquoise dot with the same characters next to it." He leaned closer and placed his finger above the dot he meant. At least twenty turquoise coloured pulsing planets appeared on the screen, all across the galaxy.

"Just making an educated guess here." Gus said, and pointed at one of the dots, causing the map to zoom closer to the planet he had pointed at. The planet had only one symbol changing its form next to it.

"It's almost ready, counting down for that planet," Gus said excitedly, just before the symbol stopped and the planet started pulsing with the now familiar turquoise light.

"Exactly the same as earlier!" he shouted happily for being right and looked around the table. Then his eyes stopped near Jon. "And what is that weird T-Rex looking palm print?" He pointed out.

"This one?" Jon asked and placed his palm on the large print.

Eye-blinding bright turquoise light surrounded them, followed by a loud crackling sound, the kind of sound you hear when an electric circuit is shorting out.

CHAPTER 4

CREATURE

"**O**uch! My eyes and head hurts!" Gus shouted and held his hands in front of his eyes, trying to see his own fingers.

Both were leaning against the table, trying to find some balance.

"What?" Jon shouted back. "That cracking sound messed up my hearing! And my head feels like exploding, here in the front and somewhere in the middle of my skull." Jon pointed to his forehead.

"Mine too." Gus rubbed his forehead with his fingers, as if it would ease the pain on the other side of his skull.

After a few minutes they both calmed down, testing their senses.

"I'm OK," Jon said. "Are you OK?" He turned to Gus who was still counting his fingers.

"Getting there. My head still hurts. What just happened?"

"I touched that palm print and *that* happened." Jon pointed at the T-Rex-like palm print on the table.

At the same time, the planet on the screen pulsed turquoise for ten more seconds before fading out. A new set of symbols appeared next to it. On the table, the sphere and crystals still stood in their places, glowing the same turquoise light as before.

"Like I said, a counter." Gus pointed out as symbols changed.

"I don't know why, but the air smells different," Jon said. "Maybe our senses got knocked off with that thing. Now what?"

"I don't know." Gus seemed confused. "I will study this table a bit more. Could you go and see if there is a way out from here, like ladders or something?"

"Sure thing." Jon flicked his mobile phone back into torch mode. "Maybe I'll find my flashlight while I'm at it." He turned, threw his satchel over his shoulder and headed towards the opening they came in from.

Gus moved stars and planets around the table like one possessed. He zoomed in and out, then moved to the next constellation. He zoomed into a planet with only a few alien symbols changing next to it. When leaning closer to examine the symbol, he heard Jon's voice from outside, "I found a way out, and you are not going to believe this."

Jon waved his light in Gus's direction to show the way. To Gus, it reminded him of a firefly flying in circles. Gus also turned his mobile torch on, picked up his satchel, and headed towards Jon. He reached the opening and saw Jon standing only a few metres away from him.

"I thought you said you found a way ... what the hell?" He was struck with an impossible view, while his ears were filled with various sounds of insects, animals and night birds.

"Sir, the way out, as requested," Jon said, moving his arm towards the scene in front of them. It was dark, but there were trees, lots of trees. "And look up." He pointed up with his index finger next to his face, creating a suspenseful gloom on his face with the mobile's light.

Gus looked up and his brain scrambled to make sense of what he was seeing. There were stars. Gus and Jon were no longer underground. But it was not the stars that made his brains twirl, it was the clear sight of three moons, all different sizes.

"Either we've been breathing some serious hallucinogenic mould, or we are not in Vancouver anymore." Jon and flicked off his mobile torch, looking serious. "And that means I can forget finding my flashlight."

For several minutes, both stood and stared at the moons, taking it all in.

"Not what you see every day, or night, is it?" Gus said, his eyes still fixed on the three moons in the sky.

"At least now we know what that table is for, right?" Jon said, in hope of Gus knowing the answers.

"Right ..." Gus answered and looked at Jon. "It did bring us here, wherever here is. And it happened after we chose a turquoise pulsing planet and you touched that palm print." He gave Jon a piercing stare, one like a parent would after the kid had done something wrong.

"Oh. Right. Sorry about that," Jon responded with a fake smile. "What's done is done, but we wouldn't have *seen this* ..." He gestured with his hands, as if he had a serving plate in his hands. "Ta-da!"

"Okay, fine. It's pretty damn awesome."

They fist bumped.

"Can't be angry with you. This is something I've been dreaming about for my whole life." Gus took a deep breath.

The thick forest in front of them was noisy with at least a dozen different bird sounds, thousands of insects, and some animals making sounds reminding them of pigs and squirrels. Somewhere near a branch snapped and leaves shook, making Jon and Gus stand a bit closer to each other. High above them in the sky a large creature glided silently in front of one of the moons. It had bat-like wings and a long beak.

"Looks like one of those Jurassic era birds," Jon managed to say, when a ten times larger flying creature with the wing span of a 747 appeared from one side and snatched the Jurassic era bird with its massive alligator-like mouth. In two gulps, the bird was gone. Once the bird had disappeared down the creature's throat, it let out a loud shriek that echoed through the air. Jon and Gus froze.

"Was that a ...?" Jon asked.

"A dragon?"

"Sure looked like one."

"Sure did."

"They seem so much nicer in the movies."

Both remained frozen for another five minutes.

"You think it's safe to move?" Gus finally asked without moving his lips.

"Probably not," Jon answered. "I will try to find something to burn ... for a campfire." Jon continued when Gus said nothing. "If the same laws of animal instincts work here as on Earth, we should be safer with fire."

"Sounds good." Gus looked around nervously as if something, anything, would soon come and snatch him for a meal. "I will go back inside and take a look at that table. Maybe figure out how we get back home." He turned and headed back inside the dome structure, slower than running but much faster than normal walking.

About ten minutes later, Jon returned holding his arms in front of him, piled up with dry branches and smaller pieces of wood he had found near the dome.

"Gus?" he called out when he got closer to the dome.

"I'm here," Gus shouted back from inside the dome.

Jon dropped the pile of wood at the entrance and headed deeper inside.

"Anything?" he asked.

"This is definitely alien tech," Gus stated the obvious, while studying the pieces they had placed on the table before. "A bit too dark to see any details on and around the table. Maybe we'll have better luck in the morning."

"I will start a fire by the entrance. We can camp inside the dome, just to be sure we are not becoming the dragon's midnight flyby snack," Jon said and got to work on with fire starting.

After creating a small circle on the ground from stones he found lying around, Jon knelt down and started working on wood logs. With his Swiss Army knife, aka MacGyver knife, he peeled thin layers of wood flakes which curled up nicely when he slid the knife barely a millimetre under the surface of the wood. Once he had enough curly wood shavings to make a fist-sized pile, he took out his flint kit from his satchel and scraped firmly against the surface of the magnesium block with an iron blade belonging to the flint. He continued until a small pile of magnesium dust spread out on the curly wood. Then with the iron blade, he tapped sharply against the magnesium block, creating sparks, which flew onto the pile of magnesium dust. After few sharp taps, the magnesium dust ignited into flames. Gently, he laid more curly shavings on top of the flames and at the same time blew softly on the fire. The fire grew bigger, burning faster with every curled shaving. One piece at the time he added smaller branches as kindling. Increasing the size of the pieces of wood, he added more and more until finally, the larger wood pieces caught fire. Using wrist-thick pieces of wood, he created a square shape and in the middle he placed down the two largest pieces he had next to each other, leaving a centimetre wide gap between them. Between the gap, tongues of flame came to life, burning the large pieces slowly from the underside. Gus and Jon sat down against the dome entrance pillars, facing each other, keeping some distance from the warm, bright fire. The temperature was quite warm, even though it was night.

"Can you believe this?" Gus asked, looking first into the dome and then up to the night sky with three moons.

"Absolutely amazing," Jon said. "Like a dream, but not a dream. No-one is going to believe us."

"Imagine the possibilities." Gus looked up to the sky. "Interstellar travelling right from our back yard. This is going to change everything. I will study more about that table in the morning, and we will figure out a way to get us back."

"Sounds like a plan." Jon dug into his satchel. "Hungry?" he asked. "I have some protein bars here. Chocolate with nuts, or strawberry with fruits?"

"I'll take the strawberry one," Gus answered, and Jon threw him a bar with red and white packaging. "Thanks."

"I also have some water if you're thirsty." He shook the military style flat canister, which sounded almost full.

"Jon?" Gus said instead.

"Gus?"

"Can you tell me more about your missions on Earth? When you were part of the commandos?" Gus asked, knowing it was a difficult time for Jon. "I would guess your oath for silence does not apply on an alien planet?" He smiled.

"I guess not," Jon answered with a smile, happy his friend had not fished for too much information about his missions in the past, even if Jon himself had told little pieces now and then. He was more than ready to finally share the burden. "How about something cold, while we are on this alien sauna planet?"

"I'll take anything you have. But that sounds perfect."

"Okay then. How about a story, when I almost froze to death?"

Based on Gus's face expression, he could continue.

"So, it was an early winter morning, near the arctic circle. It was minus twenty-five, and it had been snowing non-stop for weeks. I was returning from picking up some important gear for our base, located twenty kilometres away. Morning was almost upon me and it had stopped snowing. I drove a snowmobile through the forest, the important gear in a backpack on my back. There was so much powdery snow, that if you jumped off the snowmobile, you would sink down to your waist. Because of that, every turn had to be perfect or the snowmobile would sink. And if that happened, it could take an hour to dig it out. No too sharp turns and not too much throttle. Also, every stop had to end on something solid under the hot slide rail mechanism. Otherwise it would melt the snow and freeze solid before continuing. Everything went fine, until my engine died.

"I tried to restart it by pulling the start cord, but the engine wouldn't start. I jumped off from the seat and sunk waist-deep into snow. I dug myself to the front of my snow mobile and opened the hood and the smell of gasoline filled the air. I left the hood open and tried to start the engine. Again, the engine belt moved, but it wouldn't start. I jumped off and peeked into the engine compartment. I took out my flashlight, the very same one I just lost in Vancouver, and I could again smell gasoline, but this time there was gasoline on the snow, colouring it slightly pinkish. Checking all the tubes, I discovered one of the gas lines was loose. I took the glove off from my left hand and pushed the tube back in place with my bare hand. After closing the hood and jumping back on the seat, I pulled the start cord a few times and on third the engine started. I gave a bit of throttle and the snow mobile moved slowly forward. Only when I increased speed, the engine died again. While standing above my seat, I reached over the handlebars and pushed my bare hand inside the hood. I could feel the same line was loose again. I pushed the tube back into its place and started the engine like before. But then, before giving more gas, I pushed my hand back into engine department and held the tube in place while opening the throttle. For the next fifteen kilometres I leaned over the handlebars and held the tube in place with my left hand, while giving gas and steering with my right. Not the most comfortable way of travelling I must admit."

"What do you mean fifteen kilometres? I thought you had twenty to go? And what did this have to do with freezing to death?" Gus asked sceptically.

"Well, I wasn't back at my camp yet. I cut the engine and took a break. The sun was coming up and the natural scene around me was absolutely amazing. Not a sound, except for my breathing and the ticking sound from hot engine parts. Mature pine trees, only three metres tall, their branches hanging heavy with snow, and the sky painted in pinkish-blue, creating a halo around a rising sun so dim you could look at it with your bare eyes. My breath was a thick white frosty steam, freezing on my white jacket collar as well as my eyebrows. I managed to drive a little further but the engine died again, this time for good. By this time, I was at a lake I was supposed to go around. My fuel gauge showed empty. I had leaked gas all the way. I took out my vacuum packed map made of paper and it gave me two options – I could walk in deep snow for several kilometres, or walk across the lake, which would cut the trip to two kilometres instead of five."

"So which route did you take?" Gus asked, leaning forward. He was no longer sweating.

"The lake."

"Of course you did." Gus shook his head and leaned back against the dome pillar. "But why didn't you have skis with you, or snowshoes?"

"Not standard issue." Jon shrugged.

"So, with my rifle in front of me, and the equipment on my back, I approached the lake one heavy step after another, sinking into snow almost waist deep. The lake surface barely had any snow on it due to gusty winds blowing across it. I first tried the ice with my right foot and then added more weight on it. It felt solid. I decided to push ahead. In the middle of the hundred-metre crossing, I heard this ominous low thumping rumble that echoed around me. The sound reminded me of a closing thick vault door. I took few more steps, when the same sound echoed across the lake again, this time followed by a higher cracking sound, right below me."

"And?" Gus demanded, leaning now almost over the fire between them.

"I managed to say, 'Oh crap' out loud when the ice broke under me. I remember how the water pressure around me pressed my clothes and my boots against my skin. First, everything seemed fine, no cold, no wet or shocking death. Luckily, the gear on my back got stuck on the ice edge, preventing me from falling completely through the ice, stopping me right under my arm pits. I had spread my arms on top of the ice, to keep me from falling deeper. About five seconds later, water found its way through my clothes, relieving the pressure and soaking me with ice-cold water. My waterproof boots also started to fill with water."

"So, what did you do?" Gus's face looming again over the fire.

"I will continue after getting more firewood." Jon pretended to get up.

"No!" Gus yelled.

"Fine." Jon smiled, he had managed to trick his friend. "I threw my rifle as far as I could ahead of me. I then wiggled out from the heavy equipment and pushed it as far as I could towards the rifle. I placed my hands on top of the ice and pushed myself upwards. With the help of the equipment harness in front of me, I pulled myself out of the water. The cold didn't bother me that much, maybe because of all the adrenaline in my system. Instead of getting up, I spread my weight as wide as possible, I rolled away from the hole, keeping my arms above me. And every time I had a chance, I flung my rifle and the equipment on top of snowy ice, further towards my heading. After ten metres or so, I stood up and tested the ice with few small hops. I collected my gears and moved forward in fast pace, sliding my feet forward one after another."

"And you were not cold?" asked Gus in shock.

"I was freaking freezing," Jon said. "Now the adrenaline wearing off, I could feel my body temperature dropping fast. My feet felt sharp tingles before going fully numb. The wet clothes felt like fire instead of ice. The refreshing cold had changed into painful torture. I knew that the only way to keep myself alive was to keep moving. If I were to stop, I would get hypothermia and die. With no help in sight for a couple of kilometres, I started to run, forcing myself to move my legs and arms like a robot, ignoring the piercing pain from the cold that made my muscles stiff and painful to move. Screaming in my head, I kept going, knowing of having almost a two-kilometre run ahead of me. After crossing the lake, I found the road leading to my base. I kept running until the water in my boots became warm. I actually felt better. I could feel my toes again. My own body produced enough heat to warm my feet. During the last kilometre I had a full out-of-body experience, ignoring all the pain, the panic, the tiredness, the temptation to stop running and lie down into a curl and fall asleep. I finally arrived at the base, shoes filled with warm water, and clothes as hard as an exoskeleton. I had arrived, but there was no medical unit there, or anyone else for that matter. The base was deserted. I dropped my gear at the entrance and walked straight into the shower. First, I kept the water cold, and in stages within half an hour, I turned it warmer to match my body temperature. I was safe. I made it."

"Holy shit," Gus said, looking at his friend with concern.

"Yep. And to this day, because of the exposure to extreme cold, I can't tan here around my mouth and chin." Jon pointed to the area which Gus now realised was a lot paler than the rest of Jon's skin.

"True," Gus said, looking at Jon's face. "I have always thought it's just some skin thing."

"Nope, and that's the story behind it. I also have the same with my feet, which since then are constantly cold.

And I didn't get off that easily, just by taking a shower. I got horrible pneumonia in the following days that lasted weeks."

"But you made it." Gus took a deep breath and offered fist bump over the fire, to which Jon responded right away. "And I don't mind anymore if it's so hot in here." He laughed.

After an hour and a few stories later, Jon pulled out his phone and took a picture of Gus sitting behind the fire.

"Good idea." Gus reacted to the flash. "We need some proof about all this." He pulled out his phone and took several photos of Jon, sitting on the other side of the fire. "Say cheese."

Both stood up and started to take as many photos as they could. Gus several took photos of the table and the crystals, while Jon took photos outside from the dome and the moons.

"Selfie with the triple moons!" Jon shouted from outside.

Gus ran out and they posed smiling for flashing selfie pictures with the alien sky. On the fifth selfie, an ear-piercing sound came from somewhere in the forest. It sounded like a bear's roar, but much, much louder, so loud in fact that the trees moved from the sudden change in air flow.

"What the hell was that?" Jon asked, placing his phone back to his pocket.

"I don't know, but whatever it is, it's big. But it sounded like it's far away." Gus held his phone in front of them and took another picture with a flash, creating a temporary light beam up into the sky. This was instantly followed by another roar. This time, the roar was followed by thumping sounds that made the ground shake. The ground shook so hard it made T-Rex thumps seem like mouse steps in comparison.

"Computer, end program!" Gus shouted into air, expecting their reality to disappear around them and return them to the *Enterprise's* holodeck.

"Operator, we need an exit." Jon followed Gus's lead, expecting someone, anyone at all, to answer and provide them a quick getaway from whatever virtual world they were in *Matrix*.

Nothing happened.

"Well, worth trying." Gus raised his shoulder.

Another roar blasted through the forest, sending leaves flying from the trees. A roar, both Jon and Gus recognised to be already much closer. The moon closest to horizon suddenly disappeared. A large outlined shape of a creature blocked the moon. All Jon and Gus could see were six tall legs, reaching ten times higher than any tree, moving slowly step by step, each step shaking the ground with level twelve on the Richter scale. The creature's long horizontal body had no visible head. The dragon they saw earlier came out from nowhere and glided over the creature. Jon and Gus jumped when several long tentacles appeared from the middle of the creature's back and pulled the dragon into its dark outlines. The creature stopped and shook its upper body like a dog after a swim. The air filled with a noise that could have been thousands of trumpets playing different tunes at the same time in. A cold shiver ran down Jon's spine.

"Let's get out of here!" he shouted, and they both bolted back inside the dome.

The creature moved again, directly towards them. The next two thumps were so strong, it made both of them lose their footing and crumble on the ground, only a few metres from the table. They crawled towards the table like a couple of toddlers. They grabbed the edge of the table and pulled themselves back up.

"Pick a planet!" Jon shouted.

"Which planet?" Gus shouted back.

"Any planet!" Jon shouted and pushed a turquoise dot at the edge of the table, revealing all the planets that pulsed with the turquoise light. "That one!" He shouted and pointed at the planet closest to him. Planet and its solar system zoomed closer. Gus touched the pulsing planet. Nothing happened. Outside, trees cracked and fell from whatever approached them. The approaching thumping shook the ground. It was now so close that Jon and Gus had to hold the table to stay standing.

"The print! Press the palm print!" Gus shouted.

Jon did as before. Bright light and electric sound followed, and they were gone.

CHAPTER 5

NEW THATHO

Gus and Jon breathed heavily while leaning against Black Table, their eyes closed from the blinding light and crackling sounds. Both took deep breaths. The air smelled fresh, like recently watered plants.

"Are we dead?" Gus asked, his eyes still shut.

"I'm not sure," Jon replied, and carefully opened his eyes. "We are good." He blinked his eyes, trying to adjust to bright daylight. There was no headache this time.

Gus also opened his eyes. It wasn't dark anymore, but bright as a day. The black dome around them was half missing, allowing sunshine to bathe the table in light. The pillars where the entrance used to be were both gone. The dome now looked more like an amphitheatre, or a quarter of a sphere. Places where the dome was broken had uneven sharp surfaces.

"I don't think your flashlight is here either," said Gus with a snorting laugh, and he walked away from the table. Jon followed with a frown on his face. The further they walked, the clearer a view they got. They found themselves standing on an edge of a platform, up on a small mountain. Looking carefully over the edge, below them everything spread green as far as the eye could see. Thin layers of cloud floated here and there, and birds flew in small flocks before disappearing into the forest. Both to their left and right, the mountains spread as far as the green did.

"Okay," Jon said and led them across the broken dome to the other side of the platform.

Once on the edge, all they could see was dark blue water, sharing the view with a blue sky. The vast ocean and the green land were separated with the string of mountains, like a dam wall. Large waves hit far below against the mountain wall, pushing a spray of water up with the wind.

"No multiple moons at least," said Jon, hoping for Gus to say something. "Also, no monsters after us. So far so good?" Still waiting to hear from Gus, who had pulled out his tablet, now staring at it like he was hypnotised. "Earth calling Gus, literally,"

"I'm here," Gus finally answered. "That table is somehow making us travel to other planets in our own galaxy. And if we don't figure out how, and fast, we might get into serious trouble," he said and walked back to Black Table. "I will crack this in no time." He pulled out all sorts of cables and adapters from his satchel. "May I borrow your MacGyver knife?" he asked, holding his hand back, waiting for Jon to deliver.

"I'll look around," Jon said and handed his knife to Gus, who still looked at the table instead of Jon.

"Thanks. You'll get it back." Gus examined the table with his hands, looking for more clues to what they were dealing with.

"I'll be back for lunch!" Jon shouted before losing the sight of Gus, who had knelt behind the table.

The small mountain platform they had arrived on was flat only around the dome, with a steep drop either towards the water or the green territory, divided with a string of mountains continuing in both directions. While walking along the edge of the green side, Jon noticed small steps going downwards. He turned towards the dome to tell Gus of his intentions, but then turned back instead and head down.

After twenty minutes of fast paced descent, he arrived at another platform, finding only more steps heading down. Jon walked closer to the platform edge where the steps continued and saw something odd a few hundred metres below him, something that appeared like rooftops. From some rooftops, smoke rose up. Jon and Gus were not alone.

From Jon's military time he knew that proper surveillance is the basis for every mission, except this time he did not have his thermal binoculars nor his rifle scope to help him out. He also did not have time to approach by stealthy crawling. The only way to scout this would be to follow the steps and see it through. Curiosity took the better of him and he decided to continue, but before doing so, he unslung his satchel and hid it next to a large stone leaning against the mountain wall. He then walked across the platform and headed further down.

The closer he got, the odder the rooftops appeared, making Jon feel nervous about them. After descending all the way down, he had lost the view of possible houses, and was now between rock formations from the mountain wall, leading towards the area he believed he had seen from above. After a few minutes' walk, the formations ended, and he came to an opening that made Jon stop where he stood. The opening was filled with people, walking around in an area that looked like wide stone paved streets. People appeared like anyone from Earth, no pointy ears nor fierce warrior faces.

Everyone was dressed in long sleeved light fabric clothes, reminding Jon of sailing boat commercials, where people wear white or beige linen clothes, sleeves rolled up while pulling the ropes or steering the boat. Along the side of streets were sturdy stone structures about twenty metres wide and a few metres high. The whole settlement seemed to be only a few hundred metres square. Beyond the buildings, the massive green forest, similar to what they saw in Vancouver, was visible. However, the air felt much more humid than in Vancouver, reminding Jon of rainforests where he had been on a few missions. He approached the people. On the way he passed something that looked like a flower garden. Each flower had a single, finger-thick grey stem and a grapefruit sized round white flower on the top. When he walked by, all the flowers bent towards him, following him like a sunflower tracking the sun.

Definitely not Vancouver, he thought, and took a step away from the flowers.

People stared at Jon with his tight lightweight beige Gore-Tex pants with multiple small pockets and darker beige knitted knee patches. His reaction to flowers that grew almost everywhere did not go unnoticed. Jon in their midst looked like a stranger which a few children had realised and now approached him.

"Ath tho, lam phe co ..." one of the kids said, looking at Jon.

"Kentho, pall om am tham," another kid said to the first one.

A piercing pain slashed through Jon's forehead, making him bend forward and hold his head. The kids around him seemed alarmed from his sudden reaction to the pain in his head.

"Parthe are you?" the first kid said.

Jon blinked his eyes, unsure if he had heard right the last two words spoken at him.

"Who are you?" the kid asked him again, touching Jon's plain white T-shirt.

Jon stood straight again. His headache eased as fast as it came, and for some reason, he understood what the kids around him were saying.

"Leave the stranger alone," a voice behind Jon said. It was a tall man wearing a grey cloak. He had light brown skin, round eyes, and grey hair reaching to his shoulders.

Gandalf, I presume? A voice in Jon's head said.

"That's quite all right," Jon said, out loud this time. "I am new to this town. I have travelled from ... beyond the water ..." He hoped the explanation would let him escape the excessive attention. To his surprise, in his mind he thought he spoke his own language, but when words came out of his mouth, they sounded alien.

"Did you hear, Dad?" one of the kids said, looking at the tall man and pulling at his cloak. "He is from beyond the water."

"He's kidding Kentho, no-one lives beyond the water," the man said, but gave Jon a curious look. "He must have travelled from one of the cities further inland. My name is Bartho Vinth, and this is my son Kentho, and these are his friends."

Jon was about to answer when a loud horn sound echoed somewhere from the mountains. All the kids except Kentho ran away and disappeared into the crowd. People around them calmly collected their belongings and disappeared into the flat structures made of stones. The structures, Jon just realised, were the housing rooftops he saw from above.

"What is happening?" he asked of Bartho, father of the small boy.

"It's Azons. They are early. We better go. This way," said Bartho, and he grabbed his son's hand, leading him and Jon past a few houses before stopping at the third one. He then turned against the stone wall and pushed a round, slightly extending stone. The round stone moved into the wall, and to Jon's surprise, a door-sized piece of stone moved aside with a grinding.

"Welcome to our home, Mister ..." Bartho waited for Jon to answer.

"Jon. My name is Jon Peterson."

"You are welcome, Jon from far, son of Peter. You can wait here until Azons have passed." Bartho said and smiled at Jon.

"Just call me Jon, and I still don't know what these Esons are," Jon said.

"Azons," Kentho corrected him, laughing. "They are from the depths." He moved his hands above his head and made a scary face.

"Okay, not creepy at all," said Jon quietly to himself. "And how old are you, Kentho?" he asked out loud.

"I am eight bursts and four skyless," Kentho said proudly.

"Of course you are." Jon nodded and estimated Kentho to be about twelve years old.

"So, Jon ..." Bartho approached Jon. "I can tell from your clothing and surprised looks about Azons, that you are not from here, nor really far from here." Bartho offered Jon a seat at the table in a room reminding Jon of a dining room.

"No, I am not," Jon said and sat down as they continued their conversation. "And I have never heard of Azons. I am also not yet quite aware of how I got here either." Jon realised he had told a bit more than he intended and studied Bartho's reaction to this.

"I appreciate your honesty," Bartho said, looking at Jon without judgement. "I believe you came here by using the Altar?"

"The Altar?" Kentho shouted. "I knew it was real!"

He placed mugs in front of his father and Jon. The last one he carried with him as he climbed on to a chair next to his father, staying up on his knees to be closer to Jon.

"This planet is called New Thatho," Bartho said, "so the Altar is real?"

"If you mean that Black Table on the top of the mountain, then yes," said Jon, impressed by Bartho's awareness.

Bartho took a deep breath and leaned backwards, feeling relief his suspicions had finally been proven right.

"The legend goes" – he leaned back on the table – "that our people also came here a long, long time ago from our home planet Thatho, by using the Altar, or Black Table as you called it. But most of our people believe they are merely stories. My family is the only one left still believing we could one day get back to our original home planet. And now seeing you, I think our home planet really exists somewhere. On the Altar itself, there are only some holes and that weird print on it. We don't know how to power or operate it. We do have old literature about markings, but nothing to connect them with. Literature also has information about our original home planet, but without the location or means to get there. We used to be a technologically advanced people, but we believe Azons are preventing us from exploring and using any technology. So, most of our achievements are forgotten among my people and turned into legends. Even the technology we have has begun to wear out with malfunctions, and we no longer have the knowledge of how to fix them."

"You *really* came through the Altar?" Kentho stared at Jon, his mind racing through all the scenarios he and his friend had come up with. "But it is nothing but a piece of stone, surrounded by rubble."

"How many times have I told you not to play there with your friends." Bartho gave Kentho a judgmental look. "What if Azons come? You would not make it back home in time."

"But they never reach up there."

"Not the point, and you know it ..." Bartho gave Kentho a serious look. "And exactly how would you know that they cannot reach up there?"

"I know, because the rocks and steps change colour just before the second platform," Kentho argued.

Jon felt a sensation of relief knowing Gus was safe. Bartho looked at Kentho and then back to Jon.

"He has always been smart, much smarter than his friends," Bartho said, and put his hand on Kentho's head, ruffling his hair. "I am very proud of him. His mother would be proud of him as well." He now looked a bit sad. "She was taken from us almost three bursts ago by Azons, while she hunted at night in the forest. We believe she went too far and didn't make it back home in time. Azons don't usually come out at night. We miss her a lot."

"I am so sorry. I can't even imagine how you feel." Jon put his hand on Bartho's shoulder and paused before continuing. "Can you tell me more about these Azons?"

Gus had unpacked all the contents of his black fabric satchel onto the rocky mountain ground next to Black Table. He had gone over every inch of the table with his hands, feeling every little crack and opening, hoping to find access to the table's secrets. After a thorough search, he gave up. Standing frustrated next to Black Table, he dusted off his knees and wiped sweat away from his forehead.

"Anyway, the whole thing is useless without these crystals," he said out loud and sat down on the ground against the table, holding one of the crystals.

Then, while holding one of the crystals, he pulled down a cable he'd left hanging over the edge of Black Table. He sat in quiet contemplation, looking into distance, while his brain processed the small clue he thought he might have. Refocussing his gaze from the distance, he noticed himself tapping the crystal in his left hand with the cable end in his right. Notions in his brain slowly locked in place. He jumped up and laid all three crystals on the table next to his series of cables, studying the crystals in more detail, sliding fingers all around them.

"YES!" he shouted out, victorious as one of the crystals opened at its top end as he bent it.

The connection was seamless and invisible to the naked eye, but it was there. The end of the crystal came off fully, revealing dozens of tiny red crystal endings. He picked up the second crystal, and it opened the same way as the first one. So did the third. Gus felt relief and hope.

"Now, we are getting somewhere." He smiled and picked up a cable he thought would be the best suited for a home-made connection.

Just before he was about to break the cable ending into parts, a loud horn-like sound echoed behind him in the green valley. Gus dropped all the items from his hands onto the table and walked to the platform edge, calling out for his friend.

"Jon!" he shouted but received no answer. "Jon!" He waited, but still no answer. "Where did you go?" Gus said quietly to himself, when another loud sound of a horn echoed in the green valley. "What the hell is that?" he muttered and heard muffled rumbling in distance.

The sound came from somewhere in the mountain string, between the valley and the water. That's when Gus saw it. A massive ball of water appeared from through a mountain pass.

"That's not possible ..." Gus could not believe what he was seeing.

It was an actual ball of water, just like tiny ones lying on a leaf in the mornings. This drop was just like them, almost perfectly round, but about a hundred-metres wide and high. From its path, flocks of birds escaped from trees and flew higher, before landing again back onto soaking wet green trees. It looked like the ball of water pressed itself against the ground, making a small portion of its bottom flat, but kept itself otherwise round. The water moved on top of the ground like someone was guiding it. When Gus struggled to understand what he was seeing, two more came through the mountain pass further away. This made Gus drop down on his stomach and crawl to edge of the platform for a better view without being seen. His heart was pounding.

The first ball of water moved in a straight line, and came to a sudden stop, while the other two passed it and started to make a zigzag pattern, trying to cover every inch on the forest below him. Gus took out his mobile phone and started recording. "Definitely not Vancouver," he said, not sure if he should feel fear or excitement. But clearly, his curiosity and science fiction mind replaced any fear he might have had.

Bartho leaned back in his chair and took a deep breath before saying, "The old legend tells us about a big war between two races dominating this part of the galaxy. One was the race we believe built Altars, and the other ones we believe to be the Azons." Jon and Kentho leaned closer, listening like it would be a bedtime story. "One dominated the surface, and the other the water. Azons were, and still are, the rulers of the water. They are both very, very old. We don't know what they want, but it seems they come on land every now and then to collect food and raw materials."

"What do you mean by collect food?" Jon asked startled, his imagination running wild, but was interrupted by a dampening sound coming from above.

Jon's ears blocked. It felt and sounded like Bartho's house was suddenly submerged in deep water. He recognised the uncomfortable feeling from diving, when ears block during a descent. As an experienced diver, Jon moved his jaw slightly forward and eased the pressure in his ears.

"They are on top of us now," Kentho said looking up. He pinched his nose and pushed air into his nose, unblocking his ears as well.

"They travel in water because they have technology to shape it. They use it to travel and harvest on the ground," Bartho explained.

Jon's wild imagination had returned.

"Are we safe?" he asked.

"We should be." Bartho said, sounding somewhat worried. "Our homes were built to withstand the weight of their water, but those who had stayed outside during Azons' presence are never seen again. That is what happened to Kentho's mother." He looked at Kentho with a smile, but Jon could see there was pain behind that smile. "Usually they stay far away from our village, hunting and collecting raw materials like minerals or organic life like trees and plants."

"So, they are basically fishing on the land," Jon said, expecting Kentho and Bartho to understand. They did not. "Where I come from, we go fishing. We use boats on the water and nets to catch fish and other marine life."

"You have been on water?" Kentho asked in awe.

"Not only on it, but I've also dived in it. That is, being inside the water and breathing air from a tank you carry with you." Kentho's eyes became perfectly round. "We do not have Azons. We do have dangerous creatures in water, but nothing that would endanger us on the land."

Kentho and Bartho were watching each other.

"We did not know such places existed." Bartho looked confused, feeling hopeful and sceptical at the same time. "We do not go beyond the mountains, to the water world. It is strictly forbidden."

"There are very deep waters that are still unknown to us, too deep you see. I assume Azons are not able to come to higher grounds either?" Jon asked.

"Not that we are aware of, no. These are the highest grounds we have seen their presence at," Bartho said, while thinking something hard. "Some of us, who still think that Altar was used for travelling, believe it is placed so high for a reason, so that Azons cannot reach it." He paused. "But how were you able to use it, I would like to know." He took a sip of water from his hazy glass mug.

"We found a Black Table just like yours on our planet, and nearby we found shattered pieces of glass or crystals, and a power source that made it work," Jon said, realising he was giving out information about him not travelling alone.

"We?" Kentho asked curiously.

"Yes, I came with my friend Gus," Jon said, realising it was too late to change his story. "He is up there right now, I hope, trying to figure out more about the table."

Suddenly the dampened sound moved on.

"I guess we are off the hook?" Jon laughed. Kentho and Bartho stared at him curiously, clearly not understanding his comment. This made Jon to scratch his neck and continue, "I will explain later."

"Amazing ..." Gus lay on the ground at the platform edge and was filming the massive balls of water moving and stopping randomly. "I hope you are okay," he said, thinking of Jon.

He got up slowly, brushed the dust off his dark blue jeans and walked back to Black Table. "You and I have some unfinished business," he said and cracked his fingers by interlacing them and then bending his hands outwards. A series of bone cracking sounds followed his movement. He then took the cable he had carefully selected earlier and cut it open at one end with Jon's MacGyver knife.

"Sorry dude, you are meant for greater things," he said when the cable's end snapped off with a clean cut.

Several smaller wires were packed tight together inside, which he peeled open, removing the insulation to expose thin metallic wires. He connected them to the small red crystal filaments found inside the main crystals by jamming the wires between the red endings and the main crystal filling, that reminded him of hardened glue. Once done, he opened software on his tablet, connected a standard cable ending with data pins to his tablet and placed the crystals in their places one by one. As he expected, the software on his tablet started displaying data.

"Now, we need to know what the heck you are talking about," he said to himself and started to write a program for alien data decryption.

Jon, Kentho and Bartho opened the thick stone door and stepped out. The air was like being in a Turkish steam room. The sun vaporised the heavy moisture rapidly, and soon the air smelled like a freshly watered forest again. This reminded Jon of his time in the army. Walking in a leafy wet forest made him always feel like he is a part of a bigger organism, Earth.

More people appeared out from the stone structures and life in the village returned to normal as if nothing had happened.

"Thank you for your help," said Jon, "but I need to head back up to see if my friend is fine."

Jon looked up towards the mountain.

"If you don't mind, we would like to go with you," said Bartho. "I am extremely interested to see how you made the Altar work."

"That's fine with me," Jon answered.

Together, they headed out from the town towards the mountain. Before they reached the steps, Kentho had taken the lead, proudly showing the way for Jon. They climbed until they reached the platform halfway. Before reaching the platform, Kentho pointed out how the colour changed on the mountain wall from Azons' water. Bartho shook his head and gave another mini speech to his son about how irresponsible it was for him to wander around the mountain. Jon used the opportunity to look for his satchel, relieved to find it where he left it.

"This way," he called to his new friends and continued upwards, Kentho and Bartho at his heels.

After an exhausting one-hour climb, they reached the platform at the top where Gus still worked with Black Table. He was looking at his tablet, removing a crystal, changing wire locations and looking at his tablet again.

"Gus!" Jon called out to him, happy to see he was okay.

Gus was so concentrated on his work he almost dropped his tablet on hearing Jon's voice. He spun around to see where the voice came from.

"Jon, so good to see you! I was a bit worried …" He put down his work and walked towards Jon.

Before reaching Jon, he came to a sudden stop when Kentho and Bartho appeared on the platform behind Jon.

"Whoa!" Gus blurted out, shocked to see people other than Jon.

"Sek Bartho ken, k'ethe vass so Kentho," Bartho said, causing Gus to experience a piercing headache. "What did I do?" Bartho looked at Jon and took a step back, looking confused and startled.

"He must be feeling the same thing I did when I met you," Jon said in the local language and ran to Gus's aid to hold his head with his hands. Gus screamed from the painful jolt piercing his head. Having experienced the same earlier,

Jon helped Gus to keep his balance until the pain receded. And as fast as the jolt came, Gus felt better again.

"What the hell was that?" Gus cried out, blinking his eyes, as if he was inserting contact lenses and trying to make them align with his irises.

"I don't know," Jon answered, still holding Gus, "but it seems, whatever that table did to us, we now can understand the locals."

Gus looked at Jon sceptically, only to see Jon as astounded as himself.

Jon nodded approvingly at Bartho, letting him know it was all okay again.

"I am Bartho, and this is my son Kentho," Bartho said again, unsure what to expect this time.

But this time, Gus understood every word.

"Nice to meet you," Gus said in the alien language, which sounded like his own. He offered his hand and Kentho jumped in front of his father, shaking Gus's hand vigorously.

"What is that?" asked Kentho with awe, pointing at Gus's T-shirt.

Gus wore a retro, faded black *Star Wars* T-shirt depicting Luke Skywalker holding a lightsaber above his head, while behind him a huge head of Darth Vader loomed. Gus had no-idea what to answer, so instead, he changed the subject.

"Jon, did you see those water ... things?" Gus asked. Kentho still shaking his hand. "I caught them on my phone."

"I didn't, but we heard and felt them," Jon replied.

After completing introductions, Gus led them all towards the Black Table. Jon stared at the video Gus had recorded on his phone. While trying to cope with what he was seeing, he reported what he had learned from Bartho and Kentho about these mysterious beings from the water.

"Azons?" Gus said and paused, looking towards the open water, "Incredible."

"Bartho has some insight about Black Table you might be interested in," Jon told Gus, who was still fixated on the water, his mind producing all kinds of creatures Azons could be. "His people used it a long time ago."

"To travel across the galaxy?" Gus asked curiously, looking at Bartho.

"Yes." Bartho sounded happy to have someone else believe in Altars as he did. "A long time ago, our people must have used it to travel from another planet. But how, I do not know. And now, I feel like we are held back by the Azons. We do not want their attention," Bartho explained. "Maybe Kentho's mother was taken because I was asking too many questions about our origins and about the Altar?"

"I understand. Perhaps I can help you with that, if you're interested?" said Gus, feeling sorry for Bartho and his drive for finding answers for the unknown. "I have learned more about it lately, but there are still a lot of questions remaining. For example, why is it allowing travel to certain planets. Also, why is there so short a time window for travelling? And who created these tables? Azons?"

All the questions Gus asked were new to Bartho, except about Azons.

"We do not know. We believe they are made by another race," Bartho explained what he knew, as he did earlier to Jon. "Our stories tell us that they were built by a race that was technologically superior. We think that whoever built them could not fight the Azons' ability to control water. Some of us believe, that for table builders, leaving the planet was their only option in order to survive. And with time, our knowledge of them became a legend, nothing but bedtime stories. Most of our people on this planet do not believe those stories anymore, but if you used it to come here, there must be some truth to it?"

Gus related to Bartho how they discovered the missing pieces that made the table operate, and how they jumped to a strange planet, only to escape a massive creature with a panic jump, finding themselves here, on the mountain top.

Bartho paid attention to every word Gus said. Kentho had climbed on top of the table and sat on the edge, moving his legs back and forth, carefully touching the crystals and wires, unable to hide his curiosity.

"How does it look?" Bartho could not hold back anymore. "The map you mentioned, with the stars."

Gus placed the power source in its dipped place on the Black Table, and a holographic map appeared above the table, partly across Kentho, who got scared and jumped down.

Both Bartho and Kentho stared at the hologram, moving their hands through the map in awe. Sometimes the map moved slightly, sometimes their hands just moved through.

"Unbelievable." Bartho could not believe his eyes. "This has been in front of us the whole time?" He felt both excited and frustrated at the same time.

After a small demonstration of how the table worked, Gus picked up his tablet.

"I managed to tap into the crystals' data flow, and I am now able to read it with my tablet device," he said. "I am already receiving what I believe is data how the table is choosing its available destinations, but there are still too many unknown variables, and new symbols I don't even know how to start translating. I used all the decryption software I have without success, and I am now writing a new one, specifically to analyse these symbols running on my screen." He turned the display towards Bartho.

"Maybe I can help," Bartho said, concentrating on specific symbols on Gus's tablet. "I have seen those symbols before. We have very old books that could explain some things." He looked at Gus, who now in turn looked curious. "Maybe we could head back to our home and investigate further?"

"Most definitely." Gus celebrated.

He removed the power source and crystals. One by one he placed them carefully into his satchel. A few minutes later all four were heading down the steps, leading back to the village.

On the way down, Jon and Gus debated what those massive balls of water were and what they should be called.

"R.B.O.W," said Gus first.

"A what?" Jon asked.

"Rolling Ball Of Water." Gus explained like it would be obvious.

"Okay, I can play this game as well," said Jon. "How about L.A.C.O.Ws?"

"Los Angeles cows?" Gus commented laughing.

"No dumb-ass, it stands for Large Amount Concentration Of Water," Jon snapped back.

"Okay," Gus kept laughing. "How about just a BOW?" he said without a laugh this time. "Just for Ball Of Water?"

"I like it. BOW it is," Jon said, and they fist bumped.

CHAPTER 6

ESCAPE

Back at the village, Jon and Gus stayed close to their new friends, trying to avoid any unnecessary attention. Just in time, Jon warned Gus about the following flowers. Gus took out his phone to take a video of them as well, but Kentho whispered to him to keep his phone hidden. When they arrived at the habitat where Bartho and Kentho lived, Bartho pushed in the round stone next to their entrance. The door moved aside, and they all stepped in.

"We better stay inside for the night," Bartho said and closed the door with a similar round stone placed inside next to the door. "Please, make yourself comfortable. I will find the books I told you about."

Jon sat down on a comfortable armchair made of wood and re-watched the video Gus had recorded. He watched it again and again and was amazed every single time. Meanwhile, Gus emptied the contents of his satchel onto the dining table. Kentho climbed on a chair, kneeling on it while reaching over the table and curiously inspecting each item before laying it back on the table.

"You really are from another world," he said, looking at Gus and the items on the table.

"We are, and now we need to know how we get back," Gus said while opening his tablet and laying crystals one by one on the table. "These are what makes the table work, and I am trying to understand how," he explained to Kentho, who listened intently.

After several minutes, Bartho approached the dining table and dropped three heavy looking dusty books on the table, making all the other items on the table jump a little.

"These should tell us more," he said and opened the book on top of the pile. Gus leaned in, but it was mainly gibberish to him. For Bartho, it was his people's old language mixed with the alien symbols that had appeared on the table.

"But you were right," Gus said, "these" – he pointed – "are same, or at least very similar to the symbols on my table." Gus switched on his tablet and moved it closer while Bartho slowly turned pages, revealing hand drawn symbols and pictures with old language descriptions next to them. Gus felt like they had just found Indiana Jones' notebook, filled with secrets.

Time went by fast and night fell. Jon had fallen asleep in the armchair he had slumped into on their arrival. His arms were crossed over his chest with his hands tucked under his armpits, locking himself into a sitting sleeping position. His head hung down and made small twitches as he dreamed them escaping the creature from the first planet they visited. At the dining table, Gus and Bartho made notes together on pieces of paper Kentho had brought them from his private stash. He and his friends used pieces of paper to send messages to each other. Kentho had come up with a secret language to keep adults unaware of their plans to meet in the forest or at the Altar, which was strictly forbidden.

"Here," said Bartho, excited for some progress.

He lay open one of the smaller books with thick leather binding. The open page had the crystal with the round ending sketched on it, surrounded with text on both sides.

"Jackpot!" shouted Gus. It was such an Indiana Jones moment he could even hear the theme music playing in his head.

"According to this," Bartho read slowly, with his index finger moving under the text following his progress. "Each crystal, as you call them, has different information stored in them, and together, they create a map of our galaxy." Bartho flipped the page.

The open section had the remaining crystals drawn on them, the triangle one on the left, and the square one on the right. There was no additional text around them. On the next page, there was the power source sphere drawn with text around it, just like with the crystal. The theme song in Gus's head went up a notch.

"This fourth object, the sphere, is providing energy to operate the … Blato …" Bartho looked at Gus and Kentho, who were leaning in to see the picture. "I assume they used Blato for what you call Black Table?"

Gus nodded in agreement. Bartho continued reading, mumbling to himself. For a second he seemed confused, he turned back to the page with the first crystals moving his finger along the text before jumping back to the page with the power source. He mumbled and then nodded.

"Without the sphere, the Black Table will not operate. The sphere's energy allows Black Table" – he looked at Gus

– "to connect to other Black Tables on other planets and then creates an updated map with the crystals."

Bartho continued reading, mumbling then repeating out loud. As he read ahead, Gus updated his algorithms to match with new information.

"I believe I know now how it works, or at least how to operate the table," Gus said and begun explaining it to Bartho and a very sleepy Kentho, who refused to go to sleep, even after several requests by his father.

"So," Gus explained, "with crystals in place the table's map service is activated. With the sphere, Black Table connects to its vast network of other Black Tables and allows us to see which planets are coming available for instant travel. Then we travel through space, for example, to this planet. The alien symbols next to the planets on the map are counters, and they count the time when each planet becomes available for travel. When the counter hits zero, there is a short period when the trip can be made, after which the counter starts all over again with a new value, depending on how far the planet is from us. Does it make sense?" Gus asked. Both Bartho and Kentho nodded back. "But why are there only few planets available for travel instead of all of them? I feel like we are missing something, something important." He paused, trying to understand what they had missed. "Maybe Black Table creates a wormhole which means by our knowledge, that space is bent to bring two points next to each other, bringing the actual travel distance down to zero. Instead of travelling millions of light years, you just step through, in theory," Gus explained, Kentho and Bartho still listening intently. "But that requires an extreme amount of energy. No-way this small sphere can do that." Gus was sure that some crucial information still eluded him, he could feel it.

"Just give me more time and I will try to make a program allowing us to see this map of wormholes, and just maybe, I can create a map to eventually get us home." Gus now sunk back to work on his tablet.

"Time to sleep, Kentho," commanded Bartho firmly.

Kentho frowned and then yawned. He dismounted from the chair and to Gus's surprise, Kentho came over to him and gave brief hug before disappearing further into the home.

"You have an amazing son," Gus said, touched by the gesture made by Kentho.

"I know," said Bartho, and gave a tired smile. "You may sleep wherever you find a place. Have clear dreams." He smiled softly and turned away to follow Kentho.

"You too, clear dreams," responded Gus. "Clear dreams, I like that," he repeated to himself quietly and sat down to finish his coding before starting simulation for his mapping tool.

Almost eight hours later, Jon woke up in the armchair. He turned his head slowly, confused before finally remembering his whereabouts. He stood up and stretched his arms upwards with a yawn. Still slightly disoriented, he saw Gus sleeping against the dining table, still sitting, his arms and head lying on the table, his tablet running simulations in front of him. Jon approached Gus, unable to see Kentho or Bartho he thought they must still be sleeping.

Gus's tablet suddenly sounded an alert with a repeating fast paced *ding* and green text flashed on the screen, Simulation COMPLETE. Gus inhaled loudly and lifted his head as if he were coming to the surface after a long free dive underwater.

"Beware of the Chinese stamps!" he shouted, his eyes still closed and drool flying from the corner of his mouth.

Jon placed his hand over his mouth to prevent himself from laughing, and whispered, "I am, I am," prolonging Gus's half-awake dreaming.

Jon pressed his hand heavily on Gus's shoulder, who opened his eyes and looked around in panic before realising where he was.

"That was a pretty intense dream," he said with a yawn, still disoriented. "A clear dream, as Bartho put it."

"I bet. You shouted out something about Chinese stamps," said Jon. "Were you working in the Chinese post office?"

Gus looked at Jon like a person gone crazy.

"Now that doesn't make any sense," Gus said, and realised his tablet was still alerting him about the completed simulation. "Oh, finally! Jon, look." He took the tablet into his hands and showed it to Jon. "I ran the data we know, against the crystal data, and used it in simulations for symbols matching different scenarios. It is supposed to give us an idea what the symbols mean."

"So, you can take us home? Great," Jon said casually, obviously not caring or understanding the complexity of work Gus had just done.

"You are unbelievable," Gus said and began to explain. "It seems there are certain amounts of what we currently comprehend as wormholes, to connect planets with Black Tables. This means, that the map is changing constantly because planets are in constant movement, just like Dr Wells explained in Portland."

While Jon struggled with the information, Kentho and Bartho walked into the room looking fresh and rested.

"Fresh day to you," said Bartho, and then instructed Kentho to collect something for them to eat.

"Good morning," Gus and Jon said in unison.

Jon rushed to help Kentho with setting edible items on the table. Gus also stood up but took a large empty bowl from the kitchen counter instead and poured water into it from a wooden pitcher. He looked around the kitchen and found a few little jars containing something similar to dried peas. He poured the floating peas into a bowl and started stirring it until the peas moved in circles. Once ready, he carried it to the middle of the dining table.

"All of you, please come here," he said, unable to resist the urge inside him any longer. "Now, imagine this bowl filled with water is our galaxy, which we call Milky Way. Now, those peas are planets and stars in our galaxy. In reality there would be much more of them, but you get the idea." He paused, looking at his audience.

Everyone nodded, following what he was saying.

"Let's say that Black Table is connected at the moment to ten planets, here, here and around here." Gus pointed out selected peas and looked again at his nodding audience.

He placed his finger in the bowl again and stirred until all the peas were moving in circles on their own.

"Now, because these peas are moving around, their previous locations are replaced with new planets all the time. This means that to be able to go to planet 'A', we need to know where planet 'A' will be later. We have to do a kind of planet hopping to reach that planet, jumping first to planet 'E', and from there to planet 'B', then to 'C', and finally from there to planet 'A.'" Gus smiled, pointing at a different pea for each letter. "These combinations change all the time due to the constant movement of our galaxy. My algorithm that just finished, is making a kind of hopping-map for us, showing what combination of planets would take us home. The closest path to Earth right now is only four planets away," Gus said, and studied his tablet again while the others looked at each other in some confusion. "Although, there is still something odd about this, perhaps another parameter I'm are not seeing." He tapped his tablet a few times and a counter appeared on screen.

"You solved the symbols?" Kentho shouted excitedly while placing the final breakfast items on the table.

"Please, eat," Bartho said, and sat down next to Gus.

"Yes, Kentho, I did," Gus answered, "and if this is correct, the route to our home starts in two hours and ten minutes. If we miss it, I will need to run a new simulation to find a new route home. That would mean completely different planet combinations to hop through."

The table had been filled with baskets of with dark bread, spiky blue fist-sized fruits, dark red small cubes, pitch-black berries, and white round flat discs.

Completely unaware what was what, Jon and Gus followed what Kentho and Bartho were doing. Following their lead, Gus and Jon mixed all items into a small bowl in front of them and ate by hand, picking one piece at the time.

"Amazing," said Gus, after tasting the pitch-black berries and quickly adding more of them to his bowl. "Tastes like liquorice. I love it!"

"Oh my God," Jon said munching a white disc. "These can't be healthy. Way too good tasting."

Gus picked up a spiky blue fruit and took a large bite. His eyes began blinking rapidly. Not to offend their hosts, he tried not to spit out the piece in his mouth. Once he was able to swallow it, he searched for water to flush down the bitter and sour taste in his mouth.

"Help ..." he cried out as tears rolled down his cheeks. "Taste that Jon, it must be *really* healthy."

Kentho and Bartho laughed so hard they had to stop eating. Jon and Gus joined in the laughter. Breakfast continued with more exciting tastings and more laughter. Even though they had just met, Jon and Gus felt like they belonged.

"At least now we have a plan," Jon said, once his mouth was empty. "Let's finish breakfast and head out as soon as possible."

Once they'd finished the long and filling breakfast, Kentho helped make some snacks and re-filled both Gus's and Jon's water bottles. While packing, both Jon and Gus asked if they could get more black berries and white discs from them.

As soon as Gus and Jon had their satchels fully packed, Bartho opened the main door and they stepped outside. The familiar fresh forest smell filled the air and people walked the streets in sunlight.

"Take it all in, Gus," said Jon, inhaling the fresh air and watching people going on with their lives.

When Bartho closed the door behind them, a loud horn sound echoed in the air.

"A BOW on the way?" Gus asked, proud of his alternative name for Ball Of Water. "It's something I came up with for Azons method of transportation." But he did not receive the attention he was expecting for his insight.

"That's odd, they rarely come at his time of the day," said Bartho, confused, fully ignoring Gus's words.

People on the streets also seemed confused. Another horn sound, this time much louder and higher in tone, blasted in the air. Bartho grabbed Kentho's hand and turned back to their house.

"They are coming fast," said Bartho. "The second tone is for emergencies."

"Can me and Jon make it back to the table?" asked Jon, surprised how the peaceful morning had turned into chaos in mere seconds.

"No. They would catch you before the first platform. We all better go back inside," Bartho said and opened the door to get them all back inside. "Hurry!"

While people on the streets ran back to their own habitats, Bartho let Kentho first and then Jon and Gus back into his home.

"We must wait it out before heading out again," Bartho said, and closed the door as soon as everyone was safely back inside. He secured the door by sticking a small wooden beam into a hole, preventing the door from moving sideways.

This time, and much faster than last time, a familiar dampening sound surrounded them from above. Azons had arrived and were now above the village.

"Who wants more breakfast?" asked Kentho, and continued by answering for himself, "I do," when no-one else said anything. He headed to the kitchen and pulled out a jar from an upper shelf.

The jar slipped from his hands and dropped on the floor, making a loud rumble as the jar bounced a few times before breaking into pieces.

"Oops," he said casually, and knelt down on the floor to pick up the pieces.

That's when an ear-piercing voice blasted above them. It was something no-one in the village had heard before, "uuuuummmmm ... da-da-da-da-da-da-da ..."

The cabinets and the table inside Bartho's home vibrated. The first part of the voice; *uuuuummmmmm* ... was so low, Jon and Gus thought they were inside of a giant subwoofer. The second part of the voice; *da-da-da-da-da-da-d* ... began low, but the tone rose up on every syllable, slowing down towards the end, like filling a tall glass with a drink. Then nothing but silence. Jon and Gus could feel their hearts beating through their chests. Gus realised he was holding his breath before he exhaled loudly. Everyone turned to look at him.

"What?" he whispered.

The loud voice repeated, sounding exactly like at the first time. Everyone stood frozen. They were no longer looking at Gus but looking up instead.

"What the hell is that?" asked Jon, whispering.

"I don't know," said Kentho. "We have never heard them speak before."

The voice blasted now for the third time, this time followed by a loud bang on Bartho's front door made of solid rock. The same door they just came in from.

"They know about us," Gus said, and everyone turned to look at him again. "I don't know how, but they know about us. About me and Jon, I mean." He paused. "Or at least they know we have a power source here." He pushed his hand into his satchel on his shoulder and felt the content. "The power source is warm, so it must radiate some frequency Azons can detect."

"Okay ..." said Jon. "Who wants to meet an Azon?" He raised his hand sarcastically. Everyone stared at him like he had lost his mind. "Nobody?" He dropped his hand.

"The tunnels," Kentho said, and pulled his father's sleeve. "The old tunnels under the house."

The voice blasted again from above, followed by another hit on the door. A small crack appeared across the door.

"Kentho is right," Bartho said. "They built these houses on top of an ancient mining site. That is where all these building stones came from. This way!" he shouted and led everyone to the dining table. "Jon, take the other end."

Bartho and Jon lifted the dining table aside and Kentho pulled away the rug lying underneath it, revealing a hatch with a handle on the floor. Kentho pulled the handle, but the hatch was too heavy for him.

"Together," Jon said, smiling at Kentho.

He and Kentho pulled it together. The hatch sprung open and fell down on the other side of its hinges. "Go. Go. Go!" Jon shouted.

One by one, they climbed down the ladder attached to the bottom of the frame. The climb was not long, only a few metres. Jon, who entered last, pulled a piece of rope attached to the hatch and closed it with a loud bang. Azons' voice still blasted from above them, but not as loud as before. Gus and Jon switched on their mobile phone torches, illuminating an earth smelling narrow tunnel heading left and right. The tunnel had no working lights. The ceiling had wooden support frames every ten metres, keeping the ceiling from collapsing. On the ground, two iron rails, only half a metre apart, run through on the ground in both directions.

"This way," said Bartho and headed into the tunnel on their left, leading towards the mountain.

They had just started walking in line, Bartho first and Jon last, when an explosion blasted behind them. Azons had made it through the door into Bartho's home. The sound of rushing water followed the blast. The hatch from the house to the tunnels was not waterproof and leaked water rapidly.

Bartho, holding Gus's light in front of him, ran at full speed followed by Gus, Kentho, and finally Jon, shining a light for Kentho and Gus. The tunnel ahead of them began ascending, and after a hundred metres, they arrived at a small opening that looked like a man-made cave. Near the cave entrance stood several broken wooden carts, used for pushing stones on the narrow rails. In the middle of the cave stood a wooden structure no bigger than two metres by two metres, and four metres high, with ropes going up from its roof structure. Above the structure, an opening continued as high as they could see with their lights.

"It's a large dumbwaiter, or an elevator," Gus said excitedly. "Everyone, get inside."

The wooden structure of the simple elevator crunched and creaked as it took their weight.

"I hope this won't come apart while we're in it," said Jon.

Once they were all in, Gus pulled a wooden lever on the side of the elevator expecting them to ascend. Above them, old wooden beams creaked, but nothing happened.

"Something is being blocked up there," Gus said, trying to get a better view upwards with his mobile's torch. "The ropes cannot move. Something is preventing the counterweights from coming down."

"I got it," said Jon, stepping out from the wooden elevator. "But I will need some help."

"I'll go," Kentho instantly said, and went after Jon.

"Kentho, no!" Bartho shouted and grabbed Kentho by his sleeve at the last second.

"Do not worry dad. I do this kind of stuff almost daily with my friends," Kentho said, with no concern in his voice.

"Fine. But be careful. You are the only Kentho I have left."

"Very funny dad," Kentho replied, and run after Jon.

Near the elevator, Jon and Kentho found several empty wooden crates lying around. Some broken, but some still in decent shape. Jon picked up several crates and piled them like a house of blocks. After they'd piled up six crates, they could climb onto a small wooden platform erected from the wall about four metres from ground level. On the wooden platform, a thick support beam had fallen off from somewhere higher and was now lying across the platform and over the ropes of the elevator, snagging them. Jon studied the two-metre gap between the wooden platform and the elevator ropes. He shook the support beam, trying to release the ropes, but they were too tangled to let go. The ropes were too far to reach, and when he stepped on the beam, it instantly tilted downwards from his weight.

"I'm too heavy for it," said Jon. "Kentho, can you get there and untangle the ropes? I will stand here as counterweight," he said and stepped onto the beam on the platform end.

"I will try."

Kentho began walking carefully along the beam, his arms spread wide on both sides to give him more balance.

A loud explosion echoed in the tunnel, followed by the sound of water rushing.

"They are in the tunnels!" Gus shouted from below.

A loud unrecognisable voice shook the beam, causing Kentho to lose his footing. He fell on his side along the beam, hitting his head hard on the edge. Before falling over the edge, he grabbed the beam in the last second with his right hand. Jon felt helpless, he could do nothing but watch. If he stepped off the beam, Kentho and the beam would crash down on the elevator roof. If he approached to help Kentho, the same thing would happen. He was out of options.

"Kentho!" his father shouted, terrified at seeing Kentho's shoes waving in the light of Gus's mobile torch.

"I'm okay!" Kentho shouted back, swinging from the beam, though warm blood ran down his cheek. Kentho used the momentum from his fall and swung himself to get a hold of the beam with his other hand. He was successful and now hung from the beam with both hands. Showing no panic, he swung his lower body and threw his right leg around the beam. Without an effort, he climbed back onto the beam, resting on it for a second like a black jaguar rests in a tree branch on a tropical day. Below him, Bartho and Gus stood in ankle deep water. The familiar but scary voice echoed from the tunnel, "uuuuummmmm ... da-da-da-da-da-da-da ..."

"I don't want to hurry you, but soon we'll be Azons' breakfast!" Gus shouted, trying to climb higher on the wall inside the elevator to keep the rising water level below him.

Kentho continued crouching forward on his knees and reached the end of the beam. He worked on the rope that ran around the beam. It didn't take him long, only a few seconds, to set the rope free.

"Got it!" Kentho shouted, when the beam gave a loud crack and snapped in half.

Feeling sudden weightlessness, Kentho took hold of the rope in front of him with both hands and stayed hanging in the air. The beam fell, landing on the elevator roof with a loud bang.

"Jesus!" Gus shouted, holding his hands above his head in protection. "Kentho?" He turned his light back upwards.

"I'm fine!" Kentho shouted and slid down the rope, landing softly on the elevator roof on his knees.

While he tried to get back up, his hand stumbled upon something with a different texture than all the wood and rope around him. He slid his hand over the dusty roof and pulled out an old leather-covered book. Without thinking further, he jammed the book into the back of his pants and got up.

"Stay there and I will help you," Jon said to Kentho, who calmly nodded back.

Jon climbed back down the wooden crates. When at the bottom, Jon placed one of the crates against the elevator. Kentho shimmied partway off the roof and Jon gently grabbed him around his waist and lowered him onto the crate. With no time to waste, they joined the others inside the flooding elevator. Gus pulled the lever again, this time the action was followed by a loud creaking sound. The ropes above them tightened, and the elevator jerked upwards. The water inside the elevator quickly drained away through cracks in the floor and walls. Slowly speeding up, the old elevator ascended, leaving the tunnels and the rising water behind them.

After several minutes' ascent, the elevator came to a stop. Another compact house-sized cave opened up in front of them. They stepped out from the old creaking elevator, which made a series of splintering sounds as pieces of wood broke away the structure.

"That was close," said Bartho, trying to see where the pieces fell, but they vanished into the black abyss before landing with a splash in the water below. Gus and Jon shone their lights around them. There were no tunnels, hatches or ladders leading out of the cave, only a door-sized rock blocking an opening to the outside – they could see slivers of sunlight through fine gaps between the stone and the mountain wall.

"Time for MacGyver again?" Jon said as he looked around.

"Who is MacGyver?" asked Kentho.

"He is a hero and a genius. You will learn all about him, I promise."

For several minutes Jon explained to Kentho who MacGyver was, and how he solved problems with whatever items he had available.

"For example," Jon said, "MacGyver would come up with a plan after seeing those ropes hanging from the cave roof near the exit ..." Everyone waited for what MacGyver would do next. "He would then use those ropes to tie up the beam that fell on the elevator" – Jon looked around – "and use it to punch his way through." He pointed towards the broken support beam on the elevator's roof and then the ropes near the exit.

"A battering ram?" asked Gus. "That could work."

Jon and Bartho pulled down the support beam from the elevator roof and carried it next to the exit. Together, they all lifted the beam with Kentho sitting on it so he could secure it with the ropes. When the beam securely hung in the air, Kentho jumped down. They swung the beam back and forth until it hit the rock that was blocking their exit. It took several swings, but finally the rock yielded. First it cracked in half and then with another powerful swing, the upper portion broke away and dropped to the ground. Bright light burst in, forcing all to shield their eyes.

"I love this MacGyver person." Kentho said, while Gus and Jon fist bumped.

One by one, they climbed through the opening and found themselves on the lower platform of the path between the table and the village. The same platform where Jon had hidden his satchel earlier.

"We made it," said Jon, relieved. "Now let me see that cut."

He knelt in front of Kentho and inspected his wound from the fall against the support beam. The cut reached all the way from Kentho's upper temple, down to his jaw. Even though there were no major veins, the amount of blood surprised Jon. He tried to hide his reaction by talking to Kentho, "That's a nasty one," he said, "but it will be okay."

Jon dug into his satchel and pulled out a pack of tissues and a small emergency kit he always carried with. He wiped the blood away with some tissues and then used antiseptic wipes from his kit to clean the wound. Kentho flinched at the sharp stinging sensation they caused. Jon switched for a new dry tissue and asked Kentho to hold it in place while he chose eight butterfly bandages from the kit which he used along the length of the gash, evenly spacing them to hold the wound closed. To Jon's relief, the bandages held the wound together.

"It really requires stitches, but these will do for now," he said.

To protect the wound from infection, he used the two largest rectangular Band-Aids in the kit, covering almost the whole side of Kentho's face.

"That was brave of you," Jon told Kentho, who smiled proudly for his actions. "You need to keep pressure on it," Jon dug into his satchel. "I might have just the thing." He pulled out his green coffee bean embroidered baseball cap from his workplace.

"Put this on it," Jon said, and adjusted the cap band to fit Kentho's head.

"Perfect," Jon said and squeezed Kentho's shoulders. "You look like an elf from *The Lord of the Rings* movie. An elf with a cap. Very cool."

"I don't know what that means, but I like it," Kentho said, and they fist bumped for the very first time.

Both smiled. They had made a connection.

"I think you all should see this!" Bartho shouted with concern in his voice, looking down from the platform edge towards the village. Others joined him to see a single massive balls of water on the top of Bartho's home. It could only reach as far as Kentho had detailed to them earlier, where the colour changed on the mountain wall. The ball of water held its position only a few metres below them. From close by, it looked like the surface was in constant movement, like there was a strong internal current. But the ball of water stood still, holding its shape.

"I have never seen one from so close before," Bartho said, and in that moment, three more massive water balls appeared in the mountain pass. They were approaching fast. Trees cracked in their path and flocks of birds flew away in panic.

"We should be safe." Bartho said. "They cannot reach up here. Also, people in the village are safe for several hours, as long as they keep their doors shut. They designed our homes to create a pocket of air, even if water is on top of them. But if this lasts much longer, they will eventually run out of air. Also, the tunnels are out of question after we led Azons there."

Three more massive ball of water rolled towards the village, slowing down once they got closer.

"That's odd," Bartho wondered.

"What's odd?" Gus asked, while dropping stones onto the water surface, as if testing how it worked.

The three new balls stopped next to the ball above the houses before moving forwards, merging with the original one.

"That!" Bartho shouted. "Run!" he commanded, as the ball of water below them began growing, reaching higher and higher. The ground vibrating voice filled the air again, "uuuuummmmm ... DA-DA-DA-DA-DA-DA-DA ..."

They all spun around and ran to the steps leading towards the top platform. They could not climb fast, but they were just faster than the rising water below them.

After a half-hour rapid climb, they reached the top, panting for air. Gus was already digging in his satchel for crystals and the power source. When they reached the table, the ball was at the height of the platform. But instead of pouring onto the platform like normal water, it continued building into a larger and larger ball of water. The massive BOW kept growing behind them. Slowly, the BOW was so big, it could keep growing over the platform. By the time BOW's round shape reached the Black Table's dome edge, Gus had already inserted crystals with his cables attached. Jon placed the power unit, bringing everything into life. Gus flipped his tablet cover over and started typing on a screen like one possessed. The BOW was now between them and the dome walls. Kentho, looking backwards, pulled Gus's sleeve. Two figures approached them from within the water.

"Hit it!" Gus shouted, and Jon placed his hand on the large palm print on the table. Familiar electric sound cracked, and turquoise light flashed. They were gone.

CHAPTER 7

U-TURN

Bartho and Kentho were sitting on the soft sandy ground, holding their heads from a piercing headache, just like one Jon and Gus had after their first jump. The Black Table dome created dark shadow inside.

"You'll get used to it," said Jon, kneeling down and offering them some water to drink. "Three more jumps and we will be back on Earth." He stood up and looked around. "Looks like this dome is in much better shape than the previous one."

The dome around them seemed intact. Light and warm air poured in from the entrance, which was identical to the one Gus and Jon had come through in Vancouver. Jon helped Kentho up, and they walked together towards the bright opening. Gus was on the other side of the table, going through his tablet, dying to know what his tablet had recorded during the jump.

Jon, Kentho and Bartho approached the entrance while shielding their eyes from the sun. Outside, crushing heat from a single sun blasted full force on them. The view in all directions was blue sky and dark yellow sand dunes.

"Gus?" shouted Jon. "We have good news and bad news!"

There was no answer. Jon knew Gus was listening, but probably busy with his algorithms.

"The good news is, that there is no water, anywhere." He paused. "And the bad news is, that there is no water, anywhere." He waited for Gus to respond. "There is nothing but sand, everywhere," he continued anyway.

"What the hell?" Gus suddenly yelled back from inside the dome.

All three turned towards the dark dome entrance. It was too dark inside to see what Gus was yelling about.

"I also have good and bad news!" Gus shouted from inside and paused. "The bad news is, that an Azon came through with us." All three outside looked at each other in horror.

"And the good news?" Jon shouted, standing outside with Kentho and Bartho.

"The good news is that not *all* of an Azon came through with us!" shouted Gus in response.

Jon, Kentho and Bartho ran back inside, but stopped before reaching the table. It was too dark to continue. Their eyes adjusted slowly to the darkness as they had for brightness just minutes ago.

"Over here," said Gus, leading them in correct direction with his voice.

As they got closer, the sand under their feet changed from fluffy and light, to wet and heavy. Their eyes begun forming shapes in the dark. The first thing they could see was Black Table on one side, then Gus in front of them near the wall, pointing down to something in front of him. That's when they saw it. It was an arm. An almost two metres long arm. The arm was cut off clean, right under shoulder, and was leaking dark blue blood, which soaked the soft sand around it. The arm itself was muscular, turquoise and the upper side was covered with some kind of thin black armour that was a similar texture as Black Table dome had. But it was an arm, an Azon's arm.

Everyone stood quietly, just staring at the arm for several minutes, until Jon broke the silence.

"You should keep it," Jon said, and poked Gus with his elbow. "Maybe for your science fiction collection? It would look great above the fireplace."

"But I don't have a fireplace," Gus replied, confused.

"Seriously? *That's* your problem?" Jon shook his head and gently kicked the arm. It did not move, even though everyone expected it to come back to life somehow and chase them out of the dome. It did not happen.

"Help me out," Jon said and began dragging the heavy arm closer to opening.

Bartho rushed to help. Jon lifted the heavier part, the ending normally attached to an Azon's shoulder. Bartho lifted from the middle, and two of them carried the arm out to the sunlight and dropped it on the hot sandy ground.

"Oh. My. God," said Gus, kneeling next to the arm.

The palm of the Azonian's arm was exactly like the print on the table.

"Now wait a minute ..." He stood up, and in his usual way, began walking in circles. "I thought the other race made the table, the one ruling the land?" He noticed from the other's looks they had the same assumption.

Bartho studied the arm with Kentho, turning it and touching the turquoise skin.

"It seems, by learning more, we know less," Bartho said and lifted the large palm and turned it from side to side.

"It would now make sense why they were so interested in the power source, and how they knew how to track it," said Gus, scratching his head.

"Maybe," said Kentho, "they never came as high as the Altar, because they couldn't use it without a power source? And they came after us, because they did not have one for themselves," he said to his father, who was already turning pages of one of the ancient books he had taken with them.

"Maybe," Bartho answered, going through pages in the hope to find some evidence about Azons and the Black Table. "Nothing," he said. Frustrated, he closed the book.

"Oh, I almost forgot!" Kentho shouted and pulled out the old leather-bound book from the back of his pants. "I found this on the top of the elevator." He handed it to his father, who started going through its dusty pages.

Jon, Gus and Kentho studied the alien arm more closely. Gus removed a small broken piece from the armour plating. The texture and weight were exactly like the dome material they'd discovered earlier in Vancouver.

"It looks very much like carbon fibre," said Jon, peeking over Gus's shoulder.

"Or something very similar," Gus said and touched the skin of the arm with his index finger. "Weird." He moved his finger across the skin. "Feels like snakeskin, only harder."

"Here, according to this ..." Bartho held the old book Kentho had found. "Black Table builders, those we now assume to be ..." He looked up. "Azons?" The others nodded in agreement. "Created the table network to fight" – he glanced at the book – "Swarm." He paused again and searched the next few pages for any clues about Swarm.

"Swarm? What the hell is Swarm?" Jon broke the silence and looked first at Gus, who lifted his shoulders, still walking in circles. Jon focused his gaze back on Bartho.

"Never heard of them," Bartho said.

"Okay," Gus said, and stopped pacing around. "It was Azons who created and used the Black Table. The race we thought to be the bad ones, turned out to be" – Gus paused and lifted his voice – "the nice ones? Or also bad, we don't know that. All we know is they fought this other mystery, Swarm." Gus looked at others for any correction. "And we know that with the table, you can travel between planets in an instant, but you need three crystals, and a power source. And those four items follow with the table when using it ..." He waited for someone to correct him, but he saw no reactions. "We also know that by using the table, it takes everything within the radius of the dome with it. Hence the arm, as exhibit one." Gus casually kicked the arm on the ground. "What we don't know, is why we all experienced a jolt of pain on our foreheads and inner brain after the first jump."

Jon raised his hand, as if he was back in school.

"Jon?" Gus pointed a finger at him.

"Thank you," Jon begun explaining excitedly. "I have a theory on that one from a course I took during my studies a long time ago. It was about how the human brain receives and processes information. I vividly remember how the language centre is located in the left frontal lobe, here in the forehead area." He pointed at his forehead. "It's the area handling syntax, grammar and sentence structure." Jon was circulating his forehead with his index finger again before continuing. "Then again, creating sentences and comprehending new languages, is located in a place called the Wernicke's area, which is in the left temporal lobe in the middle of our brain." He pointed his left ear with his finger.

"Impressive my friend," Gus said, and offered a fist bump for Jon, who responded right away. "Maybe the table is over stimulating those areas on the first jump and making our brains more receptive to new languages? Opening new pathways and expanding the unused areas in our brains or something? Who knows what could be possible? There are a few more things we need answers for. For example, we still don't know for sure how Black Table jumps work. We also don't know who and what the Swarm is, which even Azons were so afraid of. We have almost six hours to our next jump. I suggest we use that time to learn more about what is going on and to charge the devices under the sun with the solar charger I have with me." Gus concluded and went to pick up his tablet he'd left on Black Table.

"He's right," said Jon. "We are heading forward with enormous risk. Who knows where we might end up with on our next jump, or who might be there? I suggest we learn as much as we can from the books before our next jump. Bartho and Kentho, would you do that, study the books? Meanwhile, Gus," Jon called after Gus, "could you study more about Black Table and the arm without a body? I will scout out our surroundings. Sound good?" Kentho and Bartho nodded, and Gus shouted for okay from inside the dome.

Jon pulled out his scarf and sunglasses from his satchel and put them on for protection from the sun. The scarf he wrapped fully around his head and shoulders, leaving only his eyes and nose uncovered. He used the sunglasses to hold the scarf against his ears and protect his eyes from the glare. He looked back, noticing everyone was back under the dome. He threw the satchel over his shoulder and headed out under the burning sun. To avoid losing his orientation, he picked the highest sandy peak and walked towards it. The sand was scorching and gave on every step he took, making walking heavy and slow. Some places the sand was so soft he barely made any distance. Climbing up the sandy peak took him more time and energy than he thought it would. Jon glanced at his watch and estimated fifteen minutes of slow walk so far. Almost at the top, he pulled out his water bottle and took a small sip from it. Water had never tasted so good. After ten more minutes, he reached the peak. Taking those last steps felt like a job well done, a small personal victory. He leant forward to rest, hands on his knees for support. His heart pounded rapidly through his veins against his eardrums. He looked behind and saw the black dome far below. In front of him the horizon stretched wide, but not empty. What he saw made his skin crawl.

"Oh, crap," he said out loud and pulled out his mobile phone.

About two hours after his departure, Jon returned to the dome to find the others still busy in their tasks.

"Jon Peterson, reporting for duty," he said, sweating through his T-shirt and taking several sips from his water flask. "There's something you all should see." He removed his sunglasses and unwrapped the scarf from around his head.

When the others came closer, he pulled out his phone and showed them the pictures he had taken from the top of the sandy peak.

"There is a large dead city, just a few kilometres from here. There are also things that looked like ships, or something that used to be on water."

Jon swiped through the images on his phone and zoomed in, showing close range images of modern, but partially destroyed, triangular and spiral shaped skyscrapers. Some half-broken bridges had large, cargo-like ships under them, but instead of floating in water, they were half sunk in the sand.

"And here where it gets freaky." Jon opened a picture showing the entire horizon with the city in the middle.

Next to the city were massive, cigar-shaped black objects standing in the sand. Some were standing straight up and some were leaning slightly, like the tower of Pisa in Italy. The objects had hundreds of small bridges leaning against the sand, like petals from a dead daisy.

"Every one of those cigar-shaped objects is about half a kilometre high."

"Can't be ..." Gus blurted out, leaning closer to get a better view of the images on Jon's phone.

"Well, they can, I measured—" Jon started to explain, but Gus interrupted him.

"No, I mean, that they can't be the same as ..." Gus ran to Black Table and picked up his tablet. "I have it here somewhere," he tried to explain while the others looked at each other in wonder. "Here, I took snapshots of an article a few years ago." Gus turned his tablet around and showed them an image of the same cigar-shaped object, but in space.

"I don't understand," Jon said, looking back to his photos and then again to the one Gus had. "How can you have a picture of that same thing ..."

"The scientists on Earth named it Oumuamua," Gus began. "A high-powered telescope in Hawaii detected it in our solar system. They measured it to be four hundred metres long, and about forty metres wide. Exactly like the ones in your pictures. Scientists think it's an asteroid passing through our solar system."

"Asteroid my ass," said Jon, making Kentho snigger at his comment. "With those bridge-like things extending to the sand? I would say they are for delivering troops."

"Troops?" Kentho asked, confused by a new word he had never heard before.

"An invasion," Bartho joined the conversation. "And that's not all. I found these images from the book Kentho discovered."

Bartho opened the book and laid it down in front of everyone. It had a drawn image of a cigar-shaped object, with some ancient text next to it.

"It says," Bartho began reading, "The Swarm is relentless. The Swarm is ruthless. The Swarm consumes planets." Bartho paused and turned the page, revealing a mostly torn page with a drawn illustration of a Swarm. There was a picture of something made of tendrils and rods, or something like wires, attached to a centrepiece which they could not even imagine what it could be. That was all they could tell from what was left on the torn page.

"Phew! I feel kind of relieved," Jon said, looking at the picture.

"How so?" asked Gus, confused.

"We'll, hearing all those descriptions about Swarm, made me think it's us, humans. If you think about it, we kind of did our number on Earth already," Jon said. "And now we are trying to move to Mars. How would we be able to make Mars work, if we can't even save Earth?"

"Yes, you are right. We're not a very smart race, but we learn. And hopefully it will change for the better." Gus tried to give Jon reassurance that everything would be okay at home.

Jon handed his phone over to Bartho and walked to the dome entrance where light met shadow. On the shadow side he stood for a while, thinking. After a few minutes, he walked back and found the others still looking at the images he had taken.

"We have almost four hours to the next jump. I suggest we stay in the shadows and use the sunlight to recharge any remaining devices we have. We need to understand more about where we are at with everything."

Jon sat down against the dome wall, taking small sips from his flask. He dug into his satchel and found some black berries and white discs he had packed from the breakfast. Forgetting the Azons and Swarm for a while, he closed his eyes and enjoyed the snack, one bite after another.

"Can I rest here with you?"

Jon opened his eyes and saw Kentho standing in front of him, pointing to the sandy space next to him. "Of course you can," he replied with a smile, and offered Kentho one of the white discs from his satchel.

"Thank you," Kentho said and sat down next to him. "These are my favourites." He took a large bite from the disc. "Can you tell me something about your planet, Earth? Maybe about how you could be in the water, without Azons."

"Ok, I can tell you a story of when I was diving and chased by a shark."

"What is a shark?"

"On Earth, we don't have Azons, but there are up to one million species that lives in water." Jon said and saw how impressed Kentho was. "Most of them are beautiful and harmless, but there are some that even humans are afraid of, like sharks. I think even Azons would be afraid of sharks, the big ones at least ..." He paused. "Sharks are a fish, but they can grow to be huge, and they have a lot of sharp teeth, in several rows actually." Jon pretended to bite Kentho's arm, who pulled it away laughing. "The one I had an encounter with was three times bigger than me. Usually sharks are not dangerous, but they can be if they mistake humans as food. So, to go underwater we need to have air with us, compressed into tanks. That allows us to be underwater for about an hour, depending how deep we go. To see something underwater, we wear goggles designed for keeping water away from eyes. To move, we wear fins made of rubber. We use those fins to kick ourselves into motion." Jon demonstrated the movement of fins with his hands.

"This one time, we were over twenty metres deep. There were ten divers, and I was the very last person in the group, following to ensure no-one was falling behind. This turned out to be ironic, because I was the one who ended up falling behind."

"Why, what happened?" Kentho asked, imagining everything Jon had told so far, impatient to hear more.

"While we were going slowly forward, I thought I saw something at the side of my dive goggles. I peeked backwards between my fins and saw a large Oceanic whitetip shark, considered dangerous. This was surprising as there were not supposed to be sharks where we were. I stopped moving and kept my eyes fixed on the shark, waiting for it to swim away. It didn't. Instead, it slightly arched its back and made some fast movements towards me. That meant the shark was hunting." Jon showed the shark movement with his hand.

"So, what did you do?" Kentho asked with suspense.

"I let all the air out of my vest, which allows me to hold buoyancy in the water. By letting all air out, I sank to bottom, which was only about four metres under me. I landed on my knees, keeping my arms and legs against my body. The shark swam around me a few times and then swam away as fast as it had approached. I felt so relieved. When I could not see the shark anymore, I turned back towards to group. From the group, I could barely see the end of the fins of the last person. I began kicking hard with my fins to catch up. Because I was swimming so fast, I became out of breath. I had to slow down. While resting, I took a peek backwards between my fins and saw the same shark swimming towards me with full speed." Jon again demonstrated the shark's movement with his hands. "So, I took a hold of the closest rock on the bottom and held myself to it. The shark swam around me several times, and this time, I was really scared. All I could do was to hold on to that stone and monitor my air-gauge for how much air I had left. I really felt like the shark was looking for lunch, and I was the main course on the menu."

"So how did you survive?" Kentho asked, fully submerged in Jon's story.

"Again, I waited for the shark to swim away, which luckily it did. I then swam slowly in the direction where I saw the group last time. I found them at the depth we had been swimming at previously, near a coral wall rising from the bottom. I joined them and looked for the shark but couldn't see it anymore. Unfortunately, because of all my swimming and excitement, I had only a small amount of air left. I went to the leader of the group and used hand signals that I must return to surface. After he gave me the okay sign, I began my ascent. Now this is where it got super scary. Because of the depth I had been, I had to make a three-minute safety stop at the depth of five metres, to balance the nitrogen in my body. When I reached five metres, the visibility was so bad I could only see a few metres around of me. No matter where I looked, up, down or around me, it all looked the same fuzzy and blue. I kept imagining the shark appearing from nowhere. I have never been so afraid as I was on that moment. Not even when I dropped through ice on a lake, during a mission, which I can tell you about some other time. When I finally got to surface, I have never climbed into a boat so fast as I did this time. I did not even need a ladder to climb up. I just threw my gear over the board and swam up like a jumping fish in a rough river, right over the railing of the boat." Jon again demonstrated with his hands, which mesmerised Kentho.

"That was ... AMAZING!" Kentho shouted and lay on his back next to Jon.

Jon pulled out his copy of Dr Wells's book from his satchel and pushed his satchel under Kentho's head. Kentho thanked him and closed his eyes. Jon smiled and started reading the book.

About three hours later, Bartho called everyone to see something. Gus walked over, holding his tablet. Jon closed his copy of Dr Well's book and got up, waking Kentho at the same time. Bartho had been studying and comparing his notes with the other old books he had taken with him during their escape.

"Look at this," Bartho said. "This following text would explain how our people found a new home." He displayed the open book on Black Table and began reading what he had just discovered. "Those still alive, took a week's exhausting journey with countless jumps, and finally settled on a planet we shall from now on call New Thatho. This will be our home." Bartho slowed down at the end of his sentence and looked happily at Kentho. "This book says that our people came through Black Table escaping war on our original home planet, Thatho."

Bartho tuned away, mumbling on his own as he quietly read further, jumping back and forth between pages. Next to him, Gus opened his tablet, but then stopped like someone had used a pause button on him with a remote control. His body was fully still, and his eyes kept staring through the air. Jon moved his hand in front of Gus's eyes, but he did not blink. After several seconds, he came back to life and his eyes focused on the others again.

"It might be possible for me to get a location for your home planet, if I could get my hands on tables used for the trip. For Thatho, I mean." Gus looked at Bartho. "If your people came using the table, it would mean there should be a power source and crystals somewhere on New Thatho, right?"

"Here." Bartho found a page and began reading, "After devastating loss of life during the grand battle, our people have found haven. To remain safe here, we have destroyed the Altar and its surroundings. I hid the Altar's keys ..." Bartho looked at the others. "I presume those are the crystals and sphere?" He looked at Gus before continuing. "I hid Altar keys to look over our new home, New Thatho."

"What's that supposed to mean?" Jon asked, frustrated.

"That would explain the broken dome around your Black Table," Gus said out loud what he was thinking.

"The second platform!" Jon shouted, making everyone jump a little. "Oh my God, we walked right past them!"

He took a few steps away from the Black Table, holding his head in his hands. "When we were inside the cave, with the elevator! We even came out on to a platform with a view over your home. We came through a stone that could represent an eye, looking over your home."

"Our village is the oldest," said Bartho. "There are hundreds more, but they are all far away from the water."

"If that's true, how come Azons did not detect the power source already?" Gus asked.

"Maybe it is depleted? Those mines are the oldest and were used to mine formable rock. It is a very heavy metal, vahl. Maybe vahl is blocking their sensors?" Bartho kept guessing.

"Lead. We call it lead," said Gus excitedly. "It must be lead. A heavy metal used in our world to protect from harmful radiation. It must have blocked any radiation or signals coming from the sphere."

"I vote for going back." Jon surprised everyone with his words and a raised arm. "We will find the sphere and crystals, and then we will find your home planet." Jon now looked at everyone with a smile. Kentho raised his hand, following Jon's example, as did Bartho and Gus.

"What about Earth?" Gus asked Jon while keeping his hand still raised.

"Earth is not going anywhere. Besides, we cannot drag Bartho and Kentho away from their own home."

"The last few days have been the most scary, exciting and fun I have had, ever. This is a dream come true for any science fiction fan," said Gus, offering his fist for Jon, who responded in kind right away. "According to my simulation, if we wish to return to New Thatho, there's a jump window available in twenty minutes." He took a look at his tablet. "Get ready."

CHAPTER 8

THE EYE

Most of their devices were fully recharged and ready to go, Gus placed his hot-wired crystals back into the slots. He pulled out the power source from his satchel and placed it carefully in its place. The power source turned on its own a few times until it found its correct alignment. Light shone through the cracks in the ball, and Black Table came to life. Gus, Bartho and Kentho looked at each other, ready for the jump.

"Wait, where is Jon?" asked Gus, realising his best friend was not at the table.

All three turned around and saw Jon pulling the Azon's arm through the entrance.

"What?" Jon groaned. "Like I said, it would look really cool at home."

Everyone stood quietly, looking at him critically.

"Fine!" he raised his voice and dragged the arm back outside before returning to the others.

"Your planet should become available in ten-seconds," said Gus, watching his tablet.

Precisely ten seconds later, New Thatho begun pulsing turquoise light in the holographic map above Black Table. "Kentho, if you please?" Gus looked at him.

Kentho's face lit up like a kid in a toy store. He pushed his arm over the table but could not reach the palm print.

"Little help?" he said.

Jon walked behind him and placed his hand under Kentho's armpits. With an effortless lift, he raised Kentho high enough to reach the print. Kentho placed his own palm on it, and they were gone.

A blinding light and a cracking sound later, all four stood around the table at the top of the hill, on the same platform they had left only six hours earlier. Gus disconnected all the crystals and the power source and carefully placed them back into his satchel.

"At least no Azons waiting for us," said Gus relieved, and closed his satchel.

"This way!" Bartho called for the others to follow him to the steps leading down to the lower platform.

On the lower platform, Jon and Kentho looked down towards the village from the edge.

"Still there," said Kentho.

Jon offered him a fist bump, which Kentho happily accepted.

Gus and Bartho studied the untouched stone leaning against the entrance they had come through a day earlier.

"What? How? It's shut closed again," said Gus, looking at the massive stone jammed into the rocky mountain wall. "How is that possible? How are we supposed to get in there, when we barely got out from there?" He pushed the massive stone without any effect.

"Azons did this?" Jon asked, looking at the stone and the wall for any cracks.

"I suppose so. We will need some gear to make it move," said Bartho, standing next to Jon and studying the stone. "There are some tools at home."

"Too risky," said Gus. "Plus, the tunnels are flooded. Maybe our home as well."

"True. We will have to wait for sunset and pick up some tools we have in the utility storage. It is a cabin in the forest. It has tools used for hunting and harvesting."

"I'll go," said Jon. "Just show me where it is, and I will bring everything we need. Meanwhile, could you study for more clues from the book Kentho found?"

It was getting darker; the sun had already turned slightly orange but was still looming above the horizon where the mountain divided the land and the water. Just before going further down, Jon took a picture of the village and surrounding areas. He then marked the target location pointed to by Bartho on his picture.

"Where is your north?" Jon asked Bartho.

"I do not know what that is. I am sure I did not bring one with me," Bartho replied, confused.

"I'm sorry." Jon said. "It's the direction where your chilly wind comes from, and the time between where your sun sets before coming back up again." Jon tried to explain. "Maybe it is nothing like we have on Earth, but it would help me navigate when I would know some fixed direction."

"The north won't work," said Gus. "If we are in the southern hemisphere, the cold comes from south."

"I didn't think of that," said Jon, confused.

"You should be able to see the peaks of this mountain, even through the trees in the forest," Bartho said, looking at the picture Jon had taken. "You can use it as your north."

"Great," Jon said and made a few extra marks on his picture before putting his phone away. "I would guess it will take me three hours at most. See you guys later." He hurtled down the steps without another word.

Jon found going down the steps easy and fast, keeping his heart rate low. Once closer to the village, he stayed inside the forest but close to treeline. This way he could stay hidden, but able to see anyone approaching from the village. It was almost dark now, and the forest grew louder with insect and bird sounds. Some insects buzzed like ones on Earth, and some birds made an indistinct whistling sound. He stopped and pulled out his phone. The picture he had taken from the mountain view showed him the way; in front of the mountain was the village with the utility cabin further in the forest. On the left side of the village ran a river, flowing away from the mountain at an almost perfect ninety-degree angle.

Jon figured if he kept the village on his right until he reached the river running parallel somewhere on his left, he could follow the river until he was adjacent to where the utility cabin was located, Then he would head in his imaginary west towards it and reach the place Bartho had described as the utility storage.

After joining with the river, he kept pacing forward along the riverbank which was raised almost two metres above the rushing water. Counting his steps, he kept his mobile torch at his feet, trying not to raise any suspicions. After four hundred steps, which he had estimated to be as much as crossing the village, he stopped. Then, standing with his back to the river, he raised both arms from his side, creating a direct line through his shoulder line. He aligned his arms to match with the river. When in place, he looked straight ahead. He had found his heading. Jon begun pacing forwards, trying to walk as straight as possible.

Only a few minutes later he could see a dim light looming ahead between the tree trunks. He had found the utility cabin.

When Jon got closer, he saw a light-grey building, similar to the buildings in the village, but twice as high and several white doors made of solid stone on its outer walls. Jon knelt on one knee and studied the area for a while. Just when he was about to stand back up, a door opened and three people came out. It was two men and a woman, all carrying enormous sacks on their shoulders, heading back to the village after closing the door behind them.

Simultaneously, from the village's direction, two women approached. They were carrying similar, but empty sacks on their shoulders. The arriving pair greeted the other three and entered through a different door.

Jon checked the timer on his phone and decided he still had time to wait for them to come out. A few minutes later, the two women exited, carrying equipment that looked like hunting weapons. They said something to each other and parted their ways, going in different directions into the forest.

"This is it," Jon said to himself and stood up.

With no-one nearby, he hurried towards the facility but slowed down when approaching the nearest door. It was the door which the three people had come out of earlier. He pushed the round stone in the wall and the white door slid aside. He stepped in.

The room was dimly lit and there were straw baskets on the floor filled with items that seemed like potatoes to him. On the walls hung tomato-shaped blue vegetables.

"Not this one," he said and walked out.

Jon pushed the round stone at the next door, which the two women had come out from. The door opened, and he stepped in.

"Jackpot," he cheered quietly.

The walls hung with all kinds of tools, nets and ropes. He quickly went to them and picked up a small shovel looking device, several ropes and a sharp tool that could hack rocks into pieces. On the opposite wall hung a backpack made of soft beige linen, which Jon pulled down and opened. He placed the selected tools and ropes into the bag. When ready, he threw the bag on his back and stepped out. The door closed back into place behind him. When he saw no-one nearby, he pulled out his phone and switched the display on. He studied the picture he had taken from above and estimated the direction he should take.

Back to the river, he thought and slid the phone back into his pocket.

After his first step, a horn sound blasted through the air from far away.

"Azons? Again?" he wondered out loud. "Great, they were not supposed to come out at night."

The horn sound blasted again, making Jon realise he should start running, and so he did. With his phone in his pocket, the forest was already pitch black and he couldn't see a thing. But this time, all he had to do was to run towards the river and then head back to village, by keeping the river on his side. Joh felt quite confident he would reach the river at some point, even if he didn't run a straight line. This time, speed was the essence, not the direction.

Running at full speed in a forest covered with random large trees and short vegetation, Jon kept his steps short to prevent stumbling and injuring his knees. To protect his face, he kept his arms pointed straight forward, his right arm at his face level and the left arm in front of his stomach. In daylight this might have looked weird and out of place, but now it was essential. When branches hit his higher hand palm, Jon adjusted accordingly by dodging his head. He kept running awkwardly between smaller trees with his arms as his sensors, so far avoiding bumping into any larger trees. From time to time, the ground disappeared from below his advancing foot, which he supported instantly with the other leg. And when the supporting leg was not there on time, he landed on his support leg's knee, but kept his back straight without bringing down his arms. He just got up and kept going.

After the third warning sound, all insect and bird sounds ceased, like someone had pressed a giant mute button on the forest-life remote control. As scary as it felt to Jon, it also helped him. He now could hear the river rushing ahead of him. Just when he felt relief from knowing he had the correct direction, something smashed into him, hard.

Jon stumbled down with his attacker and they fell over the edge of the riverbank and plunged into the knee-deep water, Jon landing on his hands and knees. Water instantly soaked his hiking pants, but his feet stayed dry, thanks to his relatively new, waterproofed hiking shoes. The water temperature was cold but bearable. He got up fast and pulled out his mobile. He switched on the torch mode to see who had attacked him.

To his surprise, a woman stood in front of him, looking astounded and covered in leaves and small branches. She was as tall as Jon, and she had long black hair in a ponytail. A hunting bow was crossed over her chest and one shoulder. Jon recognised her right away as the one leaving last from the utility storage.

"Hello," said Jon, before remembering what was going on. "We've got to go, now!" he shouted and turned his torch on the river surface, waving his light towards the village. "The river leads to the mountain, but we must hurry." He began climbing out on the utility cabin side of the river.

"We can't, not anymore. It is too late!" she shouted and grabbed Jon's hand. She looked around as if to remember where she was. "There's a place. This way," she said and let go of Jon's hand before she began crossing the river, going further away from the cabin.

Jon thought about his options for two long seconds. He lifted his satchel over his head and followed her deeper into the river. In the middle of the crossing, the water reached all the way to their chests. After a dozen of steps, the river got shallower again, and they could pick up the pace. On the other side, the riverbank was flat, unlike the one they had fallen down from.

"This way," she said.

Jon pulled his legs forward, but the water made it feel like he was in slow motion. Once they made it back on to dry land, the going became easier and they could speed up to a run. Jon estimated their heading to be about a forty-five-degree angle between the river and the mountain wall. He had no other option except to follow the mysterious woman. Jon kept his mobile phone torch pointed forward to show the way. Though it didn't look like she needed help. All Jon could see was her back and her legs running at a fast pace. Smaller plants and tree branches flew aside as she stormed forward.

After a time that felt like forever in the dark, they arrived at the rocky mountain's wall.

"Now what?" Jon shout out in frustration. "We are trapped!"

It was like she didn't hear him. Meanwhile, the familiar sound of an approaching BOW rumbled right behind them. Instead of explaining to Jon what to do next, she kept studying the wall carefully. Jon looked behind in horror. He could hear the mass of water approaching and saw how the tallest trees further away had disappeared into a wall of water. Jon turned his head back to the mountainside, only to see the woman had disappeared.

"Here! Come! Now!" She appeared through a bush growing against the mountain, revealing a narrow opening in the wall.

"I'll be damned," said Jon relieved, and pushed himself after her through the opening.

The air smelled earthy and wet. They were inside of an old abandoned mine. Jon raised his mobile's torch. They were in a small but high chamber. There were rocky steps near the wall, leading higher inside the chamber. They kept climbing up until they were higher than the hole they had come through.

"This should be enough," said Jon, turning to his rescuer. "We are now higher than the entrance. It should create a natural air pocket." Jon pointed his light towards the flooding entrance, followed by a loud dampening sound of the BOW hitting against of the rocky wall outside with full force. The water level inside the chamber rose rapidly, but stopped at their feet, just as Jon had predicted.

"Impressive," she said. "Now, exactly who are you and what is that, and what are you doing with our tools?" She first looked at Jon with narrowed eyes, then pointed at his mobile phone and then leant her head to see the backpack Jon was carrying. She raised her eyebrows without a smile. For Jon, it felt like he'd been caught red-handed.

"My name is Jon." Jon turned the light into himself. "Nice to meet you?" he introduced himself but got no response. "I am an explorer from far, far away, and I need to borrow these tools to help my friends in trouble. And this," Jon turned his mobile phone in his hand, beaming the light all over the walls, "is my light." He paused, not knowing what to say next.

There was an awkward silence.

"My name is Julith," she finally said. She placed her hand on the middle of her chest and bent her head slightly downwards. Jon answered in kind. "I was supposed to work tonight, but for the second time in my whole life, Azons have granted their presence during the night. Very unusual," she added.

Jon could hear dislike towards Azons in her voice.

"Yes, Azons! I have heard about them," Jon said cheerfully, realising this time he was aware of them, unlike when he had met Bartho and Kentho for the first time.

"Why are you smiling? Azons are evil and brutal race," her voice changed from dislike to hate and loathing.

"Not smiling," Jon corrected, dropped his smile and raised up his arms in front of him in as a sign of surrender. "Happy to know *about* them," he said carefully. "Are they though, evil?" he asked, now knowing more than the villagers did.

"Of course they are evil. Our legends say they control us and destroy worlds," she said in shock at Jon's comment. She looked at Jon's modern, factory-made hiking pants and shoes. "Who are you, really? And why are you dressed so funny?"

Jon realised he could not tell her more, nor explain his origin, so he shone his mobile phone torch around them instead.

"Do you think there could be another way out?" he asked, trying to change the subject.

Changing the subject seemed to work. Julith took a deep breath and followed Jon's light.

"Over there," she said, pointing to the only wall with a flat surface, the rest of the chamber had still mining pickaxe marks all over it.

They walked closer and studied the flat wall. It was an old mural, filled with art and old text. The colours had mostly faded, but still visible was a depiction of four people standing behind a table which Jon recognised right away as the Black Table. All four had something in their hands, but the shapes and colours were too far gone. Above the people was a faint text which took Julith's attention.

"That's odd," she said, looking at the text. "I recognise it as our old language. I suppose it was our ancestors who came here that made this chamber."

"How do *you* know about his place?" Jon asked in return.

"I found it one day during a hunt. My arrow missed a full-grown Phirvi. The arrow flew into the bushes we came through, and when I came to look for it, I discovered this chamber. I never gave it another thought, not until now when we had nowhere else to go."

"Lucky us, and lucky Phirvi," Jon replied, wondering what a Phirvi might look like.

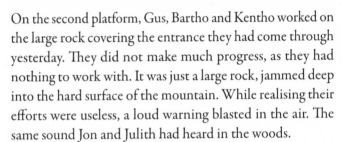

On the second platform, Gus, Bartho and Kentho worked on the large rock covering the entrance they had come through yesterday. They did not make much progress, as they had nothing to work with. It was just a large rock, jammed deep into the hard surface of the mountain. While realising their efforts were useless, a loud warning blasted in the air. The same sound Jon and Julith had heard in the woods.

"Azons?" Gus asked in surprise. "I thought they did not come out at night?"

"They must have detected our arrival or the power source, like they did last time," Bartho suggested.

"Of course! Why didn't I think of that?" said Gus, kicking himself for the obvious mistake they had made.

"What about Jon, is he going to be okay?" Kentho asked, worried about his new friend.

"Let's hope he heard the warning and finds some cover," said Gus, also sounding worried. "He is a survivor."

In the cave, Jon and Julith studied the mural, which seemed to be the only clue for their survival options.

"I recognise these symbols and characters," Julith said, moving her hand on the flat surface. "It is describing a journey through darkness." She used her lungs to blow dust away from the surface, while Jon shone the light from his phone.

"Here," Jon said, and revealed a symbol. "I have seen this before." He pointed his light on a symbol he had seen on Black Table screens.

"It means safe," Julith said, and paused. "Yes, now it makes sense. It roughly says; Journey through darkness, new home, protected, safe, no more journey." She jumped to a lower part of the surface and continued; "Passage left behind, burning through the barrier, find a new home." She stopped, appearing confused.

"Could it be," said Jon, "that the first part describes how you got here, and the second part explains how you would get away from here," Jon tried to explain, without sounding sure about it and without revealing he already knew what those words meant.

"What do you mean by you?" Julith wondered, looking at Jon curiously. "And what was left behind, and which barrier is burning? I do not understand," she continued, agitated.

"I think we are looking at it." Jon moved his light around the mural. "I think this mural is the barrier. Look, here."

Jon shone his light along the finger-wide indented groove surrounding the flat surface. The grooved line had a strange colour. When he moved his finger over it, the smooth and slightly silvery colour transferred to his finger. Jon smelled it and pulled his finger away from his nose due to the metallic smell.

"I think they made the surrounding border from magnesium." He took out his Swiss Army knife and scratched the silvery surface into his hand.

"I don't know what that word is," said Julith, studying what Jon was doing.

"It is a heavy alloy, and it reacts with fire," he explained and poured the small pile of dust he'd scratched off from the groove on the ground and pulled out the fire starter flint from his satchel. The flint had two parts, a magnesium block and an iron blade, used to shave magnesium from the block. He knelt down and poured the magnesium dust on the ground. He held the iron blade against the rocky ground and moved it over the pile of magnesium. The sparks from the iron blade jumped around, some of them landing on the magnesium dust. The pile lit up instantly into sparkling white flames, which died as fast as it had ignited. Julith jumped backwards.

"Parkh!" she shouted, and Jon looked up at her. "It is parkh!" She smiled, looking back at Jon. "We use it for starting fire and throw it into flames in celebrations."

"Parkh," Jon said, and smiled back. "Shall we see if the parkh will set us free?" Jon asked.

Julith nodded. Jon moved closer to the mural and looked at the clear silvery grooved line.

"Here." He held his hand at the groove, near the left edge of the mural. "Step back. This parkh is a lot stronger than the parkh we have. At my home I mean," Jon said, grinning at from Julith.

He placed his flint blade partly on the parkh, and partly on the painted mural stone. Then, with a fast pressing movement, he slid his hand downwards. The wall ignited. It begun with pure white blinding light, then followed with crackling and popping as small pieces flew all over the chamber. White flames followed first the groove around the mural, and then spread through the ancient texts and symbols. Both Jon and Julith knelt down, shielding their eyes with their hands as the wall got brighter and brighter, popping more tiny explosions around them. Then the popping and crackling stopped. The air smelled like burned metal. Both dropped their hands from their faces, just in time to see the mural glowing from the heat and still intact through the smoke, before it crumbled into small pieces on to the ground.

"All right!" Jon shouted, switching his mobile's torch back on, and offered Julith a fist bump. Julith looked at Jon's fist and then shook it briefly before letting go.

"You are an interesting man, Jon," she said.

There was tunnel where the mural used to stand. A tunnel smelling of smoke and earth. They stepped through, first Jon, then Julith. Almost tripping, they found steps hacked straight from the mountain itself. Jon pointed the light towards the steps. They led upwards. Behind them, the sound of rushing water grew louder.

"There must be an opening up there," said Jon, pointing his light further upwards. "The water begun rising after we broke the mural. That means the air pressure has changed, allowing water to continue rising." He turned his light behind them. The water kept rising, slow and steady.

"We must go," said Julith, and pushed past Jon, pulling his sleeve after her, heading upwards inside the mountain.

They climbed for a long time. Jon checked his phone and estimated they'd been climbing for half an hour. The air was difficult to breathe. The smoke from the burned mural followed them as they kept going. The climbing route took 180 degree turns five times, until finally, the narrow tunnel widened and ended with another chamber. Both supported themselves with their arms against their knees. The climb had exhausted them.

"Can you see an exit?" asked Jon panting, trying to get air into his lungs. He looked at Julith, who shook her head, her hair covering half of her face. She was already standing straight up, leaning against the rocky wall.

Jon, used to physical exertion, could not believe he had trouble keeping up with Julith. He forced himself to stand up. He placed his hands on his lower back and pushed his hip forwards. There was a loud crack coming from his hip.

"Are you okay?" asked Julith, now approaching Jon.

"Getting there," Jon replied embarrassed and begun showing his mobile's torch around the small chamber.

At first glimpse, it seemed like there was nothing else than the steps they had come up from, but as he moved his light around, he noticed a small box on the ground against the wall.

"No way!" Jon shouted, his imagination had taken over.

Memories from Stephen Spielberg's movie *Goonies* played through his mind. He approached the box which turned out to be no bigger than a large mailbox. It was not a treasure chest from a pirate movie. It had eight corners and a flat lid. Jon knelt next to the box and began studying it with his light. There were no visible locks or hinges.

"Now what?" he said frustrated, expecting some hard mystery to be solved to get it open.

"What is it?" Julith asked, kneeling down next to Jon.

"I don't know," Jon said, shining light all over the chest. "Another mystery?" He carefully pulled sand away from around the box, trying to find clues and booby traps.

"It is merely a box," Julith said and opened the lid by pressing it down from the top. The lid opened when she released the pressure. "We still use boxes like these," she said casually.

Jon felt stupid, almost idiotic.

Julith lift the lid all the way open, and they saw a yellow lump glowing back from Jon's light. Jon pressed the yellow lump with his free hand. It was soft, slightly warm, and he could feel something inside. Jon gave his light to Julith, who curiously turned the mobile in her hand a few times, before shining the light back towards their find. Jon slid his hands in between the sides of the box and the lump. He kept pushing deeper under the soft material until his fingers met. He smiled and tried to lift it. His smile dropped. The lump barely moved.

"Holy crap," he said in surprise. "It's some kind of fabric with something in it, and it's really heavy."

"Here, let me help." Julith placed the light against the box and pushed her hands also under the fabric, just like Jon did.

Together they lifted the fabric out from the box. They laid it on the ground and begun unravelling the fabric to see what it hid. After pulling away the last folded fabric corner, three crystals and a sphere were laid out in front of them.

"Yes!" Jon shouted, lifting his hands up in victory and making Julith fall on her side.

"I suppose you know what those are?" Julith asked. She pulled herself back up and picked up a crystal.

"I do, and I will explain to you later, but we really need to go." He collected all four items into his satchel and stood up.

"Wait a minute ..." he said, lifting his satchel up and down with his one arm. "This is not so heavy ..." He looked at the yellow fabric on the ground for a second and then dropped back down on his knees next to Julith.

He grabbed the fabric from one of its corners and lifted it up. It did not flap or move like normal cotton. It was the size of an extra-large T-shirt and it moved almost snake-like and felt heavy.

"Oh, my God," said Jon in shock, still holding the corner of the fabric. "This is made of gold." He burst out a laugh and offered it to Julith.

"Interesting ..." she said, holding it from one corner with her both hands. "It is made of very fine threads of vahl, sewn like a fabric. I have seen nothing like it." She studied it closer. "Vahl is an exquisite mineral. We use it to cover other surfaces. It has qualities other rocks do not, and very resistant to other materials."

"It's so coming with us," Jon said, smiling like a crazy person.

He threw the fabric over his shoulder and slowly stood up. The fabric was heavy, but instead of complaining, Jon giggled like a little child. Julith stood up, shook her head, but said nothing.

"Now ..." Jon said. "We should find an exit." He turned his mobile's torch around the chamber. The sound of running water echoed from the tunnel they'd climbed out from. They could also feel the air pushing out from the tunnel. It reminded Jon of railway tunnels in major cities. As a train approached a station, a massive amount of air moved in front of it, making platforms feel like wind-tunnels.

"I have an idea," said Jon, holding one hand on the light, and one on the fabric on his shoulder. "Could you throw some sand into air?" He looked at Julith and pointed his light towards the sandy areas on the rocky floor. "The air should move the sand towards the exit, and away from the approaching mass of water."

Julith did as asked, and like magic, sand flew towards the wall opposite from where they had found the box.

"Again," Jon said while they got closer the wall. "Again."

Sand took off from Julith's open hand and flew into the wall. It literally flew into the wall. Jon walked closer to where it all disappeared. The wall felt solid. Just when his mind refused to understand what happened to the sand, he saw it.

"Here," he said in relief, and Julith also walked closer.

Behind the wall there was another wall close behind it creating a narrow passageway between them. When looked at straight on, the first wall concealed the passageway perfectly, making the viewer believe there was only one wall.

Jon peeked into the opening between the two walls and saw night sky at the other end. It was not far, maybe four metres away. The narrow passage was just wide enough for them to go through. He took a deep breath and pushed himself into the passage. Julith followed him. Both had their hands in front of them, their palms touching the wall, while their backs slide against the other wall behind them. After four metres, the passageway ended. Jon stopped right at the edge, realising there was a long drop if they continued. He could see a BOW looming under him and over the village.

"This is the view over the village," he whispered when Julith bumped into him, pushing him out from the narrow passageway.

With one foot dangling in the air, Jon desperately looked for something to hold on to. His right hand fumbled uselessly against the mountain wall. Just when his balance leaned towards a fall, Julith grabbed him with both hands and pulled him back to safety.

"Thank you," Jon whispered, afraid that Azons could hear him.

Jon studied the foot-wide ledge at the end of the passageway. It extended along the face of the mountain, leading to their right. Carefully, they both exited the passageway, facing the mountain, with only their toes and soles of their feet on the ledge. As they came out from the mountain wall passage, Jon realised how the exit looked like an iris of a cat's eye. The black narrow vertical slit stood straight up and the mountain wall around it changed colour slowly from dark to light. The eye was invisible from the village, but it tirelessly looking over the valley and its habitants.

On the lower platform from Black Table, Gus, Bartho and Kentho were looking down from the edge. A BOW had arrived and now loomed on top of the village against the mountain wall.

"What are the Azons doing?" Kentho asked his father.

"Do not worry Kentho, we and everyone in the village are fine." Bartho tried to calm Kentho down, who seemed scared.

"But how does Jon get back here?"

"I don't know. But I am sure he is safe somewhere. He will join us once Azons leave," Bartho said.

"Are they going to leave though?" Gus joined them. "We have a power source and nothing to block it with. And as long as we cannot get in there," Gus pointed to the massive rock blocking the cave entrance, "we cannot hide it."

Kentho sat near the edge and tried to watch for any sign of Jon. In his peripheral vision, something to his left moved. He turned his head and saw a light further along the mountain wall, moving in circles and straight lines, like someone had caught a star and waved it around.

"What is that?" Kentho called to the others and pointed towards the mountain wall next to them.

Bartho and Gus walked closer to edge, trying to get a glimpse. It was definitely a light, moving randomly in a small area.

"Is that you guys?" a voice said from the light's direction.

"Jon?" Gus shouted with surprise and relief.

"Yes!" Jon shouted with relief in his voice too. "Look for a narrow ledge on this side of the platform." He meant the narrow ledge they walked on with Julith.

Gus put on his mobile's torch and pointed it towards the wall. There was a ledge, but without knowing what it was, it looked like a natural formation on the mountain wall.

"Found it!" Gus shouted, Bartho and Kentho joining him.

"Help us out, the ledge is getting narrower," Jon called, his voice now coming from much closer.

"Us?" said Gus and looked at Bartho and Kentho.

Jon edged along the ledge with his face and chest hard up against the mountain wall, his satchel and the golden fabric on his shoulder. His light was directed towards the platform, making him and Julith just figures behind the light.

"Here. Take my hand," Gus said, and got a hold on Jon's hand, pulling him closer onto the platform and to safety.

"Thank you," Jon said, feeling relieved he had found his friends again. He dropped his satchel and the fabric on the ground and turned around to help Julith. "Here is my new friend," Jon said. "She's saved my life twice already." He reached towards the ledge to pull Julith on to the platform. Gus lifted his light to see her face, when Kentho suddenly shouted, making Gus drop his phone.

"MUM?" Kentho shouted so loudly his voice bounced back from the mountain walls and echoed in the valley. He launched himself towards his mother.

"Kentho?" Julith said casually, but slightly surprised, without seeing him properly. "What are you doing here, aren't you supposed to be at home, sleeping?" she said in a motherly way, unaware what Kentho and Barth had gone through after losing her.

"Julith? Is that really you?" said Bartho in disbelief. Kentho burst into tears and wrapped his arms around his mother's waist, with no intention to let go ever again.

"I don't understand ..." she said confused, holding Kentho's head between her hands. "What happened to you?" She seemed puzzled. "You are much taller, and you look older?"

Kentho squeezed her with all his strength. Bartho joined them, now looking at Julith the way she did at Kentho just seconds earlier.

"Oh crap ..." said Gus quietly from the sidelines, looking at Jon who stood only a metre away, admiring the unexpected reunion. "What happens now has already happened. And what will happen is happening now," Gus rambled. With his palms on his head, he began walking circles in his usual way. "How did I miss this ..." He pulled out his tablet and began tapping the screen in panic.

"Julith? Mum?" said Jon out loud.

"Yes Jon, this is my husband Bartho and my son Kentho. Or at least I think they are," she said confused. Both Kentho and Bartho were hugging her like they had not have seen her in years, which they hadn't.

"You died, almost three flashes ago," Bartho said, holding her face between his palms and looking deep into her eyes.

"Don't be silly," she responded and laughed nervously. "That is not possible. I'm right here."

Jon made an awkward smile and turned around to find Gus while Bartho recounted to Julith what had happened since her death until Jon and Gus's arrival.

"What the hell is going on?" Jon whispered to Gus.

"That's it! That's the unknown parameter!" Gus stopped pacing and turned around, shouting, "The missing piece has been *time*!" He approached the group. "The table is not using worm holes to bend distances: it's using *time* to bend distances."

Gus typed parameters into his tablet and started a new simulation with the Black Table interface he had made in an Impossibly short amount of time. Only ten-seconds later, his tablet gave a noise notification for the completed simulation.

"Of course ..." He read the results. "How could I be so reckless?"

"Of course what?" asked Jon, trying to interrupt Gus's next rambling monologue.

"It is a miracle we are still alive." Gus hid the code and brought the simulation results into view. "Look." He turned and held the tablet display towards others. "Now do you understand? What happens now has already happened. And what will happen is happening right now." Gus looked everyone directly into their eyes, one by one, and then pointed up to stars in the night sky above.

"No offence, but you sound bat-shit crazy," said Jon, without a hint of sarcasm in his voice.

"My missing parameter was time," Gus explained. "I assumed I knew how Black Table works. We could have ended up millions and millions of years back or forward!" Gus shouted and collapsed to sit on the ground with the tablet in his lap. "I could have killed us all ..." He continued mumbling and holding his hands on his head.

"But you didn't, did you?" Jon knelt next to Gus, calming him down. "And now you know the exact value of the missing time parameter. Now you can get us home."

"True." Gus lifted his head. "Me and Bartho must go through the code again, find the exact time. Most likely New Thatho months and years are not the same as Earth's." He got up full of excitement again. "Did you at least find the tools for removing that rock?" He pointed at the massive rock leaning against the mountain wall, hiding the wooden elevator chamber.

"Yes, but we found something even better." Jon had a broad smile.

"Dynamite?" Gus said excitedly, wearing a wild grin on his face.

"No Gus, not dynamite." Jon dropped his smile and lifted his eyebrows, thinking his friend would need some sleep. "We found crystals and another power source." He smiled and pulled two crystals out of his satchel. "Ta-da!"

"That's it ..." Gus grabbed one crystal in his free hand. "And that's why the rock is still in its place two years from now. We never had to open it to find the crystals." He gave the crystal back to Jon, who placed it carefully back into his bag.

"And check this out." Jon picked up the golden fabric off the ground. "The sphere and crystals were wrapped in this." He passed it to Gus, whose hands dropped under the weight as soon as Jon let it go.

"What the ...?" Gus blurted out as the fabric dropped to the ground with a thumping sound. Jon pulled out his phone and turned the light on. Gus bent down to lift it back up.

"Use the Force, dude. Use the Force ..." Jon imitated Yoda while Gus lifted the fabric and opened it.

"It's made of gold," Gus said right away, admiring how the fabric felt and moved. "Never seen anything like this. It contained the crystals and the power?"

"Yes, wrapped like a newborn baby."

"That's why Azons never detected it."

"What do you mean?" Jon felt confused. "I thought it had to be lead."

"Actually," Gus said, "lead and gold have similar properties. Gold is even more dense than lead, so even better for blocking radiation, as well—"

"Are you telling me this sucker is radioactive?" Jon interrupted, alarmed.

"Not radioactive, radiating," Gus explained. "Everything around us is radiating a different frequency, that is how we are able to see and feel things. Actually—" his words were cut short when another sound of the warning horn echoed in the air.

"I think we know what that means," Jon called out for others. "They are after the power sources, we better go."

They began climbing back to the Black Table platform, Kentho in lead and Gus second. Far away, more warning horn sounds echoed in the air. During the climb, Gus shared his time bending theory with the rest.

"So, on Black Table's interface," Gus said, "the turquoise pulsing planets are sharing Black Tables somewhere in their timeline, in their past or in their future." Gus stopped for a second to take a breath before continuing. "And when you select a planet, there is a limited time to make the jump. We jump to another table that existed or will exist at the same place where this table used to be, or will be."

"Amazing," Bartho said, while climbing in front of them. "Instead of bending space, it bends time? Connecting the same locations together with time?"

"Exactly," Gus said happily, noticing how easily the others had picked up the new information.

"Like the peas in the water?" Kentho joined conversation.

"Exactly," Gus said. "Black Table's interstellar navigation system stores their location. I think ..." Gus stopped climbing. "Like catching a bus, waiting for the correct one to pass you by."

"A bus?" Kentho said to himself, but let it go this time.

"And why the domes?" Kentho asked.

"I'm guessing Azons need water for their jump, and the dome helps keep the form. Just a guess," Gus tried to explain, realising he still had many questions about Black Table.

On the platform, Kentho pulled at his mother's sleeve, and recounted what he had learned from Gus and what had happened to them in past twenty-four hours.

"I will make the crystals ready," Gus said and began working with the table.

Jon joined Gus, while Bartho, Kentho and Julith embraced their extended time together.

"Do you think she died two years ago?" Jon asked Gus, who pulled out cables and attached them to the crystals Jon had discovered. "Or were we here, and that's why she was 'taken' by Azons?"

"I think what happened to her, happened now," Gus said, sounding sure. "Bartho said Azons came that night and took her. He also said Azon's appearance at night is extremely unusual." He continued while working with the cables, two crystals in place already. "And the only plausible reason for Azons to appear during that night, is their interest in our power source. Hence, we were there."

"So, did we steal two years from their lives?" Jon looked worried. "And because of us, they had to go through losing a family member?"

"That, I do not know," said Gus, interrupting Jon. "We don't know what would have happened if you hadn't run into her in the forest. Without her, you would not have found the second sphere and crystals. And without you, she might have been taken by Azons ..." Gus paused working for a second. "To me, it feels like everything went as it should have. We are all here, alive," he said and placed the last crystal into its place.

"I'm not angry to you," said Kentho, standing right behind Jon and Gus, eavesdropping.

Both Jon and Gus jumped from his sudden sound of his voice.

"Jesus," said Jon, startled. He turned around, looked at Kentho and put his hands on his shoulders. "I am so sorry, Kentho," Jon said, with all compassion he had in him. "We both are."

"I'm not," Kentho said smiling. "Without you, I would not have my mother now. And you didn't come here to hurt us, you came here by accident."

"That is almost true," Jon said. "We ..." Gus interrupted him with a sharp kick to his ankle. Jon looked at Gus, who shook his head discreetly.

"Better if we don't know it all," Gus said, smiling at Kentho.

He placed the last crystal into place and pulled out the power source from his satchel. One by one, Gus attached his homemade interface to the crystals. "I am looking for planets from where jumps were made this way. If it's not your original home planet Thatho, then at least it would be the next best choice to look from."

Everyone gathered around the table while Gus moved planets and solar systems. From the valley echoed familiar voice, "uuuuumm ..." Which Jon finished, "Yes, we know ... da-da-da-da-da-da-da ..."

The sound continued, just as Jon had predicted.

"Will you check on Azons?" Gus asked Jon, who took off immediately and ran closer to edge, where enormous balls of water merged into one gigantic one.

"They are doing the merging thing! Three BOWs merging into one!" Jon shouted and ran back to group.

Gus now had all three crystals hooked up with his wires. He placed the power source in its place, which did its usual spin before settling, bringing the table into life. Julith gasped and pulled herself behind Bartho, who calmed her with the information about how the table worked.

"Here we go," said Gus. "Our galaxy takes about 230 million years to go full circle. If we want to travel to the other side of our galaxy, we would have to set time parameter to 115 million years." He tapped his tablet, revealing zero planets with Black Tables.

"I guess the network does not reach so far?" asked Jon, watching Gus's tablet screen over his shoulder.

"Looks like it," Gus commented and scrolled his tablet parameters. "That one," Gus said and pointed at a planet in a solar system with two suns and about a dozen planets surrounding them.

"You sure?" Jon asked seriously, making Gus turn and look confused.

"What do you mean, am I sure? Well, I can't be sure ... But I'm sure there is a Black Table ... I ... I ..." he began rambling again when Jon interrupted him.

"I'm kidding." Jon laughed.

"Hilarious," Gus responded. "Thirty-seconds." He returned his attention to his tablet.

Kentho began climbing higher on the side of the table to reach the palm print.

"Kentho, no!" Julith shouted, looking worried.

"It is okay Mum, it is safe," said Kentho smiling at his mum, who put down her hands and nodded approval.

Kentho waited for Gus's command.

Their target planet with two suns began pulsing turquoise light accompanied by the countdown symbols.

"Now," said Gus and nodded to Kentho. "Say bye-bye to Azons my friends!" Gus shouted happily.

Kentho put down his hand. There was familiar electric crackling sound, a flash of light, and they were gone.

CHAPTER 9

AZONIA

With a bright flashing light and a loud electric crackling sound, Jon, Gus, Kentho, Bartho and Julith appeared in a new dome. They all leaned against the table, disoriented from the jump. While Julith held her head from the piercing pain which the others had experienced earlier, Gus quickly hid the power source and crystals in his satchel just before four guards entered the dome in formation. They were all as tall as the tallest basketball player on Earth, with long muscular arms and long sturdy legs, which made their torsos appear oddly short. The guards had matching uniforms made of a material similar to that on the severed arm they'd left on the sandy planet. The armour material was mixed with white fabric, covering most of their turquoise skin. Their heads were covered with something resembling a helmet, but shaped unlike a human's, being an oval shape but on the horizontal plane. The narrow visors for their eyes stretched from one side to the other and immediately reminded Gus and Jon of Robocop or the

Cylon's helmets in *Battlestar Galactica*. On the guards' hands, integrated around their arms between elbow and wrist, were things Jon immediately recognised as weapons of some kind.

"Say hello to Azons," said Jon, sarcastically.

The guard in lead exchanged words with the rest of his kind, and in unison, the four guards moved into a perfect line, pointing their integrated weapons to everyone except Kentho.

"Ammmmm, alavillaa, maillaa," spoke the second guard from the right.

Jon and Gus looked at each other. Jon took a step towards the guards. All four guards moved their weapons for more accurate positioning and thin beams of green light caused rotating green dots to appear on Jon's chest. Jon swallowed and hoped his hunch of what he was about to do would not get him and his friends killed.

"uuuuummmmm ... da-da-da-da-da-da-da?" Jon voiced, trying to imitate the sound they kept hearing on New Thatho. Jon tried again, "uuummm stop ... da-da-da-da-da-da-da we come in peace."

Jon understood his own words, as the over stimulated language learning centre in his brain came into play after hearing more speech from the guards. The guards turned to each other, confused.

"Aaaaaaaa ..." said all Black Table arrivals together, all except for Julith, as they realised the truth about their previous encounters with Azons. Jon and Gus looked at each other with a grin as they both recognised the mistake they had made. Azons were not trying to kill them, but to stop them.

"So, *that's* what it means," said Jon, feeling embarrassed.

The green rotating aiming beams of light disappeared from Jon's chest as the guards lowered their weapons. Jon looked at his group with a wide grin.

Two guards in the middle stepped aside, opening a path which the recent arrivals began walking through. Trying to avoid close contact with the guards, they kept bumping into each other as they rubbed shoulders all the way out of the dome. Outside of the dome, a crowd of aliens grew larger, trying to get a look at what went on inside the dome.

Only minutes earlier, the air had filled with the sounds of arriving authorities to take control of an unauthorised Black Table activation. From above, between the two highest spiralling buildings, four egg-shaped silvery pods the size of a two-story house, arrived with a harmonious humming sound. The pods hovered above the dome for a second, and then landed between the crowd and the dome, leaving the dome exactly in the centre of the pods. Once perfectly aligned, the pods sent a turquoise beam to each other, erecting a tall wall of light between them, high enough to conceal the dome from the curious crowd.

At that moment, the guard walking behind new arrivals made a gesture with his long arm, pointing to a bridge like path leading into the closest silvery pod. All five approached the pod and hesitantly walked inside along a bridge extending from the pod. Inside the pod, a dozen seats against the wall waited for passengers. Large seats surrounded a space in the middle, divided by the entrance and stairs leading up to the next level inside the pod. Before heading to the pilot room on the upper level, the guard made another hand gesture for them to take seats. Jon and Gus sat down on one side, while Kentho, Bartho and Julith on other, facing Jon and Gus. Once seated, the quiet humming sound grew louder and louder. The pod's extended bridge towards the Black Table dome slid back inside on to the floor. Once the bridge had retracted, a pod-shaped shield moved from between pod's outer hull, concealing the exit like a sliding door. At the same time, solid harnesses came down over the passengers, automatically stopping when enough pressure applied against their shoulders.

"Welcome to the latest theme park ride at Universal Studios," said Gus, holding the U-shaped support that landed on his shoulders and reaching down to his chest. "Keep your feet and arms inside the vehicle at all times," he said, looking nervous.

"Are you okay?" asked Jon, worried his friend might lose it.

"Nope," Gus replied, while taking deep breaths.

The humming sound grew louder with a tone rising higher and higher. Then the pod took off. Jon and Gus could feel the acceleration, but it did not match with the speed. Right after take-off, the walls of the pod turned semi-transparent, revealing amazing view over a modern alien city and surrounding ocean.

They had arrived on a planet covered mostly by water. Hundreds of silvery cities rose from a chain of islands. Around the islands, lagoons and massive reefs coloured the ocean surface with every shade of blue and green. The planet orbited around two small suns and had a colourful orbital ring made of countless small particles. The suns' own gravity made sure they could never escape each other, instead they displayed a never-ending powerful dance around each other. From the planet's view, the suns were now almost in alignment, the closer sun revealing only a small section of its dance partner. In awe, Jon pointed out to Gus how each shining city with their tall spiral buildings stood on tropical islands with a diameter of several kilometres. Around the cities, tall green trees cast shadows over white sandy beaches.

"Would you look at that," said Jon. "Looks like the Great Barrier Reef in Australia, or the islands of the Maldives, only much bigger and with alien cities on top of them ..." He could not believe his eyes. "This is so surreal!" He looked at Gus, whose face had changed from Irish reddish-white to slightly greyish-green from his fear of heights.

Only five minutes later, the humming tone faded and then stopped. The shoulder harnessed moved back up and released the passengers. The outer hull door made a small hissing sound and slid aside into the pod's wall. From the floor, a walking bridge pushed out and lay firmly against the ground outside of the pod. Jon and Gus looked at each other and stood up, the others following their example. They walked towards the door, expecting the pilot to come down before reaching the door, but the pilot stayed out of sight. With Jon and Gus in lead, they reached the pod exit. Warmth from the sun and the fresh air from the ocean hit them like an invisible wall. Both the warmth and wind felt nice on their skin.

"Oh, my God. Look!" said Gus, seeing the double suns and the orbital ring. "There are two suns." They continued walking down the short bridge, the others right behind them.

The pod had landed on the top of a building on the other side of the city. Next to the building they stood on was another tall building connected by a long walking bridge. Once all five were standing on the building, the pod behind them began humming and flew away, its bridge and door closing automatically as it rose. They looked around, there were no exits except for the long walking bridge towards the neighbouring building.

"I'm taking a wild guess here and assume that's where to go next?" said Gus, and led them forward.

"Flying eggs?" Jon wondered, as they began crossing the bridge.

"It seems they have mastered gravity manipulation," Gus answered, and watched the pod flying further away.

"Flegs. That's what they are. Flying eggs, Flegs," Jon said proudly, realising he got to name something. "Flegs it is," he decided, when no-one challenged his suggestion, although part of him knew the others were not even listening but paying attention to the alien world around them.

When approaching the halfway point two figures appeared from the opposite building's entrance and began walking across the bridge. One figure resembled the guards from the dome, but without a helmet, weapons or armour.

"It's a genuine alien," Gus said, offering a fist bump to Jon.

"We are the aliens here, but yes, it is," Jon replied, and responded to the fist bump Gus offered.

The second figure looked like a female human, with a similar appearance to Bartho, Kentho and Julith. She had short, light-brown hair reaching just over her ears. Her clothing was even similar to the beige and white linen people on New Thatho wore. Jon could not ignore a feeling he felt when he saw her. There was something special about her. Something that took Jon's attention and made his heart pound faster. Both parties kept walking until they faced each other from a few metres away. Everyone came to a full stop.

"Welcome," said the turquoise skinned tall alien with a low trembling voice and held his arms across his chest. Jon and the rest responded with the same gesture. "We do not get many visitors through the Blato." The alien released its long arms and continued. "My name is Uzano, and this our home planet, Azonia. Our security force told me you offered a peaceful approach."

Uzano, like the guards earlier, had tall sturdy legs and long arms with three-fingered hands. Uzano's head looked like an evolution from crossing dolphins and Velociraptors from the Jurassic period. His enormous mouth reached from side to side, and his eyes were big, black and round like a dolphin. With the turquoise coloured smooth skin, it was apparent their origins were aquatic.

"Check this out," Jon whispered to Gus, and took a step forward.

"Greetings," Jon said calmly, "my name is Jon. It is an honour to meet you." He held out his arm with his fist closed in front of him.

Uzano looked at his female companion and then responded in kind, giving Jon the very first interstellar first-contact greeting with a fist bump. Behind Jon, Gus held back from laughing as hard as he could.

"These are my friends, Gus, Julith, Bartho and Kentho," Jon introduced. "We come from planets Earth and New Thatho, and we are looking for a resting place for a while."

"New Thatho?" Uzano's companion, who kept studying them, suddenly broke her silence. "I'm sorry. My name is Nova." She looked directly at Bartho and his family, ignoring Jon and Gus. "So, the tales of New Thatho are true?" she asked. "Please, let us continue inside the capital." She turned around and began walking towards the building she and Uzano had left from.

Before going inside, Gus noted that how the walls of the building were made of something similar to solar panels. They filled every floor with flowers, plants and homes for colourful flying insects and birds.

At the end of the bridge they walked through an entrance into a room with walls of glass. The floor was pure white, as was the ceiling, both emitting bright light. Once everyone was inside, the glass door behind them closed. Without a sound, the room broke away from the building and hovered through the air. Beyond the glass walls they could see the whole silvery city with crowds on streets below them.

"We are in an elevator," Gus commented out loud on the obvious. "We might have made a mistake."

"What do you mean?" asked Jon, thinking back to understand what the mistake was.

"Telling everyone we are from Earth."

"How so?"

"Well," Gus explained, "every time Earth gets into trouble, it's because someone goes out there and tells where they are from and where Earth is located."

"You are not wrong, my friend." Jon gave a suspicious look towards their new hosts. "Let's keep Earth's location to ourselves, for now," he finished and gave a small, hidden fist bump to Gus.

The crowds on the ground and on the long bridges connecting buildings were mixed with Azonians, people like those in New Thatho, and some aliens that Gus and Jon had not yet seen before.

"And we are back to Comic Con," Gus whispered to Jon. "Azonians look almost as if T-Rex and a dolphin had a baby."

"And they probably think the same of us," Jon replied quietly. "Instead of T-Rex and Dolphin, they think monkeys and some worm had a baby." Jon moved his index finger like a worm in front of Gus's face.

"Our race is called Azonians," Uzano said, noticing how the recent arrivals stared at him. "We have a dozen other planets as our home. We have developed an ability to live in the water as on the land, and we live three times as long as our friends here." Uzano turned to Nova, who smiled back.

"That's right, *old* friend," she said. "What you see out there is thousands of years of friendship between several races." She looked outside where the crowds became smaller as the round glassed room climbed higher.

When up high, which Jon estimated to be at least half a kilometre, the room slowed down and approached near the top of the highest building. A door the size of the room they were in, opened on the side of the building and let the room in with millimetre precision.

"We have been called to a council meeting. You can join us if you like," Uzano said, when the room came to a stop.

"Kind of risky, isn't it?" asked Jon. "You've just met us." His human habit for paranoia had taken over and he was not able to understand why someone would trust new arrivals so quickly.

"Are you telling me we cannot trust you?" Uzano asked with a calm, low voice.

"No. I mean yes, you can trust us. I mean ..." he tried to explain, fighting with his instincts and logical thinking.

"Relax," Uzano said and smiled as they walked pass several guards. "We have been monitoring your jumps for some time now. And our scans show no weapons of any kind on you, except for the power source and three crystals in your friend Gus's possession. Also, we believe you might have information we could find useful."

Gus's face turned red while others pretended to look elsewhere, anywhere else.

"That went well," Jon whispered to Gus, grinning.

"But at least now we know for sure," Gus whispered back. "Know what?"

"That the gold is shielding any radiation or frequencies that the second power source and crystals might emit." Gus winked his eye to Jon, who tried to wink back, but closed both eyes instead of one.

In the Operations room at the top of the council building, ten Azonians and ten Thathonians sat around a circular table. Uzano directed the new arrivals to stand to one side against the wall. An Azonian stood up and started the talks. His clothing was similar to Uzano's except instead of white fabric, he wore coppery red. He also wore armour.

"We have a reason to believe that Swarm is spreading in sector three," The coppery armoured Azonian said, and a colourful three-dimensional holographic map appeared in the middle of the room, highlighting Swarm's presence on the map. "We cannot wait any longer, we must strike now."

Gus and Jon looked at each other upon hearing the word Swarm.

"I agree," Uzano replied. "The Swarm already has sectors one and two. Today, we have witnesses from sector three." Uzano turned towards the recent arrivals standing at the wall, causing everyone at the table to whisper to the person sitting next to them while looking at the new arrivals.

"Right, sector three ..." said Gus, trying to catch up why everyone had turned to look at them. He looked at Uzano, then Nova, and then at Jon and Bartho, who both raised their shoulders in a shrug.

"We detected jumps on three planets, maybe four. The fourth seems to have a defective Blato. All four Blatos are located in sector three," said Nova, sitting next to Uzano but looking directly at Gus.

"Right, Blato ..." Gus realised seconds later that Blato was just another name for Black Table. "We didn't notice any Swarm activity on New Thatho, if that is what you mean by those vessels that look like big sticks?" Gus tried to explain, remembering now what they discovered in the book Kentho had found. The book with pictures drawn of Swarm and of massive cigar shaped vessels, like those detected by the Hawaiian observatory. "We don't really know anything about Swarm, who they are or what they want, but we saw those long blunt vessels on a planet along the way. Jon took pictures of them. I can show you the planet on your galactic map."

Gus pulled out his tablet, switched on the display and searched for the sandy planet and its solar system.

"Here, this one." Gus showed his tablet screen for Uzano, who then slid his massive right palm over his left arm between elbow and palm. An interface turned on, on top of his arm.

"That's so cool. It's like in the movie *Predator*," Jon whispered and pulled his sleeve. "Remember, when the creature laughs nastily just before blowing itself up with the mini-nuke?" Gus nodded in agreement.

Moving one of his three fingers above his interface, Uzano shared the sandy planet's location on the main map in the middle of the room.

"We call those vessels Anthers, and this planet is Sagawe, located here at the edge of sector three. Meaning there is still time to act for New Thatho." Uzano looked first at Nova and then at the three new arrivals from New Thatho, who showed signs of relief at the news.

"Could you show us the entire galaxy, and how you share the sectors?" Gus asked carefully, feeling like he was out of his league in the present company.

Uzano made another movement above his personal interface, zooming the main map into the familiar Milky Way view and then cutting it into six sectors like a cake. Of the six, the display showed two sectors greyed out.

"What? One third of the galaxy is just, gone?" Jon asked loudly, his brain unable to accept the fact there was something worse out there than constant wars on Earth.

"Not gone, just without life as we know it," said Nova. "Swarm is an enemy we have fought for ages, and with ages I mean across time."

Jon and Gus knew she was talking about Black Table.

"The Blato has a vast network," she continued. "That network is not for travelling, but an intelligence counter measure to be aware of Swarm's movements ahead of them. Messing with time can be more dangerous than Swarm. With small actions in our past, we might erase ourselves from existence."

"Swarm is not a traditional enemy," said Uzano. "You cannot negotiate with it, nor intimidate it. It feels no fear, remorse, anger or love," he said, making the recent arrivals feel uncomfortable again. "It is more like a lethal disease of the galaxy, a natural phenomenon without evil intentions. It just keeps spreading, and we have no cure."

"How come our home planet has not noticed half the galaxy losing life?" asked Jon, feeling anger about everything he had learned so far, unaware he had just slipped out information about Earth.

"It takes a long time for light to reach your planet," Uzano explained calmly, "which is why you will not see the changes in real time."

Jon looked at Gus, who confirmed it by nodding. He had a hundred percent trust in his friend and found no reason to question the explanation any further. The anger inside him did not ease, just slowly changed into sadness and a sensation of fear for people on Earth.

"So how do you fight it?" Jon asked, feeling defeated.

"With everything we have got." Uzano said. "The best weapon is the Blato network. But creating the network has involved countless sacrifices. Before the network had sufficient data, we made all jumps blind, not knowing where the jump might lead. We lost a lot of explorers, millions to the vacuum of space or the inside of stars and planets."

Everyone around the table crossed their arms in front of their chests and bent their heads to honour the ones lost.

"We would like to help if possible," Jon said without hesitation, knowing their help would also help Earth.

Jon, Bartho, Kentho and Julith nodded in agreement.

"Gus is a genius when it comes solving technical problems, and our race on Earth has experienced war far more than we would like to admit." Jon paused, realising he had just given out the name of Earth. "We do not yet master space travel, but our imagination covers every possible intergalactic war you can think of," Jon said, feeling his fear change into hope. He felt there was no obstacle they could not conquer.

"In that case, your help is welcome, and we thank you for it," Uzano said and slightly bowed while holding one arm across his chest.

"Thank you all." Nova stood up. "Let's convene again in three days. Meanwhile, we will analyse Jon's pictures and send a scout team to study Anthers for anything new we could use."

"I would like to join the scout if possible," Jon called out to Nova before she turned away from the table.

"Very well. Come back here tomorrow at the same time. I have arranged accommodation for you all in this building. Uzano will show you where. I suggest you get some rest."

Before turning away she gave a slight smile which Jon thought to be the most beautiful smile he had ever seen, causing his heartbeat to increase. He was in trouble and he knew it.

Everyone around the table got up and walked out until only Uzano and the recent arrivals remained.

"This way," he said and lead them out.

CHAPTER 10

THE TRENCH

Uzano led the visitors to their private units, one floor below from Operations. The units resembled normal apartments like on Earth, with high ceilings and wide balconies looking across the city towards the ocean. Jon and Gus had their own apartment next to the New Thathonians with a shared balcony.

"Would you have believed in Portland, that this is where we would end up?" Jon said, leaning against the balcony railing and looking over the alien city to the ocean in the distance. "I can't believe we woke up in a Portland hotel only few days ago."

Gus joined him at the railing. To their right, a glass door slid aside and Kentho, Julith and Bartho stepped on to the balcony, gasping at the view.

"How are you doing, Kentho?" Jon asked Kentho, who looked exhausted.

"Just tired," Kentho replied, yawning.

"What are your thoughts about all this?" Jon looked at Bartho and Julith.

"Overwhelmed, relieved and excited," Bartho said. "Overwhelmed about all this," he repeated and nodded towards the city below them. "I'm also worried what will happen to New Thatho if this Swarm gets there." He paused. "But then again I feel relieved that Azons on New Thatho are not a threat to the families and friends we had to leave behind. I also feel excited about what we could learn about Thatho, our original home planet, and if we can go there."

"We won't let Swarm reach New Thatho," Jon said with determination and placed his hand on Bartho's shoulder. "But first, we need to learn more about this Swarm."

"Guys?" Gus had pulled out his tablet and was staring at it intently. "With the new data from the Black Table here on Azonia, I could create a similar map of our galaxy with sectors like we just saw in Operations. We are now in sector three, as is New Thatho." He paused and turned display towards his friends. "But Earth is, or should I say was, in sector two."

An hour later, both apartments had fruit and water brought to them for refreshments, which all found to be in need for. After Kentho tasted the exotic fruit, he headed to bed, exhausted. Jon also lay on the bed in the apartment he and Gus shared. All his muscles ached from the past few day's running and exploring. He pulled his satchel closer and found the book signed by Dr Wells. He turned his head and saw Gus, Bartho and Julith, gathered on the balcony, talking theories about Swarm and debating the best course of action. They waved their hands and shook their heads.

Feeling exhausted, Jon placed the book on his chest and crossed his finger on top of it. He closed his eyes, took a few deep breaths and fell asleep.

In his dream, he was on Santa Monica beach boulevard in California. The sun was shining, and a warm wind was blowing from the sea, carrying the sound of waves breaking on the shore. People were biking, kick boarding and jogging past him. Some played beach-volley over a net erected on the sand. Two small kids were building a sandcastle, running sometimes to the waterline to fill their small red buckets with water. Along the boulevard, street buskers performed for money. Jon looked up to the sky and noticed black clouds approaching. Something was in the black clouds. They were not filled with water particles, but with billions and billions of small bug-like flying organisms instead. It was Swarm. Everything became dark around him. Swarm covered the sunlight, turning everything on its path into dust with a single touch. Jon stood in the middle of everything, but the Swarm did not touch him. People began running and screaming. There was nowhere they could hide. One by one, people puffed into dust. A little girl stood crying next to her sandcastle, the red plastic bucket still in her hand. The ocean behind her turned black.

Jon woke up with breathing heavily and looked around. The balcony was empty and Gus was not in the room. Jon removed the book from his chest, put it down on floor, turned on his stomach and fell back to sleep.

Gus was heading for Operations. He also felt exhausted but could not sleep until he knew more about Swarm. After a few wrong turns, he located the room they had assembled in earlier, one floor above. In the room, he emptied the contents of his satchel onto the table where Uzano had sat, including the extra power source and crystals he was carrying inside the golden fabric. He studied the round pillar in the middle of the room where the larger three-dimensional map was displayed earlier. After a quick search with his hands, he found a control panel on the pillar near the floor. While humming the Axel Foley theme song from *Beverly Hills Cop*, he removed the control panel and found similar but smaller crystals as used by Black Table. He removed a few crystals, opened them from the top as he had done before, and then inserted wires from his stripped cable. He picked up his tablet and plugged in the cable from the pillar. While still humming the theme song, he typed in commands and witnessed the data scrolling on his screen.

"Jackpot!" he shouted in celebration.

He opened his simulation tool, entered recent information he had learned and hit the 'start simulation' button on his screen.

"Interesting," he said looking at the screen. "I wonder ..."

"What are you doing here?" A gloomy voice surprised Gus, making him drop his tablet. It was Uzano. "Interesting approach." He looked at Gus's way to hack the mapping interface. "You could have just asked. Nothing here is secret."

"I'm sorry," Gus said embarrassed, now regretting his actions. "I needed more information and couldn't wait. I also did not think you would willingly share information with us. Especially when you know we came from Earth, which is in the sector two, within Swarm's territory."

"For now," Uzano said with a calm voice.

"For now?" Gus asked, confused.

Those two words woke a little hope inside him, enough to push aside the horror he felt earlier.

"Your first two jumps took you almost 300 years forward in time. The Blato from your last location seems to be damaged, but based on your earlier jumps, you have ended 100 years into your own Earth's future. Therefore, the Earth you left is not yet in Swarm's territory," Uzano said. "I admit we are running out of ideas, but as long as we have hope, the fight is not over. We also believe the Blato network, or Black Table as I heard you and your friends referring to it, will still work to our advantage. Maybe even change the outcome."

"I would like to talk to you about that," Gus said. "I made a simulation tool, showing how the Swarm is behaving." Gus picked up his tablet and showed it to Uzano.

"Swarm seems to act like a river. If you place a stone to prevent a river flowing towards you, it will find a way around it and eventually continue. In some places, you created a dam. But the dam can never be big enough, and Swarm keeps building up and eventually flows over." Gus looked at Uzano, who agreed so far.

"There must be a source where Swarm is gaining its vast energy." Some place or a reason enabling the massive growth, something must feed it, somewhere here." Gus pointed to a location on the galactic map. "The river must start somewhere."

"That region is not accessible to us. Every new Blato delivery attempt has failed. We have no option but to jump there blind with tools to build a new Blato and dome. Once a Blato is built, it will connect to the Blato network, making jumps safe and accurate. So far, no-one has ever returned from the region where Swarm originates. We are no longer sending our people there to die."

"Have you tried traditional space travel?" Gus asked.

"Not an option, it is too far from here. By the time we reach it, Swarm would have taken over the entire galaxy. We do not know how to handle Swarm anymore, except for trying to stay out of its way. We do not know how it thinks. We do not conquer or suppress other races. But obviously, only defending is no longer enough."

"Well, lucky for you, we know how to conquer and suppress others," Gus said smiling, but instantly turned his smile into a grin, realising what he just said. "I say that with regret. Our planet has more history of suffering than I would like to admit. Our race has gone through too much exploiting others and wars. But maybe we can use that for our advantage now. From what I have seen so far, I believe Swarm has a source, strengthening it. Swarm also feeds on resources that are available, whatever is available, like planets, organisms and life as we know it." Gus moved the galaxy that was displayed in the middle of the room. "But see here and here. Swarm left empty areas. Why?" He looked at Uzano, who spread his long arms.

"Either the areas are toxic for Swarm, or there is nothing for it to gain," Gus said and zoomed closer to the galactic map, showing an enormous area between sectors one and two that was avoided by Swarm.

"We call that area of space the Trench." Uzano waved his large palm over the hologram. "There is nothing but dark matter pockets and black holes."

"And there lies our solution," Gus said. "Now we know Swarm's natural enemy. We just have to make ourselves too bitter for Swarm to digest."

For the first time, Uzano looked like had Gus surprised him with fresh information. He studied the galactic map and then Gus, looking curious.

"I believe I have a plan," Gus said and offered his fist for Uzano, who responded with his massive fist.

Before they exited the Operations, an ominous figure listening to them left in a hurry from behind the door.

Jon woke up from his nap when Gus entered their apartment unit.

"Oh, my God, that was some scary dream," Jon said, still feeling tired, sweating from the dream he had. "Where were you?" he asked, realising Gus had just returned. "Don't tell me, on an adventure to find some food for us?" Jon pulled himself into a sitting position and stretched his back by stretching his arms side to side over his head. He felt like someone had beaten him all over with a baseball bat. The entire room was spinning.

"Not really, but I saw a place on the way. I think we could find some food there," said Gus, receiving a thumbs up from Jon.

"You know the feeling, when travelling," Jon said, "and you wake up in the middle of the night in some unfamiliar place, but your brains thinks you are at home?" He looked around. "Take that feeling and multiply it by a million." He held his head between his palms. "Never thought I would say this, but this intergalactic travelling is really messing with my head."

"Let's go and find something to eat," said Gus, his brain still reeling from what he and Uzano had found out. "You will feel better after some food. I will ask if Bartho and his family would like to join us."

Gus went back out through the main door and a few seconds later Jon heard him knocking on their neighbour's door. Before he knew it, they were all at his door, waiting for Jon to join them. As Jon had fallen asleep with his clothes on, he merely put on his shoes and walked out.

The common dining hall resembled a large food court, like the ones at shopping centres on Earth. There were fresh food dispensing counters along two long walls, all offering fruit and some kind of jello in unique colours.

"Lunch is on me," Jon offered, after realising it was all for free. "Personally, I have always wanted to try pink jello," he said sarcastically and put two small plates with jello on his tray, right next to a small white pineapple-looking fruit.

Kentho followed his lead, and Jon realised it.

"You see Kentho, my mother used to say, you can, and should, taste everything at least once." Jon tried to wink but managed to close both his eyes instead. Kentho looked at him curiously.

Once they were all seated, Gus recounted everything he and Uzano had discovered in the Operations room after Uzano caught him sneaking around.

"Dark matter and black holes?" Bartho repeated after Gus finished.

"Yes," Gus said. "We could use Black Table network and the Trench somehow to control Swarm. Now eat your jello and we'll get back to this tomorrow. We all need some proper sleep." Gus finished what had collected for dinner.

On returning to their apartment doors, they all said good night before entering their units. Because of his earlier nap,

Jon had trouble falling asleep. Instead, he continued reading his book from Dr Wells.

It was late at night, when Jon approached Gus, who was deep asleep on his stomach. Jon poked Gus on the shoulder and whispered into his ear, "We need to talk."

Gus flinched. He sat on the edge of his bed, having the same difficulties as Jon earlier to remember where they were. He got up slowly, wearing only boxers and a semi-dirty T-shirt. Once awake, Jon led him to the furthest point of the balcony from New Thathonian's, to be sure no-one could overhear them.

"Listen," said Jon, whispering. "At the tunnels, when Kentho fell off the beam, he hit his head hard. You saw the blood, right?"

"So?" Gus said confused, still sleepy and disoriented.

"Later, I cleaned and fixed his wound, and then placed a baseball cap on it." Jon said, standing right in front of Gus, and acting like he was sharing the mysteries of the Universe.

"I'm going back to sleep now," Gus said out loud and turned around to head back inside.

Jon stepped in front of him and looked around to see if anyone had heard them.

"I believe Kentho and Dr Wells are the same person," said Jon, biting his thumb nail while waiting for Gus's response. Gus's response came in a form of Eddie Murphy laugh from *Beverly Hills Cop*, accompanied with a smile and raised eyebrows. Still laughing, Gus tried to walk by, but Jon held his arms against Gus's chest and looked into his eyes.

"No, hear me out. The scar." Jon said. "It looks identical to the scar Dr Wells had." Jon looked for any reaction from Gus, who was still not responding, but at least was now listening, tilting his head on a side. "He recognised us at the

Comic Con. Think about it, his reacted with surprise, and he was smiling with tears in his eyes. He recognised us. And then there is the book Dr Wells wrote."

Jon pulled out the copy Dr Wells had signed with the mysterious coordinates. He opened the very imprint page with the publisher and author information. "Dr Wells's full name is Kevin Bart Wells," Jon said. "Kentho Vinth, aka Ke-Vin. And his second name Bart, as from his father, Bartho?" Jon looked at the book and felt doubt rising in his mind. "I know it sounds crazy ..."

"Actually, it doesn't sound crazy at all," said Gus, looking rather serious and surprising Jon. "It makes all the sense in the world. Think about it. Instead of bending space to bring two locations next to each other, Black Table is using existing places, but in different times. Distance to travel is nothing when time is bent. Movement of our galaxy takes care of moving planets. Think about it. Where were we at lunch time?"

"Just on the floor above us. Not that far," replied Jon.

"No, we were thousands and thousands of kilometres away. With this technology, not even theoretical wormhole is needed."

"If that is true, are we now in the same place we started from? Where Earth used to be?" Jon looked confused.

"Exactly!" Gus shouted and instantly covered his mouth, paused and then continued. "But no. Because the longer we stay in one place, the position changes. You remember Dr Wells's presentation? Everything in space is hurtling forward at high speed, all the time. He also seemed very off during the presentation, remember? He kept looking into the crowd like he was looking for something ..."

"Or someone?" they finished the sentence together.

"When he walked off the stage, he seemed worried and puzzled. He must have been looking for us." Gus looked at Jon into his eyes.

"Kentho is so Dr Wells," they said again the same time and fist bumped.

"But if that's true, Kentho being Dr Wells," Jon theorised, "that means that we, they, or just Kentho, will eventually end up to Earth."

"You are right." Gus looked first troubled, but quickly relieved. "Again, what happened has already happened. And what will happen has also already happened," he rambled, as Jon was still trying to digest the logic behind Gus's words. "We must trust that statement. Us being here is proof it will happen. Kentho gave us the coordinates for Black Table in Vancouver, which he will discover one day by travelling there. When and how, we need not know, because we know it already happened."

Jon made a mind-blowing gesture with his hands expanding away from his head.

CHAPTER 11

BETRAYAL

The next morning, Jon and Gus woke up with a knocking on their door. Both of them were too sleepy to react, Jon merely grunted out a sound that had no words.

"Uzano and the others would like to see you in Operations as soon as possible!" Nova shouted through the door.

"Coming!" Jon called back as he was finally able to produce a coherent word.

He forced himself to sit on the side of the bed and yawned while stretching in his usual way.

"I feel like I slept a year," he said to Gus, who looked exactly like Jon, hair all over the place and pillow prints on his face.

A few minutes later, all five visitors found themselves walking together towards the Operations room. Just like before, the round table in the room was filled with Azons and Thathonians. Uzano stood next to Nova, who was seated.

Jon, Gus, Bartho, Kentho and Julith took up the empty area near the back wall. Someone from outside closed the door.

"My fellow Azonians," said Uzano, "yesterday, after our meeting, our guest Gus came up with an alternative theory we should look into." He offered the room to Gus, who hesitantly walked forward.

"Hello again. My name is Gus, and ..." Gus struggled, unaware of any protocol he should follow.

"Please Gus, just show us what you showed me yesterday," Uzano said calmly.

"All right," Gus said and continued walking into the middle of the room. "I have studied the behaviour of Swarm against the table network data." He nodded towards Uzano, who opened the galactic map with six sectors and Swarm's progress.

"As you can see, Swarm is spreading like a plant, looking for energy to consume. Unfortunately, we and our homes are the energy it needs." Gus moved his hand around Swarm's blackened territory. "Swarm starts here, or that is the current assumption." Gus nodded to Uzano, who moved his massive finger above his personal arm interface, zooming the map into a point where Swarm originated from.

"Now, according to Uzano, this area is unexplored, but I believe it is exactly where we should go," Gus said. This set the audience murmuring and shaking their heads. "I tapped into Black Table data and compiled a simulation, based on the history of the building of the table network."

"To be clear, with Black Table, Gus means Blato," Uzano said, letting the rest understand what name the recent arrivals had gotten used to.

Uzano then started the simulation Gus had given him earlier. The Milky Way galaxy in the middle of the room returned to a time when it was still filled with stars and life. Also, millions of turquoise Black Table indicators disappeared.

"Please pay attention on the map," Uzano said as he let the simulation run forward.

On the enormous galactic map, light begun disappearing from the stars and blackness spread, covering almost the entire first sector. Slowly, turquoise dots began appearing into the map, representing Black Tables that Azonians and Thathonians were building. As the Black Table network grew, so did the Swarm.

"If I am right, the harder you fought Swarm, the more it grew. Is that right?" Gus asked, allowing the simulation to progress.

"That is right," Nova said in return. "We have stayed a step ahead of them, but Swarm always overcame whatever we do."

"Swarm spreads wherever you set a Black Table?" Gus asked like he already knew the answer.

"Correct," Nova answered.

"My theory is," Gus explained, "that Swarm is feeding on tachyon radiation." He paused and looked around the room, which now was in total silence. "You need Tachyons to power Black Tables. Am I right? Tachyon particles are faster than light, therefore used in Black Table technology?"

At the back wall, Jon looked at his hands and then wiped them against his pants, just in case he had tachyon radiation poisoning, which he did not.

"That is right," Uzano said. "That is also how we detected your power source, with tachyon sensors."

"This is nonsense! If, and only *if*, this theory is correct," roared the large Azonian, who had also spoken the day before, the one wearing armour with copper red fabric, "then it means we have been feeding it this whole time?"

"That is correct." Gus said calmly, knowing Uzano would share his view. "That would be the reason New Thatho is still untouched, even though it is right at the edge of Swarm's territory. They never used their table. But to verify this theory, we have to visit Sagawe. We need to bring an energy source near one of the Anthers and see how it reacts to tachyon radiation."

"That is extremely dangerous, and even if it is true" – Nova stepped in without taking sides on the argument – "it means our advantage with Black Table network would be lost. We could never use it again."

A loud murmur spread across the room.

"Maybe so, but with so many planets at risk," Gus said, "we need to see this through." He looked at his friends, who stood by the back wall, all were nodding their approval to his words. "If my theory is correct, it would also mean that even if Black Tables gave an advantage in the beginning, they later led Swarm and helped it spread. When you thought you could jump to planets ahead of Swarm, it unintentionally led Swarm to those planets. Or at least that is what the data is showing." Gus paused. "There's another thing, Mr, Sir ..." Gus said awkwardly and looked at the big Azonian wearing the copper red armour.

"My name is Muro. I am the commander of our security forces," Muro roared and stood up, crossed his arms over his chest and made a small nod.

"Commander Muro," Gus said and offered a fist bump, which Muro accepted by following Uzano's example from the sidelines. Jon chuckled from the back of the room.

"Commander Muro, would it be possible to modify one of those Flegs?" Gus asked.

"Flegs?" Muro became irritated again.

"I'm sorry, one of those flying egg-shaped silvery pods, to make it space travel capable and to include an active Black Table in its cargo space?"

"Never thought of that, but I believe it could be done," Muro replied and looked at Nova, who nodded. "It will be ready in a few days' time."

"Wow, really? That's fast?" Gus grinned at Jon. "I expected weeks or months."

"Let's get to work!" Uzano declared and switched off the map from his arm interface. "The team to Sagawe will leave right after nourishment."

The rest of the Azonians and Thathonians got up, crossed their arms over their chests, nodded and then walked out from the room.

About an hour later, Uzano and Nova came to pick up Jon and Gus from their apartment. Bartho had decided he and his family would stay behind, taking a long-needed rest and a chance to enjoy the city.

Uzano and Nova led Gus and Jon to the same transport room they used on arrival. The glass-walled room hummed and exiting the building. It descended towards a launch pad at the edge of the city next to the ocean where several silvery Flegs stood a few centimetres off the ground.

A few minutes later, Gus and Jon stepped out of the glass room and looked around before entering the Fleg.

Above them, the massive particle ring surrounding the planet sparkled.

"So beautiful," Jon said, admiring the colours the ring reflected. He had only ever seen one in pictures.

"I am glad you like it," said Nova, "it is our neighbour planet, Zudon. Or what is left of it." She looked at Jon and Gus, who were struck hard by the news. "It was our last resort to avoid Swarm reaching Azonia. We had to blow it up after Swarm Anthers entered Zudon's atmosphere and plunged into Zudon's terrain, just like in your pictures of Sagawe. Luckily, we had detected Anther's approach almost a year before, and we evacuated everyone to here on Azonia. But we lost a lot of homes, mine included. After the explosion, fine remains of Zudon spread in all directions, much of it pulled into our orbit." She paused before continuing, "It is beautiful, but a painful reminder." She looked up with sad eyes. Jon and Gus didn't know what to say, so said nothing.

After a Fleg ride of a few minutes of, they arrived at the Black Table dome. The dome was still protected with a white wall of light from the three pods that had stayed behind. Jon, Gus, Nova and Uzano exited from their pod, which landed inside the walled area. Two large Azonian guards wearing copper red suits waited for them at the dome entrance. Both carried Black Table power sources with them. Only these power sources were much larger than what Gus and Jon had seen so far. Both also had weapons, that seemed to be offline at the moment, integrated to their arm interfaces.

"Muro sent these two guards to guarantee our safety," Nova said as she led the group past the guards, into the dome.

"Great," Jon said out loud after passing the guards. "I only wish they wouldn't wear red," he whispered to Gus, referring to *Star Trek* TV-series, where any unnamed crew member wearing a red uniform wearing almost always end up dead during away mission.

Once they were all in, the two guards followed them with a loud thumping sound from their sturdy legs and enormous feet.

"Hi, I'm Jon, what are your names?" Jon said, turning towards the massive guards following him, but received only grunts and sneers that revealed hundreds of small teeth in perfect rows in reply.

Gus held his breath, impressed how Jon had no fear of the massive aliens.

"They seem nice," Jon said and looked casually at Gus while shrugging his shoulders.

At the table, one guard handed Uzano three deep red crystals, and a basketball-sized power source.

"What is that?" asked Gus, looking at the significantly larger power source.

"This will allow us to jump directly to Sagawe, without bending time," said Uzano, waving for Gus to come closer.

Gus instantly jumped forward, unable to resist learning more about the different coloured crystals and power sources. Meanwhile, Nova set the new crystals and power source into their usual places.

"The power needed for a direct wormhole jump is so enormous, it will deplete this power source completely. Therefore, we brought another one for the return trip," said Uzano, pointing towards the second guard carrying a second power source. "One of these power sources was used to blow up Zudon, the planet which is now surrounding our planet as an orbital ring. The one you saw outside just now." He turned towards the guard with the second power source. "So, handle them carefully."

The guard nodded and pulled the extra power source closer to his chest. A three-dimensional map lit up above the Black Table.

"Here we go," Nova said and selected Sagawe from the table's interface.

With the help of the stronger power source, Sagawe pulsed in a dark red colour, instead of turquoise. Also, the palm print on the table had changed colour to dark red. Without further warning, Uzano placed his enormous hand on the print, and they were gone.

Jon and Gus felt like their surrounding reality was pulled through a narrow pipe. Everything around them became distorted. A stream of lights stretched past them like disco lights after a dozen tequila shots. It reminded Jon and Gus of their visit to the Magic Kingdom park at Disney World in Florida. They had taken a ride on a rollercoaster called Space Mountain, where they sat in a small bobsleigh inside a space themed building. The two-seater bobsleigh then dropped straight down along a pitch-black underground track. The only thing they saw were lights stretching out and passing them. They knew they were going fast from the wind on their faces and the G-forces they felt when the sleigh rocketed along the track. Just like the rollercoaster, Black Table jump ended, and the world around them returned to normal. It was dark inside the dome on Sagawe.

"That was brutal," said Jon, holding himself up against the table, feeling seasick. All three crystals glowed red, giving the room a ghostly atmosphere. "Are you sure we are on Sagawe?" he asked loudly. "The table feels different, wet, warm and slimy" – he smelled his hands after touching the table – "and it smells absolutely horrible."

"Maybe," Gus mumbled, covering his mouth with his hand, "it's because I just threw up on it." He gasped for air as he leant over, hands on knees, spitting the foul taste out from his mouth.

"Oh, gross!" Jon shouted. He dropped to his knees and used the fine sand underfoot to wash his hands.

"What happened?" Gus asked. "Why do I feel sick?"

"When bending time," Nova explained, "the distance is nothing and jumps are relatively pleasant. But when bending space, we are travelling through two points in space pulled together by the Black Table. Because of that, you feel like it has pulled you through a narrow passage. You probably get used to it. We rarely use them because of the amount of energy required. That sphere would have powered our cities in Azonia for ten years. Therefore, this mission's approval did not come easy."

Outside of the dome was dark, which Jon commented to be to their advantage due to high daytime temperatures.

"If I remember correctly, the city is located forty-five degrees that way." Jon pointed out towards the peak he had walked over earlier.

While everyone looked at the peak, Jon discreetly kicked sand on top of the Azonian arm lying on the ground next to entrance. It was the same arm Jon had dragged out a few days earlier, although it now looked dried out, like many years had passed since their last visit.

Uzano ordered the guard with the spare power source to remain at the dome and for the other guard to accompany them to the city.

After a half hour hike, they reached the same peak as Jon did a few days ago. This time the walk felt easier without the scorching sun. Only the soft sand under their feet made for heavy going, but the night desert wind felt pleasant, like air-conditioning. At the peak, Jon panted and pointed towards the area where he saw the city and the Anthers. Uzano lifted his left arm interface in front of him and made slight movements on top of it with the large fingers of his right-hand. A three-dimensional holographic map appeared above his interface, showing the destroyed city and Anthers, just like Jon remembered.

"That one," Uzano said and pointed to the closest Anther. He made few finger movements above his arm interface and a ten-metre-long red line appeared above the sand. As they walked forward, the line always stayed in front of Uzano, showing the way around ruins and larger rocks in the way.

"That's so cool," said Jon. "Would have needed that in New Thatho, and in a dozen other places."

When they were only hundred metres from the Anther, Uzano disabled the automated path finder and turned on a light on his arm. The light was so powerful it illuminated the remaining distance to the Anther like it was a sunny day.

"It's massive," Gus said in awe. "But I don't see any propulsion system of any kind."

"As far as we know, they do not have any," Nova replied. "It really is like an organism. The Swarm is launching these Anthers from somewhere and they travel through space without guidance and power. They then pierce through a planet's atmosphere and plunge onto the surface, releasing millions of tiny insect-like organisms that consume everything and everyone in their path. But something is different here on Sagawe. Usually there is nothing left, not even ruins. Good, that we came to investigate." She looked up at the Anther exterior and bridges that resembled flower petals, leaning down on to the ground. "There is our way in," she said and took the lead. Meanwhile, Gus pulled out his smart phone and began recording everything he saw as they approached the entrance. His phone light was just enough to examine the Anther's exterior hull. At the entrance, Jon slid his hand against the hull.

"Feels like stone," he said, studying the surface.

"Oh, my God!" Gus said loudly and pulled Jon's hand off from the wall. "Don't you remember any alien movies?" He continued recording Jon touching the wall again. "You should not be touching things with your bare hand. And especially, we won't stay to watch any alien eggs hatch." He sounded furious and turned the phone's camera towards himself. "Oh, look at that, what could it be … something is moving in a huge alien egg, on some scary spaceship … Jesus!" Gus shouted angrily as he re-enacted the scene from *Alien* with hand gestures.

"It's a wall. Not an alien egg," Jon defended himself while Gus turned the camera back to him.

"Friends, please," Nova said. "Can we concentrate on the matter at hand?" She pointed her light towards the dark interior of the Anther.

Uzano shone his powerful light through the entrance, revealing spider-like webs crossing from wall to wall within the space inside. There were millions of webs, all a few centimetres thick. From them hung millions of round egg-looking pockets which were the size of stretched bowling balls.

"I freaking knew it!" Gus shouted desperately. "Looks like eggs to me!" He further re-enacted the scene from *Alien* by placing his hand under his T-shirt and then pushing it forward, stretching his T-shirt like something trying to get out all the while making groaning sounds. When he saw his impersonation was failing to impress he decided to get back into serious-mode. He took several steps back, still holding his phone's camera towards the eggs. "Looks like the web is protecting the eggs from velocity changes and from the Anther's impact on the planet's surface?" he theorised.

"That would make sense. We have never seen the inside of an Anther before," said Nova curiously and walked closer to an egg attached to web.

At this Jon opened his eyes wide in shock and looked at Gus, who held up his hands in front of him, his palms facing upwards. "Just hold on," Gus said, stopping Nova before she reached the ball and pulling her back. "Uzano, do you have anything we could use to study them from afar?"

"I do," Uzano said and stepped forward. With a few finger movements over his left arm interface, he produced a 3D model of the object. "Whatever it is, it's dead now."

The object rotated above his left-hand interface. Uzano nodded to the guard who came along with them. Hesitantly, but as ordered, the guard approached the egg-shaped object and cut it off from the web with a laser tool he enabled from his left-hand armour. He pulled the egg off from the web and laid it on the ground. Using the same thin red laser beam, he cut the egg open. The egg opened with a cracking sound. Gus and Jon held their hands in front of their mouths to prevent any alien attacks towards them. Nothing happened.

"Interesting," said Nova. "It is dead." She knelt next to the egg and studied the remains closer. "Maybe the people of Sagawe used some kind of bioweapon that destroyed everything living?"

"Maybe they didn't know what they used and destroyed themselves in the process?" Uzano commented.

"When I took the pictures, few days ago" – Jon stepped closer carefully – "I didn't see any signs of a battle. It seemed more like everything and everyone had simply vanished."

"Let's look further, maybe there is something else to learn about Swarm," said Gus. "I and Jon will head this way." He walked deeper into Anther, Jon right behind him.

Above them millions of webs and eggs crossed wall to wall, layer after layer.

"There is no cockpit, crew or anything that would control this vessel," Gus said sounding disappointed while recording the surroundings with his phone. "It's just a massive means of delivering, something. Something able to spread and kill everything on its way." He suddenly felt amazed and afraid at the same time.

"So, Swarm's goal is to consume everything and spread?" Jon asked, already knowing the answer.

"Well, yes. It sure sounds like a galactic cancer, doesn't it?" Gus said. "Without having a hidden agenda or strategy. It just grows like a plant, but on a massive scale."

"What the hell! How is that possible?" Jon shouted, standing at the wall opposite from the entrance, furthest away from Gus.

"Why, what did you find?" Gus ran towards Jon, who stared at something on the wall with his own mobile phone's torch.

"It's a NASA insignia. NASA made these," said Jon, now pointing his light away from the wall and into Gus's face.

"What, where?" Gus shouted in shock, shining his own light onto wall, unable to see anything on it.

"Nowhere! Don't be stupid!" Jon laughed and pulled down the light from Gus's face. "You should have seen your face though. Priceless," he said, and he imitated Gus's facial impression, mouth open and eyes wide open, trying to find the notorious cross.

"Very funny," Gus responded slightly agitated. "But the scary part is, I believed it for a second."

"Everything all right here?" asked Nova, with Uzano and the guard right behind her.

"Everything is okay," said Gus, trying to avoid annoying their hosts any further. "Jon thought he found something, but it turned out to be nothing," he continued and gave stink eye to Jon. "I think it's time to test the theory we came here for." He pulled out the heavy golden fabric, hiding the power source inside. "If my theory is correct, Swarm should react to the tachyon radiation this power source is emitting."

Gus knelt down and revealed the power source. He placed it on the floor, only a metre away from the opened egg. He folded the golden fabric and put it back into his satchel. Now all they had to do was to wait. It was dead quiet. A few minutes passed, but nothing happened. Gus still knelt next to the power source. He pulled out the golden fabric from his satchel and unfolded it.

"Nothing," said Nova. "I guess we are back to ..." She paused, for the floor under the power source began dispersing neon green light in all directions, making it look like the floor had a thin neural network, spreading neon green pathways further and further.

"Okay, that should be enough," said Gus, and picked up the power source. "I guess our tachyon theory has merit. And I guess we should get out of here, right now."

"I will take that," said the guard, who stepped forward and reached for the power source in Gus's hands.

"Thank you, but Gus can manage. You can stand down," said Uzano casually, expecting the guard to obey.

The guard unexpectedly swung his massive arm into Uzano's face instead, making Uzano grunt and fly to the ground a few metres away.

"What are you doing?" shouted Nova to the guard, who was now pointing his integrated arm weapon towards her, making her take a step backwards.

"I have orders from Muro," the guard stated and took the power source from Gus, "to protect Azonia and the Blato network. My orders are to leave you here. I am sorry." The guard fought his mixed feelings from acting against his own people for the first time in their history.

"So am I," said Jon, and blinded the guard momentarily with his phone torch, before launching into him with full speed and power.

Knowing the guard was much stronger than him, Jon plunged his right shoulder into the guard's left knee, making them both crumple and fall. The guard grunted from the pain in his knee, dropped the power source, turned on his side and aimed his weapon directly at Jon, who had landed face down on his stomach. In a panic, Jon grabbed the power source rolling next to him and smashed it into the guard's weapon interface. The guard's interface emitted small yellow sparks and shut down. In anger, the guard took a swing at Jon, who caught the enormous arm with both hands and wrapped his legs around it. Jon then yelled out as he pulled, twisted and squeezed the guard's arm as hard as he could until he heard a loud pop, followed by the guard's roar of pain. The struggle was over. The guard's interface was malfunctioning, his left knee was throbbing, and his right arm was dislocated. Jon let go his hold and pushed himself away from the guard. Gus and Nova helped him up, while the guard stayed on his back, moaning while cradling his arm.

"Don't mess with a commando!" shouted Gus at the guard.

"Commando, who has had no coffee for days!" Jon shouted after Gus.

"Yeah!" Gus confirmed Jon's words. "And don't wear red on off-world missions!" A statement which confused Uzano and Nova.

Jon and Gus fist bumped, and then helped Uzano up, who held his head and checked if it was bleeding. It was not.

"I do not understand," he said, still feeling dizzy from the blow. "Muro has always put Azonia first."

"Maybe he thinks this is the best course of action," Nova said, holding Uzano. "Maybe ..."

"Guys, what's happening?" Gus interrupted her, looking upwards.

Neon green light was spreading rapidly along the web constructs through the pathways in the floor and walls.

"Not good!" Jon shouted, pointing down instead.

Gus turned his mobile torch towards the power source, realising it had cracked from the impact against the guard's weapon interface, and was now leaking thick turquoise liquid. The liquid was emitting high levels of tachyon radiation, waking up the Anther. Gus followed the neon green light with his phone, realising the video recording was still on since their arrival. The light spread everywhere, exposing millions of webs and eggs. They had no choice but to leave the broken power source and make a run for it.

"RUN!" Gus shouted as he watched his second worst nightmare come true.

Ever since his parents died, his worst nightmare has been to end up homeless. The hatching alien eggs, on an abandoned alien ship, stood firmly in second place. Jon and Uzano helped the guard up and supported him from each side while heading out. The eggs buzzed like a beehive whenever the neon green light reached them.

At the dome, the second guard stood at the entrance, holding the second, larger power source in his massive left hand. He looked nervous, not knowing how the experiment went. Then, from the top of the highest sand peak, he heard shouting. The guard enabled his 3D viewer towards the peak. Two figures ran down the sandy slope, fell down rolling and then ran again. A moment after, three more figures appeared. From those three, two figures were supporting the third. The guard enabled the weapon integrated into his left arm. When the three last figures reached the bottom of the highest dune, a swarm of unknown organisms poured over the peak after them.

"Start the Blato!" Nova shouted, while running ahead with Gus.

The guard hesitated and raised his weapon beam towards Nova and Gus instead.

"We know about your orders!" Nova said, panting and taking deep breaths. "You must start the Blato, or we all die, and so will Azonia!"

The guard grunted, lowered his gun, spun around and went inside the dome carrying the second, large power source. Gus and Nova were almost at the dome while Uzano and Jon had slowed down. Fatigue from supporting the injured guard's weight was taking its toll.

"We won't make it," the injured guard said, pain piercing his knee. He compared the distance to the dome with that of the approaching Swarm behind them. "You must leave me."

"We will make it," Jon said, pushing himself forward, his feet sinking into the sand from the extra weight they carried.

"I am sorry Uzano, for going behind your back," the guard moaned and pushed himself away from Jon's and Uzano's supporting grip. "Go!" he yelled and fell to the sand.

Jon and Uzano stopped for a second, thinking through their options. There was nothing else they could do. Without the extra weight, they sprinted towards the dome. A low buzzing sound grew louder as a mass of Swarm piled up above the guard they had left behind. The guard stood up, roaring with pain. He found balance on the soft sand and took a look at his approaching death, a cloud made of small organisms, humming towards him. His weapon was destroyed, but the display on his interface still worked, signalling the horrors closing in. With a painful roar, he used his massive middle finger to unlock access to a restricted command menu. When ready, his interface turned red, waiting for his final confirmation for self-destruct.

"For Azonia!" he shouted and laid down his finger.

At first there was no sound. Long shadows extended in front of Jon and Uzano as they ran when a bright white light flashed behind them. The light burned so hot it created a vacuum where the guard had stood, sucking all the air and sand from his surroundings. Then with a massive explosion, reverse pressure pushed everything away from the origin, spreading a massive pressure wave of air and fire in all directions. The explosion burned the approaching Swarm halfway up to the sandy peak, and the following pressure wave pushed the rest back over the top. Jon and Uzano could feel the heat before the pressure wave knocked them to the ground. They got up fast and looked back. There was a small crater where the guard used to be. The sand at the centre of the crater had melted into waved glass, still glowing red from the heat.

"We've got some extra time." Jon said. "Let's make it count."

More Swarm poured over the peak again. Inside the dome, Gus had just finished the table setup, when a loud explosion shook the dome. The dome wall had protected them from the shock wave.

"What the hell was that?" Gus asked, holding himself against the table.

"Sounded and felt like the self-destruction in our arm interfaces," the guard inside said seriously and walked out to see what had happened. "Where is Mazon?" he said to himself, looking for his guard friend, but saw only Jon and Uzano approaching fast.

The guard lifted his gun and fired it towards Jon and Uzano. Arm-thick beams of turquoise light of energy flew inches past Jon and Uzano, blasting into the cloud of Swarm behind them. He fired again and again, giving Jon and Uzano more time.

"Be ready to jump!" he shouted back towards the Black Table.

Jon and Uzano were only metres away with Swarm right at their heels. The guard walked backwards into the dome, firing to keep Swarm away.

"Now!" he shouted, and Gus placed his hand on the palm print.

Jon and Uzano jumped forward. They flew headfirst inside the dome. There was a bright flash, and they were gone.

CHAPTER 12

POLITICS

The mission team pulled through the wormhole and arrived back to Azonia with a flash of light and a brief crackling sound. From their headfirst dive into the dome, Jon and Uzano hovered in the air for a split of a second, before dropping to the ground. A faint cloud of sand dust puffed into the air when they landed coughing and moaning. Gus again felt nauseous and held himself against the table. Nova stormed out of the dome and ordered the pod pilots to assist.

"We need to move," said Uzano, slowly standing up with assistance from the pilots. "We have Muro to deal with." He wiped the sand dust off his clothes.

As Nova, Uzano, Jon and Gus were back on board one of the Flegs it took off. During the flight back to the city, Uzano tried to make sense of what had happened. "Muro has always been protective over Black Table network but taking measures like these are extremely rare among Azonians," he said.

"It's called politics," said Gus, who was pressed tightly under the shoulder safety harness.

"Politics?" Nova asked, confused. "We don't have that word."

"Lucky you," Gus said. "In politics, a person or a group of persons, are driving forward issues that are benefiting mostly themselves. Unfortunately, on Earth, politics seems to be more important than people's health and happiness."

"That's awful," Nova responded in shock. "Why would anyone place themselves in front of their people?"

"Based on our experience of politics," Gus said, "Muro is afraid of losing something important. Based on his reaction during the meeting before our trip, that something in this case could be the Black Table network. So far, the Black Table network has given him a feeling of control over Swarm. We must convince him the recent discovery is much more important than his personal illusion of control. We should approach him carefully and make it sound like it is his idea. I am guessing he does not understand what Earth's politics are capable of. Now, this is how I think we should approach ..."

Gus continued explaining his plan while the Fleg slowed down. After a slow approach, they landed softly onto same platform they had taken off only a few hours earlier. Before entering the glassed room ride towards their building, Uzano told the pilot to call an emergency meeting. Everyone in question should join them in the Operations room.

The room with glass walls gained altitude rapidly until it reached the destination level next to highest building in the city. Like before, the room integrated with the building and came to a full stop, allowing its passengers to exit.

"Operations in ten minutes," Nova said, parting ways with Gus and Jon.

After three wrongs turns, Jon and Gus found their living unit. Instead of entering, they walked past and knocked on the neighbouring door. After few taps on the door, Kentho opened it.

"Jon!" Kentho shouted and gave a big hug to Jon, and then to Gus. "Why are you so dirty, again?"

"Nice to see you too, kiddo," Jon said and hugged him back while Bartho and Julith entered the room from the balcony.

"How did it go?" Bartho asked, Julith standing next to him.

"Not good," Jon said.

He recounted everything that had happened on Sagawe. How Swarm had reacted to the power source, how Swarm multiplied instantly and how they were betrayed by Muro and his guards.

"They did what?" Julith asked in shock. "I thought they saw Swarm as much as a threat as everyone else."

"And that is why there is an emergency meeting in Operations in a few minutes." Gus stepped in. "We need to stick together. At this moment, I only trust you guys and Jon. Maybe also Uzano and Nova. They seemed as shocked as we were by Muro's actions. But we have to be careful."

A loud chattering filled the Operations room. Azonians and Thathonians were exchanging theories about what had happened on Sagawe. As before, Uzano, Nova and Muro took places next to each other. Gus, Jon and the New Thathonians stood at the back near the wall.

"Quiet please!" Nova raised her voice, and the room rapidly fell silent. "The Sagawe mission has given us fresh information about Swarm, Black Table network ..." she paused, "and about Muro." She turned her gaze towards Muro. "Could you please explain yourself and what happened on Sagawe?" Nova sat down. Jon leaned his head towards Gus, watching the reactions of those in the room. Half of the audience appeared surprised, the other half did not.

"I guess now we know who is supporting Muro," he whispered. "Those who did not look surprised."

"You got that right," Gus responded.

Muro stood up, looking troubled. Conflicts were not new on Azonia, but acting behind someone's back, was.

"Everything I have done has been for Azonia," Muro said, defending himself with a hint of embarrassment. "I will *not* let some strangers from another world come and destroy our hard work and ability to fight Swarm."

Muro waved his hand towards the wall where Gus and his friends stood. Some at the table nodded in agreement with him, and some looked confused, still unaware of what had happened on Sagawe.

"The Blato network is our only chance to fight Swarm!" he continued, appearing more confident now. "Swarm has spread too wide, and we cannot just give up our network merely based on some crazy theories by those same strangers!" he roared louder when he noticed some agreement in the room. "So yes, I gave my guards orders to seize the power source from the visitors and leave them at the planet."

The last words dampened the chatter in the room. There was a moment of perfect silence, and then the rest of the attendees began talking over each other. Some seemed to blame Muro for wrongdoing, and some argued for defending the Black Table network.

"You all need to know what happened on that planet," said Gus, who walked forward, straight to the room's interface. He attached his phone to interface with the same cabling he had hacked the crystals with. He switched on his smart phone display, selected saved videos from his photo gallery, and began playing the footage he had recorded during their mission.

"As soon as we reached the Anther, we realised it to be dormant or dead. At least, our sensor did not detect any life upon our arrival. The Anther also did not contain any technology to explain how it can travel through space. The only conclusion would be they are launched from somewhere towards inhabited planets, while Swarm remains in a dormant state throughout the journey. It's not like there was a captain's log or anything else similar left behind to explain their status," Gus sounded frustrated and pointed out on the video how Jon touched the walls and how the removed egg was empty. "We don't know what happened on that planet, but there was no life, nothing." He gave a dramatic pause. "At least not until we took out a tachyon power source, used for Black Tables, Blatos." He paused the video image where the intact power source stood on the ground, and neon green pathways had spread around it.

"That proves nothing," said an older Thathonian man, a supporter of Muro.

"Oh, but this does," Gus said and let the footage continue, where Jon smashed the guard's weapon with the power source. "So far, Muro's guard was doing what he thought was right. As was Jon, protecting the rest of us as self-defence."

The video showed the struggle which ended with a loud pop, Jon dislocating the guard's arm. The sound made the audience groan with grimaces of empathic pain.

"Here," he explained, "when the power source broke and tachyon radiation poured out, the whole Anther came to life." Gus played the video to the end, showing how the entire ship glowed green, and the eerie sound echoed from Swarm eggs. The footage ended after he had shouted to make a run for it. The audience in the room looked shocked. The chattering began again.

"And now for the solution part," Gus whispered for Uzano, who took over.

"Quiet. Please!" Uzano's deep voice roared calmly. "Muro's guard did what he was told to do. But he also saved our lives." Uzano switched the image to the three-dimensional green scanned version, captured by Uzano's arm interface while they escaped. "When Swarm was advancing on us, we would not have made it while carrying the injured guard, commander Mazon, from the second fleet." He bowed towards Muro. "Here you can see how fast Swarm grew, and all because of that minor power source." He paused. "And here commander Mazon" – Uzano looked at Muro – "pushed us away and sacrificed himself to give us a chance to make it back to the dome which we did, to bring you these facts." Uzano let the recorded scan play to the end, from Swarm's horrific approach, to commander Mazon's self-destruction, and until the moment they barely made the jump.

The room fell quiet again. Gus stepped into middle again.

"To beat Swarm, we have to work together, not against each other," he said, everyone now looking at him, their doubts cast aside. "Your Blato, to us known as Black Table network, might still be the key to doing so."

"Explain," said Muro, leaning forward and looking interested.

"The table network and the long range data suggest that while Swarm is gaining energy from tachyon particles, it is avoiding any black hole activity," Gus explained and pointed towards the Milky Way galaxy map Uzano had switched on as planned.

Uzano zoomed into the area avoided by Swarm. The area they called the Trench, filled with dark matter and black holes.

"Maybe we can use Black Table network to make our galaxy toxic for Swarm. At least for the time being, until we find a way to study its source, located right here." Gus pointed to the location from where Swarm spread from, waiting for Muro to jump in, which he did, just as Gus had predicted. The plan was working.

"Maybe we could mask the Blato network's tachyon radiation with black hole radiation?" Muro said. "It would push Swarm away from planets, instead of being called to them. Meanwhile, we will work on a means to reach Swarm's source, with the resources Gus suggested earlier," Muro said, now standing with enthusiasm.

His supporters nodded in approval, as did those who had found his actions questionable.

"That's an excellent idea," Uzano said, while others around the table also seemed pleased with the idea. "Maybe you and Gus could come up with a plan. Anything you need is at your disposal."

"We will get right to it," said Muro boldly, but then paused, looking ashamed. "I am sorry about what happened on Sagawe. I honestly thought you were here to harm us and our network." He looked at Gus and the rest of the mission team.

"Everything is okay," Gus said. "There must be a reason Azonians and people of Thatho has always worked together. Maybe Earth would fit in there as well?" Gus offered Muro his fist for a fist bump.

"You will, and you already do." Muro smiled with his hundred teeth sparkling in a long two rows.

He responded to Gus's fist bump in kind, launching the Operations room into cheers.

Minutes later, Gus followed Muro, Nova and Uzano to plan their next move against Swarm. Jon, Bartho, Julith and Kentho set off to their apartments. Jon, not feeling comfortable at the thought of being alone, asked Bartho if he could hang out with them. Before Bartho had a chance to answer, Kentho and Julith warmly welcomed his request. In their apartment, Kentho asked if he could bring Jon something to drink. Exhausted and thirsty, Jon slumped into a couch in the corner. The couch was much more comfortable than it looked.

"Do you think they can stop Swarm?" asked Kentho, sitting next to Jon and offering him an enormous glass of water.

"Thank you Kentho," Jon said with a smile and took the glass from Kentho. "I have my trust in Gus. He, if anyone can come up with a plan that works ..." He paused and took a long sip from the glass. "His top priority is to keep us safe. Us being also you and your parents."

"Can you tell me more about Earth." Kentho lay on his back next to Jon, using Jon's leg as a pillow. "Is it like New Thatho?"

"Earth is beautiful, just like New Thatho," Jon said. "There are millions of unique animals and insects, but no

Azonians. We have tales about the city of Atlantis, which disappeared into the ocean. That could have been habited by Azonians, but there is no proof of any kind. I asked Gus to find out why on New Thatho people are afraid of Azonians, and why you cannot understand them. Maybe he will come up with some answers."

"So, what did you do on Earth? Gus told me you were some kind of soldier, is that true?"

"It is, but it was only a small but exciting part of my life."

"How was it exciting? Did you hurt people?" Kentho could not believe Jon would hurt someone.

"I didn't hurt anyone if I didn't have to." Jon did not feel comfortable thinking Kentho would find him evil.

"Would you hurt Muro?"

"Muro is not bad. He is just afraid. That makes people, and Azonians do horrible things."

"Tell me something of what you did as a soldier, please," Kentho begged.

"Fine." Jon smiled, finally giving up. "I can tell you a war-game story, when I was doing a night recon mission on enemy forces."

"What enemy, I thought there are no Azons on Earth?" Kentho asked.

"It's complicated on Earth. There are so many people, with so many beliefs, with limited resources. Conflicts among us are constant. We have over four thousand religions. Can you imagine that? And every one of them thinks theirs is the right one, making them ready to do anything to protect their faith. We have become our own enemy."

"That is just nuts." Kentho shook his head. "And what is a recon? What is a war game?"

"A war game is how soldiers practise their skills, so the enemy is not a real enemy, but another team, often from a different country you are friendly with. A recon is a mission where the goal is to find out about the enemy, their resources, their strength, anything you can find out, but only by observing them," Jon explained. "In this war game we were hiding behind the enemy lines, only few kilometres from their base. I was sent on a recon to find out more about them."

Kentho was now paying one hundred percent attention to every word coming out of Jon's mouth. He was enthralled.

"The enemy camp was in the forest, with two simple unpaved roads leading in and out. The forest had trees much like on New Thatho, but much smaller. A lot of ferns and moss grew on the ground. To reach the camp unnoticed, I had to crawl the last two hundred metres." Kentho looked confused. "That is almost as wide as your town in New Thatho," Jon clarified, and Kentho focused back on the story. "To approach without being detected, approach in a direct line towards the enemy. Never go sideways, or they can see your movement." Jon displayed with his hands how to approach. "Also, avoid young trees and larger ferns. If your body touches them, they shake like someone would wave for attention," Jon kept explaining while Kentho imagined himself amid a forest, crawling closer, just like Jon had.

"When I was in visual range, I lay still for an hour before continuing. I used that time to count vehicles and the number of people in the camp. After being sure I was still undetected, I continued my approach slowly, choosing my path through the shadows. My orders were to do a vehicle and head count, but I had to know more. I had to know if they were a threat," Jon said with suspense, making Kentho sit up cross-legged, his back against the couch.

"So, what did you do?" he asked, eyes wide open.

"I continued," Jon answered. "I approached their thin wire fence in a shadow cast by their command tent. I pulled myself under the fence and crawled closer to the tent. I could hear people inside planning something, but I couldn't make the words."

Kentho sat on his knees now.

"I used the shadows to crawl closer to one of their tarp covered utility vehicles that had six enormous wheels. I stood up, and was about to look under the tarp, when I heard steps close by. I dropped down on my stomach and rolled into the shadow, trying to be as still as I could. Two guards walked by the truck towards the command tent, their feet marching only one metre away from me. My heart was pounding like crazy and I was sure they would detect me. I even saw it in my head, how they would discover me lying there. By the time I decided I should run for it, they had passed by. I was safe. I suppose they couldn't imagine someone on the ground in the middle of their camp," Jon paused, seeing Kentho holding his hand in front of his mouth.

"Then what? Did you escape?" Kentho asked, unable to remain still.

"I did not. As soon as those two guards disappeared, I pulled the vehicle tarp ajar and jumped in."

"You did what?" Kentho shouted, making his parents on the balcony turn their heads.

"Once inside, I switched on my small flashlight. The same flashlight I lost on the way to New Thatho. I really loved that little light. So many memories ..." Jon looked up, pretending to forget he was telling a story.

"What was in there?" Kentho stood on his knees and shook Jon from his shoulder.

"Wooden boxes containing food and medical supplies," said Jon casually.

"What? That is all? No weapons or other malicious objects?" Kentho sat back down, sounding disappointed.

"Nothing dangerous or malicious," Jon said smiling. "I jumped out from the vehicle and made my way through the shadows away from the enemy camp, still undetected. From the extra intel I had gathered, our enemy not being an enemy, but troops supporting their people in need. We did not advance on them but moved deeper into enemy territory instead."

"Where? What happened next? You must tell more." Kentho was pulling Jon's free hand, begging.

"Some other night, kiddo," Jon said and shook Kentho's hair. "How about I tell you a story that happened a long time ago in a galaxy far, far away ..."

Kentho lay back down on his back, imagining whatever Jon was telling him next. He fell asleep only ten minutes into the story where a man and a droid were looking for a Jedi Master called Obi-Wan Kenobi.

Jon stayed up with Bartho and Julith, discussing on the balcony what had happened in the past twenty-four hours. Together they watched an amazing sunset, displayed by two suns drifting over the horizon. Even after sunset, the orbital rings around Azonia shone bright against the black night sky filled with stars. The moment did not need words. All three just stood in silence for half an hour. It was something none of them had experienced before.

Finally, fatigue overcame him, and Jon returned to his unit. He threw all his clothes into the ionisation chamber Uzano had advised them to use for cleaning and disinfecting their clothes. He then walked into the hot shower he had been missing since the morning they left their hotel room in Portland. While standing in the shower, Jon laughed out loud. Something like Portland felt light years away. He kept laughing, because he realised Portland was, in fact, light years away. After a long, relaxing shower, he fell on the bed, noticing Gus was not back yet. He fell asleep as soon as his head hit the perfectly soft pillow.

Four days went by without a single sign of Gus. On the fifth morning, Jon woke up from his bed, unsure if he was still dreaming or not. Gus was asleep on his stomach in his bed with all his clothes on. His left hand hung free. This time, there was an interface similar to Uzano's attached to Gus's arm between his wrist and elbow.

Jon dressed and walked over to Gus, happy to see his friend again. Jon gently poked Gus's shoulder until he groaned and opened his eyes halfway. Gus's eyes made several random circles before focusing straight forward.

"Good morning! Good to see you buddy," said Jon, standing right next to Gus's bed.

"Good morning, buddy," Gus mumbled, barely moving his mouth, letting the words slip through his lips.

"I'm thinking about breakfast, want to join?"

"Sure, I'll catch up. You guys go ahead," Gus said, his lips moving slightly more now.

Jon walked out and knocked on their neighbour's door. Julith opened it and smiled when she saw Jon.

"Hi Jon, did you dream clear?" Julith asked happily.

"I dreamed very clear. I had a wild dream though. I was inside one of those BOWs we saw in New Thatho, but I was using it to race against other BOWs," Jon said, looking confused. "Anyway, Gus is back. Ready for some colourful jello?" He said with a smile when he saw Kentho.

"Yes, we are. How about Gus?" Julith asked.

"Gus is back?" Kentho shouted excitedly.

"He is, but he just woke up. He will join as soon as he is able, and hopefully he'll tell us what's going on," Jon replied and held the door open, saying good morning also to Bartho as they all walked out.

At the breakfast table, surrounded by many other breakfast tables full of Azonians and Thathonians, Gus finally joined them.

"Morning guys," Gus said, still sleepy and disoriented.

Jon noticed Gus's clothes were now also clean. His red Puma sneakers were bright red again, and on his T-shirt, Luke Skywalker and Darth Vader in the background were again distinguishable.

"Where have you been?" Bartho leaned over the table, whispering, when Gus set down his tray full of blue and orange wobbling jello.

"I've been working with Azonians on our next move against Swarm." Gus sat down, leaving Kentho between him and Jon. "It has been crazy few days. It's something I can't explain you must see it for yourselves. After breakfast, I will take you where I have been working, in the depths." He made ominous movements with his fingers in front of his tray.

"Uuuuu ..." mumbled Jon, while trying to swallow the purple jello in his mouth. "I mean, we are happy to go with you, but a word about you being okay would have been nice."

"Sorry about that, everything was so hectic, and the time just flew by when working on our new Black Table ship." Gus accidently let slip his news.

"Black Table ship?" Kentho put down his jello eating tool that looked like a spoon.

"You'll see. Let's finish our breakfast and I'll take you there."

The rest of the breakfast was not as relaxing as it used to be. Everyone was keen to know what a Black Table ship was. They were all ready to go with in minutes.

Ten minutes later, all five stepped into the hovering, glass walled elevator. Gus stood near the entrance and made a few selections on the transportation interface. The room took off silently, exiting from the top of the highest building.

While they descended and passed other tall buildings, the edge of the city with a wide beach came into view.

"Oh my God," said Jon, looking down at their heading. "It's a BOW!" he shouted and turned to the others, pointing down. "A Ball Of Water, right there!" He waved his hands excitedly.

They joined Jon and looked down through the glass wall. There was a BOW, just like on New Thatho, but this one was much smaller. The BOW held its form outside of the water, reaching halfway up on the pure white sand.

"Are we going to ...?" Jon asked but paused. "Yes, we are," he replied to himself.

The room with glass walls landed on the sand between the green vegetation and the BOW. Gus operated the room's interface, giving them an exit. He then led his friends across the soft sandy beach, and walked right through a thin, waterfall like barrier, into the BOW. The others stopped outside of the barrier, hesitating on going through it. All four stood at the watery barrier when Gus's hand appeared through it and waved them to continue. Together they stepped through the water.

"How is this possible?" Kentho asked in awe. They were in a large tunnel surrounded by water.

Gus made practiced movements with his right hand above his new interface, and the tunnel behind them merged with the walls as they walked further. After a minute of slow walking, the dry space around them expanded to a size of a two-storey house. They were now in the middle of the BOW. Bartho, Julith and Kentho held each other's hands. The city on the land side was still visible, but fuzzy from all the surrounding water. With his arm interface, Gus made another change and the surrounding water began moving in circles. There was almost no sound inside the BOW from the water movement.

"We are now in the middle of the BOW," said Gus. "First, we get some distance away from the city. Then we go deeper, much deeper." He passed his fingers above his interface, making the BOW move, first off the beach, and then sinking into the ocean, still holding its form. "We are going to an Azonian base, down on the ocean floor. It is at a depth of fifteen kilometres."

"Fifteen?" Jon asked nervously. "Isn't the deepest place on Earth eleven kilometres, at Mariana Trench? There is no way we will survive the pressure." He stood right next to an inner wall of water, which kept moving around them like a river. "And how are we able to stand on this?" Jon looked down at his feet, which did not sink.

"We are okay. It is something they call Aquatic Pressure Manipulation," Gus said. "It allows them to maintain this BOW's pressure anywhere it goes. And, because the BOW is a hundred percent of water, it is not affected by the weight of the ocean. Impressive, to be honest. There is even no need for decompression." Gus looked at his feet. "And the floor, they manipulate the water particles to vibrate so intensely, it feels solid. Just like water skiing without skis. If you think about it, water is a hard element when approached at high velocity. In our case, the speed is not made by us, but by the floor, in tiny separate high-speed movements."

"Amazing. Aquatic Pressure Manipulation," said Jon quietly, stamping his foot against the aquatic floor, making it splash like a puddle after a rain. "So, one could call it the APM?" he asked with a suggestive smile, now standing still.

"Sure. You can have that one."

"Yes!" Jon shouted out loud.

"While we are going down there." Gus said. "I would like to tell you more about what I have learned in the last few days. For example, now I know where they make the tables. They make them in the deepest places of the ocean. They use the weight of the ocean to compress carbon and crystal molecules to create the hard and feather-light Black Table material. They also use it for domes and armour." He showed the arm interface, which had the same material protecting the interface edges. "Then I know something about New Thatho. Why the communication between Thathonians and Azonians is not working, they don't know. It might have something to do with the New Thatho's table. The most plausible explanation is that the table became damaged, when Thathonians tried to destroy it, as was written in the old book Kentho discovered. Maybe because of that, the language stimulation for brains didn't work anymore on that specific table. Remember, me and Jon got our brains stimulated on the planet with the gigantic creature. Bartho and Kentho got it on our first jump to Sagawe, and Julith on our jump here to Azonia. Maybe the communication on New Thatho ceased with future generations, when no-one possessed the skill to teach languages. Stories about Azonians and Swarm became a legend, and as more time passed by, the more afraid New Thathonians became of Azons." Gus paused. "It is only natural to fear what we do not understand."

"Maybe Azonians became afraid to show themselves, when the gap grew bigger?" Jon wondered.

"Now, when thinking back," Julith commented, "they didn't actually hurt anyone. Maybe those random disappearances were accidents?"

"Like Julith's death by Azonians," said Bartho. "Hate and fear towards Azonians grew significantly after they took her from us. Even though she escaped them with Jon and came with us."

"Maybe we should go back and explain it to them, after finding our home planet Thatho?" asked Julith.

"I have something for both cases," said Gus, digging in his satchel. "Azonians still don't know about this." He pulled out the golden fabric from his bag and opened it just enough for everyone to see a power source and three crystals inside of it. "The fabric is concealing it perfectly," Gus said and handed the fabric and all of its content to Julith. "I want you to have this. You can use it or not, but it is your ticket home, or wherever you want to go. Hide it."

"Thank you," Julith said and placed it into her utility backpack she had taken from storage before running into Jon.

"And I also got fresh information regarding Thatho, your original home planet," said Gus, changing the subject while looking at Bartho and his family. "Or it is more about Azonian's original home planet, but it might lead to Thatho. I hacked into their Black Table archives, which is a collection in their factory database. You would not believe how many tables they have made. Millions." Gus shook his head and his arms swung around as he explained. "The oldest data they had dates back over two-hundred-million years. The Azons truly are an ancient race. Time had corrupted most of the old data, making it unreadable with Azon's technology. But with the extra time I had, I made an algorithm to fix corrupted data." He paused and his hands stopped moving around. "I found the very first table ever made …" He paused again, everyone looking at him and holding their breath.

"And?" Jon yelled after the pause stretched too long.

"It's Earth's," said Gus slowly.

"It's what?" asked Jon, astounded and unwilling to believe what Gus had said. "There is no way. We would have some evidence. Azonians would know," he said in disbelief.

"But it is, and they don't know," Gus pushed back. "They have made so many Black Tables and so many timeline jumps, it's a wonder they know what's for breakfast," he said.

"Well, that's easy," Jon replied, snorting. "Jello, from Monday to Sunday."

Kentho laughed out loud. He and Jon fist bumped.

"Hilarious." Gus said, used to Jon's sarcasm humour. "My algorithm calculated ninety-five percent probability for first table being on Earth. They lived on Earth 150 million years ago. The first tables were made a few million years later. After that, there was a lengthy period before they made the next tables, right here on Azonia." Gus paused again, waiting for Jon to get the point or come back with another joke.

"Hmm, 150 million years ago, several tables, and a break …" Jon mumbled quietly to himself with his thinking face on. "I think I got it …" he held his finger up like he always did when he got his thoughts together. "It was the end of Jurassic period, wasn't it? They lived on Earth in the Jurassic period. Hence the palm print that looks like a T-Rex's high five? Or high three?"

"Getting warmer," Gus replied.

"And they made the tables, because they knew about the approaching meteorite and what it would cause, an extinction event, wiping out the life on Earth?" asked Jon.

"Getting hotter," Gus replied again.

"And they didn't make just one table, did they? They had to make many, so they could all escape?" Jon looked directly at Gus to get the ultimate confirmation. "That would explain the Stonehenge-like formation of rocks in Vancouver?"

"Yes!" Gus shouted and continued explaining, "There are in fact seven other large stone formations apart from Stonehenge. Or eight, if we count the one we found in Vancouver. It must have been a mass escape from Earth. And then, almost two-hundred-millions years later, human mediums or persons sensitive to energies around us must have felt the power of those places. They must have buried the domes, then raised the stone formations around them. They did this all over the planet."

"Dang, now I want to visit Stonehenge." Jon sounded disappointed, realising those places would be so very different now.

"What does this have to do with Thatho?" asked Julith after Jon and Gus were finished.

"I believe," Gus said, "that the people on Earth and the people on New Thatho are the same. This means you and I are both originally Thathonians." Gus smiled. "Thathonians arrived on Earth much later, using Black Table network, a long time after the Azonians departure," Gus approached the conclusion, all four listening carefully. "That would mean that one of the Black Tables on Earth would lead to the original

Thatho planet. To know more, we would have to interface with the correct table on Earth. Maybe it's the Vancouver Black Table, maybe it's not. But now is not the time. First, we deal with Swarm, or there is no Earth left to go to."

Gus turned to his arm interface and increased the BOW speed.

Half an hour later, the BOW was submerged to such a depth that it was surrounded by black ocean. The surface above them had been bright at first but became slowly dimmer and smaller. Only a dot of light remained before it disappeared and pitch-black water surrounded them. Now and then, some big, glowing aquatic life form swam alongside the BOW before losing interest and disappearing into the abyss. They were so deep there was no light other than the light emitting from Gus's arm interface. Realising how dark it was, Gus typed into his interface, enabling a bright glow from below. The floor inside the BOW looked like thick ice, glowing with white light. The light created a bright halo around them. From the outside, the BOW looked like a giant white pearl, falling deeper into the ocean.

"We are not that far now," said Gus, looking at his interface.

A minute later, a turquoise light grew brighter from the ocean floor. Beneath them spread a massive city of BOWs. Between the BOWs were large, black machine-like constructs, using the ocean pressure to create more Black Table material.

Gus guided their BOW over the city and joined the wall of a massive BOW that was separate from the rest. Coming slowly to a stop, Gus opened the familiar tunnel from their BOW to the neighbouring one. With Gus in the lead, they walked out from their BOW into the next one.

The next BOW was much bigger and had a similar open space inside, but one the size of a hockey arena, where they found Uzano, Nova and Muro.

"Welcome," Uzano said, and offered fist bump for Jon, who gladly responded.

"Thank you," said Jon, while turning his head to look around. "This is impressive."

"Thank you. This way." Uzano pointed the way deeper into the massive dry space inside the BOW.

"What is that?" Kentho asked. In front of them stood a ship or a vessel, slightly bigger than a Black Table dome and covered in gold, making it look like a smooth golden bun with no edges or markings.

"That," Gus said, "is our next plan against Swarm."

"Is that gold?" asked Jon, not believing his eyes.

"It is." Gus smiled proudly.

"I know you like shiny things, but really Gus, gold?"

"Not only does it look good," Gus said, "it is invisible to Swarm. Or at least we hope it is."

"This vahl, or gold, as you call it," Nova stepped in, "is proven to mask all the frequencies and radiation coming from Black Table and its power source."

Bartho and Julith looked at each other, hoping this to be the case, as she was carrying the power source and crystals in her backpack.

"We believe it will make this ship invisible to Swarm," Nova said. "The plan is to take this ship as close to the point where Swarm originates form as we can. We will gather intel and do some tests."

"Not to be a party pooper," said Jon, "but doesn't Swarm originate hundreds or thousands of light years from here?"

He paused, thinking. "I don't want to be rude, but how is *that* ship supposed to get there?"

"We asked the same thing," Nova said, "and your friend Gus figured it out. He is quite resourceful."

Near the ship was an interface erected on a table-like construct. Gus walked to it and enabled a holographic 3D map of Milky Way.

"We are here," said Gus, pointing at a small constellation near the centre of the Milky Way. "As we are aware, Swarm is spread across these two sectors." He waved his arms at the two sectors closest to Azonia. "And based on Black Table network's data, Swarm originates here, at the edge of our galaxy." Gus pointed at an area at the galaxy's border. "And knowing the fact that Swarm is avoiding this area, called Trench." Gus zoomed into an area Swarm had gone around of. "It seems the Trench is naturally toxic for Swarm. Swarm is avoiding black holes and dark matter at any cost. To test it, I wrote an algorithm for Black Tables which enables them to mask their tachyon radiation with black hole radiation. So basically, to fool Swarm into thinking that Black Tables are small black holes.

"What is a black hole?" Kentho asked curiously. "How is a hole radiating anything?"

"What I know are only theories," Gus tried to explain. "And it is not so much of radiation, but evaporation, theorised by the late Stephen Hawking. He was one of the smartest minds on Earth. According to him, because of quantum effects near the event horizon of a black hole, this radiation reduces mass and rotation energy, and is therefore called evaporation rather than radiation." Kentho looked even more confused now, and so did Jon, Bartho and Julith. "We can see the effect already on Swarm's behaviour, as it is no longer advancing on planets with Black Tables ..." Gus paused. "We will get near the Swarm origin with a Black Table," Gus finished and waved his hand at the interface, making the golden ship open a doorway in its smooth surface.

The golden curvy piece of wall moved first inwards and then slid aside into the ship's hull. A large rectangular plate pushed out from the lower part of the ship and created a small ramp to walk on.

"This is so amazing!" shouted Kentho, overwhelmed with everything he saw.

They walked up on the ramp with no railings. The first section of the ship was an airlock, equipped with flight suits secured on the wall. Gus pressed a large red button near the wall opposite the outer hatch. A door slid aside into the ship's wall.

The door from the airlock led directly to a sizeable round room in the middle of the ship with another three doors leading out. Jon counted four doors all together, all opposite from one another. The wall space between the doors were full of ship control interfaces, and in the middle of the room stood a Black Table.

"Interesting," Jon said, stroking his chin. "I think I am getting the picture. You want to jump with the ship?"

"That's exactly right," Gus said. "I hacked this table to include ship and table itself for the jumps. That allows us to make jumps to reach Swarm without spending time for traditional space travel."

"And what is behind those other doors?" Kentho walked curiously closer to next door.

The door made a familiar loud hissing sound, making Jon look at Gus.

"Is that?" asked Jon in disbelief.

"Yes, it is," Gus whispered to Jon while smiling widely.

"*Star Trek* doors?"

"Yes," Gus answered excitedly and held his high hand up in a Vulcan greeting. "I had the sounds on my tablet. I made them add them for the door movements." Gus looked like he had done something sneaky.

"They are crew quarters, storage room and a pilot room," said Uzano. "We have done nothing like this before. Thanks to your friend Gus here, we have completely re-thought our technology."

"It has been like a dream come true," Gus said. "On Earth, we have imagined everything possible and made fictional stories about space travel, but we don't possess the knowledge how to make them come true, yet."

"The ship is fully tested and ready to go," said Nova. "The question remains, who is going?" she asked.

"I haven't asked Jon yet, but I would be honoured to take this trip with him," said Gus, looking at Jon.

"Oh yes, you can count me in. Wouldn't miss it for the world," Jon said and offered a fist bump for Gus, who responded in kind.

"I think we will stay behind and maybe take a journey back to New Thatho at some point," said Bartho, cradling an arm around Julith's shoulders with his other hand on Kentho's head, who looked disappointed.

"Very well. Uzano and I will also join the mission," said Nova. "Muro will stay on Azonia in case we do not return." She looked at Muro, who held his arms across his chest and bowed as a sign of trust. "You will leave tomorrow. Uzano can take you back to the surface. I will bring the ship to surface when it's fully equipped with the resources we will need."

◆———— ◆ ◆ ◆ ————◆

Back on the surface, Jon, Gus and their New Thatho friends stood against their balcony railing, looking over the capital with its beautiful high silvery buildings covered with green plant-life. A flock of birds flew from one building to another. In the distant ocean, whale-like aquatic life forms played in the water by hitting the surface with their massive fins. On the horizon, the orbital ring crossed the sky and reached behind the ocean.

"Looks like a fantasy postcard," said Gus, taking it all in.

"Absolutely amazing," Jon said, looking mesmerised, but then became sad. "That's it then?"

"It might be," Bartho said. "It has been a glorious adventure with you."

"We will miss you until you are back. And you *will* be back?" Julith insisted.

"We will miss you as well. And we will be back. Or at least I *hope* we will be back," Jon answered, unable to see the outcome of something so much out of his league. "After hearing the plan, I'm not so sure. We base a lot on hopes and theories."

"*If* we are not back" – Gus looked seriously at Bartho, Kentho and Julith – "use the power source and crystals I gave you to go wherever you want. We will also leave you a tablet with my mapping software. I will teach you today how to use it." Gus moved his attention towards Jon. "Can I borrow your tablet?" Gus whispered, before heading in with Bartho and Julith, leaving Kentho and Jon on the terrace.

"Like you borrowed my flashlight?" Jon shouted after Gus, frowning. "Well, it's not like I can stream my favourite shows here anyway," he said, disappointed, knowing his tablet had become expendable when both Gus's tablets were in use already.

Jon turned to Kentho and shook his hair.

"Are you hungry, kiddo?" he asked Kentho, who nodded in return. "Great, let's go get some jello before going to sleep."

Before leaving Kentho's apartment unit, Jon told the rest where they were heading. Gus sat with Julith and Bartho at the dining table, showing them how to open crystals and how to connect them with the wire he had made for them. The power source remained hidden inside the golden fabric, now in Julith's possession.

When Jon and Kentho returned, Gus was still explaining how to use the tablet. Seeing Gus still busy, Jon and Kentho sat down on the couch. Kentho knew this would be a perfect opportunity to learn more about Jon and his life on Earth.

"Can you tell me one more story, please?" Kentho asked and laid down, using Jon's leg as a pillow again.

"Diving or mission story?" asked Jon, ready to comply with Kentho's request.

"Mission," Kentho replied promptly.

"Okay. Have I told you yet how we were almost captured by the enemy forces?" Jon looked at Kentho with narrowed eyes.

"No. That sounds exciting," Kentho replied, imagining Jon running away from something.

"It was ... It happened in summer, in a place with lots of trees, lakes and rivers, and a lot of hills and valleys." Jon looked down at Kentho, who was already imagining the scenery Jon had described. "In was another war game. Our mission was to disable the enemy's power plant. But this story is not about that, it's about our way back, returning to our pickup point, which was far, far away. We hiked in the forest, undetected, for two weeks, when one morning, the person on scout duty returned to the camp. He woke us up, telling us the enemy was heading straight towards us. There were six of us, and without a word, everyone knew what to do. We packed up our tent and gear in minutes, and we ran."

"How long did you have to run?" asked Kentho, unable to hide his curiosity, imagining Jon pushing through branches and leaves.

"Our pickup point was still over forty kilometres away, same as a full marathon, but in a forest."

Kentho looked confused.

"Distance was the same as running around your village one hundred times," said Jon, seeing Kentho needed an explanation.

"One hundred times?" he shouted and sat up.

Gus, Bartho and Julith paused their lesson on how to use Gus's tablet and the crystals and turned to look at Kentho and Jon.

"And doing all that, while carrying our gear and weapons," Jon said, while Kentho lay back down against him. "The enemy had trucks like in that other story I told you, and helicopters, which are like these flying eggs here on Azonia, but with propellers." Jon made a helicopter sound with his mouth and showed flying with his hands.

Kentho became mesmerised.

"We ran slowly forward in the forest, pushing through branches and large plants. The first hour went by fast, and we had made a good headway. With help of maps, we avoided roads where enemy trucks drove looking for us. Just when we thought we were safe, we heard helicopter sounds." Jon made the flapping sound with his mouth. "Fortunately, the forest was too thick for them to see us, but we knew they would also have heat cameras to see through the vegetation. When we heard the flapping sound, we dropped everything and pulled out our thin mattresses. Those mattresses were made of an insulating material, blocking heat and cold. Just when the helicopter arrived, all six of us lay on the ground under the mattresses. The helicopter flew over a few times before heading away. We folded the mattresses back to our backpacks and continued our run. Later on, our path was blocked by a wide river. We undressed until we were butt-naked" – Kentho snickered at the word butt – "and placed our gears and clothes on top of our rain protective ponchos. We then tied them up tight at the top, turning them into camouflaged floatation devices. We jumped into the river. We crossed the river one by one, so that if anyone got to trouble, there would be help on both sides. The current was strong, but nothing we couldn't handle. The floating bags worked well, helped us to swim across, and kept our clothes and gear dry. Once all were across, we dried ourselves, dressed and continued our run. After ten hours, the sun began to set. We were all hungry, so we decided to have a strategic break. While three of us made food, the three others scouted the area. Once the scouts were back, we pulled out the map and studied it while we ate. There was a road we had to cross to reach our destination. Crossing the road in daylight was out of the question, but the longer we waited, the more chance there was for getting caught. After planning in detail how we should proceed, we packed our gear and headed towards the road. When we reached it, our scout returned saying the path was clear, but the enemy was approaching on the very same road.

"So, what did you do?" asked Kentho, glued to the suspense. "How did you get across without being detected?"

"We decided to become detected," Jon replied to Kentho's surprise.

"You what?" Kentho sounded confused. "That just does not make any sense," he stressed the word *any* and shaking his head.

"Just wait for it ..." Jon said, smiling. "We knew the enemy had dogs, helping them with tracking us. All the dogs need is a scent."

"Dogs?" Kentho asked.

"Dogs are these four-legged furry animals that have a wonderful sense of smell. If they get a scent from you, it is almost impossible to hide from them," Jon explained, while Kentho imagined what dogs would look like. "So, we were coming from the south, heading north." Jon showed directions with his hands. "Before getting too close to the road, we set a rifle with a full clip of blank ammunition up on the hill and pulled a trip wire with us to set it off if anyone approached the hill."

Kentho looked even more confused now.

"When approaching from the higher ground, we saw a large drainpipe going under the road. We set flash explosives on the side of the road and then crawled through the drainpipe with all the explosive's wires. Once on the other side, we walked away from the road, leaving as few signs as possible."

"How did you do that?" asked Kentho.

"We stepped on stones, branches, and as close as possible to the roots of plants and trees. "We continued as far as the flash explosive's wiring reached, which was not as far as we had hoped for, maybe twenty metres away from the road. Our survival completely depended on our plan now. The sun was set by the time we heard the enemy trucks approaching from the east. We were ready." Jon said the last three words very slowly.

Kentho was becoming impatient from the suspense.

"Then what?" he asked, his head against Jon's leg and his arms pointing straight up, demanding to know more.

"Four trucks approached our position, driving almost bumper to bumper." Jon said. "When the first truck reached our flash explosive on the side of the road, we set them off, causing the second and the third truck to collide slightly with each other. Right after the collision, soldiers poured out from the second and third trucks, advancing on the side of the road where the flash explosions originated from. It was dark, which benefited us. The enemy soldiers began searching the terrain near the trucks towards the hill where we had come from. That's when one of them walked on the trip wire and triggered the rifle with blanks we'd left up on the hill. The rifle shot the whole clip of blanks. All the soldiers ran over the road and hid on our side, shooting back up towards the hill. If our mission had been to attack the convoy, we were now in the best situation, as we were behind the soldiers and they were all looking to the wrong direction. The plan was working. The enemy soldiers began advancing up the hill. We pulled further back without being seen or heard and began running again.

We couldn't use lights. We could still hear the enemy shooting towards the hill before losing their dogs. But, because they were headed uphill, away from us, the dogs got our scent on the wrong side and began following it, all the way to the river we crossed earlier."

"That was an excellent plan!" Kentho interrupted Jon. "How did you come up with it so fast?"

"It was something I remembered MacGyver doing once."

"Again, that same MacGyver person. He is brilliant!" said Kentho, wanting to know more about this mystery man, but first he had to know if Jon and his men escaped. "So, then what happened?"

"It was getting late, and we risked missing our pre-arranged pickup. We dropped all the heavy gear like the tent, food, sleeping bags, mattresses and spare ammunition. The trees rushed by as we ran. One by one we kept falling on branches and stones. For a second, I thought I could see something when the moon came out and shone a dim light between the clouds. That's when the ground disappeared under my feet. I don't know how long the drop was, but luckily, I landed on soft moss, on my stomach with my weapon in front of me, jammed it into my face. I broke these teeth." Jon pointed to his upper front teeth.

"That is insane," said Kentho in shock. "You could have died."

"I could have, but I was luckier than my friend, who fell hard enough to break his arm."

Kentho grunted and frowned.

"When the moon appeared again from between the clouds, we could see the cliff far ahead. The cliff was our pickup point – only one-kilometre left to go. After running in heavy gear through the forest for twelve hours, we were exhausted, and we were hallucinating enemies everywhere when there was none. As a group, after jogging the last kilometre, we ignited our bright burning green light for pickup. We were safe. It took us several days to be able to walk again," Jon said and looked at Kentho, who nodded and closed his eyes. "You can do anything, if you decide to. Don't be afraid to go after your dreams. You will do magnificent things, kiddo."

As Jon took off his sweater and covered Kentho with it, he took a deep breath, thinking about the last words he just said, and if they would be true. Would the next time Kentho saw them be in Portland, a lifetime away? He felt sad the more he thought about it. He remembered now how Dr Wells searched the audience, as if looking for someone. He remembered how Dr Wells teared up when he saw them standing in front of his book signing table. He remembered how Dr Wells, Kentho, pushed the book into his hands and said his name. As much as he wanted to wake up Kentho and tell him everything, he could not. He could not risk the timeline. He stroked Kentho's forehead.

"Good night. See you later, or earlier," Jon said quietly, and pushed away the lump he felt growing larger in his throat, got up and joined Gus and his study group.

CHAPTER 13

OPERATION HAIL MARY

arly the next morning Jon woke up to a knocking on their door. Jon got up and put on his pants. Still holding his T-shirt, he walked to the door and opened it. Nova stood there wearing a white pilot suit instead of the loose linen casual outfits she usually wore. Butterflies took off in Jon's stomach.

"Good morning Jon," she said smiling, while Jon stretched on his T-shirt over his head.

"Morning, Nova," Jon replied and looked directly into her into eyes. "You look different, but as pretty as always."

"Oh, thank you," she said, blushing slightly from Jon's comment. "Ready to change history?"

"Always," Jon replied. "Only history must wait for Gus to wake up first." he said and opened the door wider to a view of the sleeping Gus. As always, Gus was sleeping on his stomach, one arm under his head, and the other hanging down from the bed.

"Gus, the Chinese stamps are coming to get you!" he shouted, referring to the nightmare Gus had had on New Thatho.

"What? Where?" Gus blurted out and lifted his head, revealing a pillow pattern pressed against half of his face.

"Wake up, buddy! An interstellar travelling in a golden spaceship is waiting."

"I'm up, I'm up."

Gus remembered where he was and what they were about to do. Full of excitement and energy, he sat up and hummed something Jon could not distinguish. Instead of guessing what it was, Jon threw him the shirt that Gus was looking for around his bed. Nova turned around, giving Gus some privacy to dress.

"The ship is ready on the lower platform, come when ready," she said and hurried away.

"We will!" Jon shouted back.

Just before disappearing through the door, she turned her head and saw Jon watching her go. She smiled, feeling something she had not felt in a long time; happiness, excitement and nervousness, all at the same time.

"Do you think we also get that kind of space outfit?" Gus asked excitedly while pulling on his now clean again jeans and Star Wars T-shirt.

"Nah," Jon answered. "I think we look like rogue space travellers in these Earth clothes. Besides, with our luck, we would get the red ones and end up blown up like the guard on Sagawe." Jon looked suspiciously at Gus. "You don't want that, do you?"

"Oh, hell no. Earth clothes are fine," Gus answered, knowing very well the red jumpers were not a joke.

"How about a quick breakfast with our New Thatho friends before we leave?" said Jon, hoping to still see Kentho before their departure.

"Sure, there's nothing like jello to start your day." Gus smiled. "Not a bad catchphrase for it?"

Jon shook his head. They collected their personal items and placed them into their satchels. Once ready, just as if they were leaving a hotel room, they quickly looked around to check they had not left anything behind. They hadn't, so they headed out.

After knocking on the neighbouring door, Kentho opened it. Gus and Jon stood outside, asking if his family would join them for a breakfast.

"Yes!" Kentho said loudly right away. "Mum, Dad, hurry!" he called out for his parents, afraid of missing time with Jon and Gus.

"We are here," said Julith. Both she and Bartho were already approaching the door. "Hi Jon, hi Gus," she said with a broad smile. "Big day?"

"Sure is," Jon replied, knowing nothing else about what was coming. "We hoped to catch some breakfast with you before we leave."

"As did we," said Bartho, closing the door behind them. "Please, lead the way."

Gus in lead, they headed for the massive area made for meetings, mingling and eating. The whole way, Kentho walked next to Jon, asking him questions about MacGyver. Before they arrived, Kentho tried to put together what he had learned from Jon.

"So, he is a man, who can build things from objects around him to use them to escape from impossible situations?" asked Kentho.

"Yes," Jon confirmed.

"And he is also using science to make things that help his cause?"

"Yes."

"And his cause is to help people?"

"Yes."

"And he lives in a house that is on the water? And he plays ice-hockey, whatever that is ..."

"Yes."

"And there is a person who cannot die? And this person is trying to kill him? Murder ... roar?"

"Murdoc. Yes," Jon answered, enjoyed seeing how Kentho imagined everything he had told him. "Why don't we get some food and sit down?"

Gus was last one to sit down at the table.

"There's nothing like the smell of jello in the morning," said Gus, causing Kentho to sniff the blue jello wobbling on his plate.

"I smell nothing," Kentho said disappointed, and sniffed again at the pile of jello on his tray.

"Exactly," Gus said, winking at Kentho, making him look even more confused.

"Don't worry, it's not you, it's the complex Gus humour," said Jon. "I sometimes don't understand it either. Just show him this." Jon made a thumbs up gesture with his hand, making Gus smile. "See, works every time."

"When are you coming back?" Kentho asked, poking his jello and realising he had lost his appetite.

"If everything goes as planned," Gus said, "we should be back in a day or two, depending on which power sources we get to use. To make the trip, we need to use the large power sources, like we did to get to Sagawe. If you remember,

Swarm is hungry for tachyon particles, which those smaller power sources are emitting. Also, all Black Table travelling is on hold until we finish our mission. We need Swarm as weak as possible."

"But you are coming back?" Kentho persisted.

"That is our goal, kiddo," Jon said, hoping to calm Kentho. "But, just in case we don't, you now know how to use the power source and the crystals. You can go wherever you want."

"We thank you for that," said Bartho. "We will most likely keep looking for the original Thatho planet. But we hope you make it back, so you can join us." He looked at Kentho. "Kentho has grown very fond of you."

During breakfast, Jon and Gus talked about their lives on Earth and how Earth had changed in the last hundred years. They told about wars and suffering, and about the beauty everywhere. They spoke about art, music, literature, and movies where anything was possible. After breakfast, they hugged and said their goodbyes. Kentho's eyes were tearing up when he hugged Jon. He did not want to let him go.

"I will see you again?" he asked, tears falling down his cheek.

"I promise you. We *will* see again ..." Jon paused when he saw how Gus shook his head discreetly. "I don't know when, but I swear to you, there is nothing I want more than get back to you guys. Remember Kentho, you can do anything you want, and you can become anything you want. You will do exceptional things—" A kick to his ankle from Gus cut him short.

Jon gave Kentho one more hug before letting him go. Trying to keep it casual, Jon felt how something twisted in his stomach and pushed up to his throat. He was not ready to let go of his young friend, not yet. To not make it even more difficult for Kentho, Jon pushed down the feelings he had. He took as deep breath as he could and forced a smile, forcing the lump in his throat to dissolve. Jon and Gus waved as they walked out from the massive hall.

At the beach, Uzano and Nova were already waiting for Jon and Gus to arrive. There was no grand ceremony or personnel to send them off, merely the golden ship that looked like a bun, and four passengers to board it. Nova and Uzano both wore matching white piloting suits with sky-blue lines on their legs and arms.

"They look like the Finnish ski team," Jon whispered.

Gus laughed and offered him a fist bump.

"We are ready," said Uzano with his deep voice. "Let us board the ship and go through the essentials." He led them up the small ramp extended from within the ship itself.

The airlock had two more matching white-blue pilot suits hanging on the wall.

"Those suits are for you, just in case." Uzano pointed at the wall.

"No helmets?" Jon asked, accustomed to seeing helmets worn on space flights.

"You will love this," said Gus, looking again like a kid in a toy store. "Nova, if you please?"

Jon turned to look at Nova, who stood in the middle of the airlock. She reached with her right hand for a button above her left collarbone and pressed it. From the embedded padding around her neck, a helmet extruded from the suit and was covering her head in a second.

"Holy ...!" Jon shouted, amazed.

She pressed the same button, but this time twice rapidly and the helmet disappeared into the padding around her neck.

"That's insane!"

"I know!" Gus smiled and kept nodding next to him.

Uzano continued with his tour and led them to the area in the middle of the ship. The round wall and the ceiling were pure white. Interfaces for ship operations filled all the wall space. There were three double doors opposite from each other, all silvery grey. Jon noticed the airlock door behind them being dirty red, larger and stronger in build. In the middle of the ship stood a Black Table, with a large power source and three crystals in their places.

"They installed your interface as requested." Uzano looked at Gus and pointed to an interface on the outer wall next to pilot room door. "We integrated your tablet between the interface and the table crystals. You should have the same access as before, but with more computing power."

"Sweet," Gus celebrated.

Uzano approached the closest silvery grey door on their right, which opened automatically when he got close. The door made a familiar sliding hissing sound when it split to two and disappeared into the walls. Jon grinned at Gus and they fist bumped.

Behind the door was a utility room. There were two large containers on the floor and a lot of secured boxes on shelves. Uzano took a box from the shelf and opened it. The box had small canisters in different colours inside. He took one of the blue canisters and held it above his enormous open palm. On the cannister he pressed a square area emitting a dim light and blue jello squeezed out onto his hand.

"One small canister contains a week's nourishment for one person," he said and placed the canister back into the box, and then the box back on the shelf. "The lower shelf, with white containers, contains medical supplies."

"I used to hate porridge," Jon said. "I would give a million dollars for one cup of it."

"You don't have a million dollars." Gus laughed.

"No, but you do," Jon fired back, making Gus lose his smile.

Uzano moved his attention to a large container on the floor and opened one of them. It had four large power sources secured in a soft bedding.

"These are all we have had left on Azonia," Uzano explained. "The remaining ones are powering our cities and underwater facilities. It takes a year to make one. We construct the power sources deep in the ocean with Black Tables, but we charge the cores up on a facility orbiting our twin suns." He closed the container and opened the second one which had eight smaller tachyon power sources, each of them wrapped in golden fabric.

"That looks familiar," Gus whispered to Jon, who immediately knew what Gus meant.

Uzano closed the container, and they moved to the next room, directly opposite the utility room, and between the pilot room and the airlock. As he approached the room, the twin doors slid open, revealing four enormous beds recessed into a wall, two on the left and two on the right. Each sleeping unit had its own light and several secure boxes high above the bed for personal items. Each unit also had thick sliding curtains for privacy. They measured every bed for Azonians, which made the beds overly large for others. Opposite the entrance was a closed round cabin-like structure. Uzano walked closer and waved his hand over the interface on the cabin wall, opening a shower space where the crew could clean themselves.

"This is ionising shower. You may enter with or without clothes," Uzano explained and closed the cabin.

Jon threw his satchel on the bed closest to him, and they moved to next room.

The last twin doors moved aside, revealing a significantly smaller space than the other rooms. It was a tiny, but wide, pilot room. The room had two seats on both sides of the entrance, and a lot of interfaces in front of them. Right in front of the seats above the interfaces was a curved blank wall.

"I hope you don't suffer from claustrophobia," Jon joked, wondering about the odd design.

Uzano pressed something on the interface in front of the larger of the two seats. Apparently, this was his seat, and the entire curvy wall in front of them became transparent. The tiny wide room now had an unobstructed view over the beach towards the ocean and felt like the largest room in the ship.

"Whoa!" Jon shouted in surprise, seeing the wall disappear in front of him. "Now that's impressive."

Jon stepped further into the room and stood in the space between the two pilot seats.

"This is so weird," he claimed excitedly, watching how the waves hit the sand below him, and how the orbital ring hugged Azonia above him.

"Gus will get you up to speed with the controls," Uzano said looking at Jon who seemed overwhelmed. "But first, we need to get going."

They all returned to table room and while the others gathered around Black Table, Nova walked to an interface nearby and enabled a galaxy map above the table.

"There are three strategic places," she explained while three locations zoomed in on the galactic map. "Azonia, where we are now. The Trench, with dark matter and black holes. And the assumed Swarm's home planet of origin and the location we believe to be the source," she said and joined the others at Black Table. "We know that Swarm is too big to take head on with its constant growth. Now Gus, if you wouldn't mind."

"Our current plan is based on the theory that Swarm is some kind of galactic plant," Gus said. "It is literally growing and somehow able to live in space. The Anther we saw on Sagawe is just its means of spreading itself. The Azonian Black Table reconnaissance told us that Anthers spread the Swarm seeds, and once it has consumed the entire planet, it attaches itself to the Swarm root network that currently spreads across two sectors. It connects Anthers to a root network through means we are not yet aware of. What we will do is to go to Swarm's home planet and figure out how we can stop it."

Jon felt like things were spiralling out of his control. All he could do was to watch and hope for the best.

"Let's go!" Nova shouted, making Jon jump a little, before she headed to the pilot room with Uzano.

Jon pulled Gus's sleeve and whispered.

"Did you see a toilet anywhere?"

Nova pressed icons on her interface and the ship gave a low humming noise. With no effort, the ship took off with a speed that seemed impossible to Gus and Jon, who stood at the pilot door entrance looking out the transparent wall in front of them.

"I would like to say, impossible, but I gave up on that word on the day we had our first jump," said Jon in awe. "How come we don't feel any acceleration?"

"We equipped the ship with inertia dampeners," Gus explained. "It prevents you from becoming a pancake when speeding up, and vice versa when slowing down."

"This ship can travel in outer space, but with limited speed." Nova stepped in, while pressing icons on the interface in front of her. "We will get some distance from Azonia as a precaution. We have never tried something like this, jumping with the ship before," she said. "It was Gus's idea to modify Black Table's effective radius to include a vessel of this size."

Jon looked at Gus in horror, who raised his shoulders and hands in response.

"We are so dead," Jon mumbled without moving his lips.

The ship reached Azonian orbit in no time. They continued towards open space, leaving Azonia and its double suns behind. After a few hours at maximum drive, Nova started reducing speed.

"This should be enough," Nova said and pressed icons on her interface. The vessel came to a full stop, and the crew assembled back in the table room where the galactic map was still rotating above Black Table.

"Okay, here we go," Gus said, crossing his fingers like he was praying, and then turned his palms outwards until his fingers and knuckles made a cracking sound. "We are here," he explained and used his hands to zoom into the galactic map, "and we want to get here, where Swarm is originating from." He first zoomed out from Azonia's solar system and then zoomed closer to the point they believed was Swarm's home planet. "To do so, we will use a large power source, to avoid the jump itself from emitting any tachyon particles that would reveal our position." Gus made a few hand movements on his interface which lit up the large Azonian handprint. "Ready?" Gus asked. Uzano and Nova nodded.

"No!" Jon said loudly, now having everyone's attention. "This is happening way too fast! Don't we need some more preparation, speeches, or something?" he said, panicking slightly and finding the feeling extremely uncomfortable.

Gus placed his hand on Jon's shoulder, who took a deep breath and nodded 'okay' for the launch. Uzano placed his massive hand on the print on the table. The power source got brighter and there was a familiar flash.

From the outside, the golden spaceship floated in space with stars in its background, when suddenly it was pulled through a tiny hole.

Crossing almost two sectors in the Milky Way galaxy, the golden ship appeared at its target coordinates. The crew felt the familiar disorientation While Jon and Gus held themselves against the table, Uzano and Nova verified their position from the galactic map.

"We are there," Nova said and walked to the pilot room and took her seat on the left. The others followed her, Uzano taking his own seat on the right. Jon and Gus stayed standing at the doorway. Nova activated the transparent wall in front of them. It was black outside. As black as it can be.

"Where are the stars?" Jon asked, looking down and up through the wall.

Nova made a few hand movements above her interface and the ship turned.

"There!" Gus shouted, seeing the Milky Way galaxy in silhouette. He and Jon used to watch it when they were small, imagining themselves travelling across the galaxy.

"Looks funny, though," Jon added. "Like something took a bite from it."

The galaxy silhouette was not long and colourful, like the one Jon and Gus knew, but missing a section which had black threads instead.

"Is that?" asked Gus in horror, "Swarm?" He pointed to the black threads spreading across the galaxy. "It's much, much bigger than we thought."

"Seems that the missing light has not yet reached Azonia or Earth," Uzano said.

"Let's see where those threads lead," said Nova.

She made the ship turn slowly towards the area where Swarm paths grew more dense and closer to each other. After a ninety-degree turn, the galaxy was again no longer visible, but fully covered by Swarm. It was impossible to distinguish the black Swarm from dark space.

"Wait, let me try something," Gus said and walked straight to the interface made just for him in the table room. He turned them all on with a hand movement. Five minutes later he returned to others at the pilot room. "Let's try this. I changed our sensors to detect empty space, instead of Swarm and stars."

Nova made a few movements above her interface to take in Gus's modifications. The see-through wall turned from black to white. All the white was the normal space within and outside of Swarm. Swarm displayed as black. The view looked almost like a black jungle with thicker and thinner roots and vines. Swarm had consumed some planets, making them look like rotten fruit hanging from tree branches.

But there was also plenty of normal space between Swarm branches.

"There. That's how we navigate. Manually," said Gus. "So far, it appears Swarm is not interested in us. The gold plating should keep us hidden. And why should it detect us, it is only a space weed after all. We need to head that way." Gus pointed to the area, where Swarm branches got closer to each other. "All roads lead to Rome."

Nova and Uzano turn their head towards him.

"Rome?" Nova asked.

"An old saying on Earth," Gus explained. "Once, Rome was known as the capital of its age. They paved roads from Rome in all directions. Hence, wherever you found a paved road, it led to Rome."

"So," Nova rephrased Gus's words, "all branches will lead to the source of Swarm?"

"Precisely," Gus said. "And if we think about it …" He paused in thought. "Swarm is spreading, right?" he asked without expecting an answer, and headed back to his interface in the table room. A few minutes later Gus returned to the pilot room and asked Nova to update her navigation view once more. She did as requested and the view changed, highlighting direction where Swarm became thinner and thinner.

"All roads lead to Rome," Nova said, looking at the view, now showing the origin of each branch.

Nova inserted a new heading, setting their ship into motion, when something massive crossed their view screen, causing their ship to shake.

"What the hell was that?" Jon shouted, holding the door frame for support.

"I don't know. Our sensors didn't pick up anything," Nova said, and turned their ship towards the object's heading, but it was already gone.

"Hundred-and-eighty degrees, please," Gus said. "Where did it come from?"

Nova turned their vessel around, shocking everyone when they saw where the object came from. Their ship was almost in touching distance to something massive and round. Uzano adjusted their position by increasing distance from the object at maximum speed.

"What in the world …?" Gus whispered, but no-one had an answer.

They looked at something round and big, now visible to their sensors as small white moon. The surface was dotted with gigantic holes. Some holes had something black in them, but they could not distinguish what.

"I have no idea what we are looking at," said Gus.

"It is also not giving any energy readings," Nova said looking at her interfaces, when suddenly one of the gigantic holes filled with something and begun pulsing neon green light.

"That looks kind of familiar," said Jon when a full-sized Anther launched from the hole.

"Whoa!" everyone shouted in unison.

"Was that?" Gus asked.

"It was," Nova replied. "It seems we found the way Swarm is spreading Anthers. This would explain how Anther's travel without propulsion." She typed into her interface, and they observed how Swarm, with a branch like structure, pulsed neon green light.

With the alternate sensor view, sailing through Swarm occupied space was relatively easy. After passing a larger group of branches, the surrounding space became clearer.

"There." Gus pointed a small bright light far away. Uzano worked on his interface and the wall in front of them zoomed closer.

"Whoa ..." Jon said, not sure what he was seeing. "What is that?"

Uzano made a few more adjustments, and their view got even closer, as if they were right in front of it.

The image in front of them looked like a crack in space, an opening, pouring white light and bursts of small lightning bolts through its constantly moving edges. From the middle of the opening, a dark organism stretched out, moving like a snake and branching into thousands of fresh pathways, reaching itself across space into two sectors of our galaxy. It was Swarm.

"That crack is massive," Uzano commented.

"It's as tall as the building on Azonia," said Gus, looking at the data scrolling on Nova's interface. "Is it some kind of life form?"

"I don't know," Nova answered. "I have seen nothing like it before."

"Well, there goes your Swarm's home planet theory," said Jon sarcastically. "We just jump there and do our thing. What could go wrong?" he mumbled to himself while walking away.

"How long until we are close enough?" Gus asked.

That was the last thing Jon heard before he vanished towards the crew quarters.

"About five days," Nova answered.

"Good. We can come up with a new strategy," said Gus.

In the crew quarters Jon pulled out his copy of Dr Wells's book from his satchel, tossed off his shoes and lay down on the enormous bed.

"Not bad," Jon said, poking his pillow into a better shape and placed it under his head. "Must get one of these for home one day." He made a note to himself and continued reading his book.

"I am aware it looks bad," Gus said entering the room and sitting on the side of the bed he had chosen for himself, the one opposite Jon's. "But if we don't do something, everything we love is in danger, including Earth, Azonia, New Thatho, Kentho and his family." He continued, while removing his shoes and jacket. "We will figure out something." He tried to encourage Jon before lying down and closing his eyes. "We have five days to get our heads together."

Three days had passed, and no-one had come up with a single solid plan of what to do next. At the end of the third day, Gus called everyone together.

"I got something!" he shouted from the table room. The others rushed in. Uzano had been in the pilot room, monitoring for any Swarm movements. Nova had been calculating theories for how much energy they would need to cut through the original Swarm branches with the ship's weaponry. Jon had been in crew quarters eating jello and reading the book, which he had now almost finished.

"What is it?" Nova asked, joining the others at Black Table.

"As we are getting closer," Gus explained, "the ship's sensors are giving us new, incredible information. Those cracks of lightning have matter, and if the readings are correct, it is made of elements which are not found on our periodic table," he said, reading the sensor data and now getting everyone's attention. "Ship's sensors have reported at least five unknown elements and a massive amount of tachyon radiation." Gus enabled an updated map above Black Table with the new sensory data. "This is the reason Swarm won't die. It has an unlimited source of tachyon particles, feeding it as it grows. A natural conduit would be a phenomenon, but this has all the features of matter and an ongoing process to feed Swarm. It is not just a source, it is a tear, created for Swarm. Somehow, that tear is producing a massive amount of tachyon radiation for Swarm to feed on. It works like a conduit between our galaxy and something else."

"A Tear it is," said Jon.

Uzano decided to ignore Gus and Jon's predilection for naming things. "What did you mean by *something else?*" he asked, confused.

"It does not belong to our galaxy, that's for sure," Gus replied with confidence. "What worries me is the unknown factor. Is it here by accident or by purpose? And if it is built, then who or what built it?"

"In that case, my calculations for cutting Swarm from the root with weaponry won't work, will it?" Nova asked with disappointment.

"I don't think it will. The Swarm would just feed more tachyon radiation and particles in from the Tear," Gus said. "This is why the fight against it has been futile. When you kill a branch, it just grows two or more fresh ones from the breaking point, like trees and bushes do."

"Then we must remove the Tear as well," said Jon.

"But how?" Nova asked. "And with what? It is way too big and strong," she said, slightly annoyed from Jon's comment, and frustrated with the situation they were in.

"If we can't kill it, we take it to something that can." Everyone was now looking at Jon, who had been silent for past days. "You said it before yourself," Jon said, "the Swarm is avoiding the Trench, which is full of dark matter and black holes."

"There are no black holes *here*, nor black matter." Nova grew more irritated by Jon's theory.

"I know," Jon said, disregarding Nova's frustration. "It's something I read from Dr Wells's book, hear me out ..." He waited until everyone was listening. "In the book, it's explained how we, star systems, and even the whole Milky Way galaxy is in constant movement."

"Yes, that is on what we base Black Table network on," Uzano commented.

"I'm afraid so," Jon replied. "And now the network is feeding Swarm. Now, you say there are no dark matter or black holes here, but there is ..." Jon paused, waiting for the others' reaction, but didn't receive one. Jon put both of his hands in front of him and pointed down to the table.

"Of course!" Gus shouted and gave Jon a fist bump. "We have been watching and walking around it every day, not seeing what it is."

"The Black Table?" Nova asked.

"Yes!" Gus shouted, unable to hide his excitement.

"But I thought it would be extremely dangerous to use tachyon power sources near Swarm?" she asked.

"It is." Gus said. "But what if we use it only once?"

"If the mountain will not come to Muhammed, then Muhammed must go to the mountain," Jon said, Nova and Uzano both watching him again in confusion. "Another Earth saying," Jon tried to explain.

"It is a phrase from a story of Muhammed told by Francis Bacon in 1625," Gus explained, making Jon look at him with wide eyes and raised eyebrows.

"How do you remember stuff like that?" Jon wondered.

"I can't help it," Gus said, looking innocent. "I have a photographic memory."

"Guys?" Nova interrupted Gus and Jon.

"Sorry," said Jon, "if we cannot bring dark matter and black holes here, we can bring the Tear and Swarm to them. For that, we use Black Table," he explained, but Uzano and Nova still looked confused.

"Even if we use a tachyon power source, it will only have enough energy to include the outer hull of our ship," Uzano grunted.

"I will explain," said Gus, and they began planning a solution to how they could beat Swarm once and for all.

Two days later their ship had arrived so close to the Tear they had to dim the viewscreen in the pilot room. The Tear was spitting lightning in all directions, while giving powerful birth to Swarm. Gus and Nova had been working non-stop on Black Table. Everyone had gathered to the pilot room and looked at the Tear with Swarm pouring out from it.

"It's huge," said Nova, looking at the Tear, which was as high as fifty floor building. "Are you sure this will work?" she asked from Gus.

"The maths is valid," Gus answered. "It should work the same way as our Black Table does when it jumps *with* the ship. If you would all, please follow me." He walked to Black Table.

The table looked exactly like before, except instead of one power source, there were three. Gus and Nova had connected two large wormhole power sources to the small tachyon one with self-made cables, switches and transformers, all piled on a tool stand next to Black Table.

"We analysed Black Table network data, and we are fifty-thousand light years away from the Trench. It would take too much power to create a traditional wormhole to take Tear to the largest black hole in the Trench," Gus explained, while showing distances and locations on the Black Table's holographic map interface. "Therefore, we will use time-based jump, and we will bring Swarm and the Tear to the Trench, which will be here in 40 million years, based on Milky Way's rotation speed."

"Then what are those extra power sources for?" Uzano asked.

"Those," Nova said, "are used to significantly boost the diameter of Black Table's field to include us, the whole Tear and a significant part of Swarm."

"Well, I have a minor problem with this plan," Jon pointed out. "If we jump with the Tear and Swarm, aren't we going to end up in a black hole with it? Wouldn't it be easier to remove the table, send it from afar with the power sources towards the Tear, and watch it being transferred to the Trench?"

"We considered it." Nova answered. "But then we would be stuck here, without a table. Also, if we jump with the Tear, we will know if our plan worked. The idea is to get the Tear and Swarm into a black hole. Not to move it even closer to new sectors."

"Still, *we* are ending up in a black hole," Jon argued.

"And because of that," said Gus, "we will jump away as soon as we see that our plan worked. But we need to be fast. The energy needed for the first jump will most likely deplete all power sources. We have to switch to a fresh one, input new settings, and jump."

"Then what are we waiting for?" Jon said with a smile. "Back to your positions, chop-chop!"

All four returned to the pilot room. Nova and Uzano took their usual seats, while Gus and Jon stood at the doorway.

"Any last words?" Uzano asked with his deep voice.

"Engage," Jon said, and pointed while holding together his middle and index finger, in a tribute to Jean Luc-Picard, captain of the *Enterprise*.

"Nice," said Gus, and they fist bumped.

"Taking us in," said Uzano and steered their ship towards the Tear.

"Look at that," Gus said, pointing to Swarm. "It is literally pouring out from the Tear. It's not evil if you really think about it. Maybe it's just a natural part of the universe. There is *so* much we still don't know about it."

"Well, we know the Tear and Swarm are not welcome in this galaxy," said Jon. "Natural or not."

"We are in position," Uzano informed them as the vessel began shaking uncontrollably. "Any closer, and I will lose the control of our ship."

"That should do it," Nova said and made multiple movements on her interface. Behind them, the table room gave a loud hum, much louder than before. Jon turned around and saw the power sources glowing a bright turquoise light. The two larger power units pushed energy through the smaller power source, making it brighter and brighter, forcing Jon to shield his eyes with his hand.

"It's now or never!" Jon shouted.

Nova pressed an area on her interface, a red light dot pulsing rapidly.

For the very first time, they could see from their view window how their surroundings slowed down. Even the massive Tear with its multiple small lightning bolt slowed down, looking more like a tai chi exercise. The long lightening arms moved slowly because of gravitational distortions created by the Tear. Swarm was also now in slow motion. Instead of coming out from the Tear as a solid branch, it broke into billions of smaller branches. Then everything around them came to a full stop. A white light flashed, followed by the familiar crackling sound when they jumped.

The Trench was silent, and apart from its eerie name, it was a natural phenomenon. The Trench had ten black holes, one large one and nine smaller ones. The nine smaller ones were in the middle of the Trench, with nothing left for their gravity wells to consume. The last one, the size of hundred suns, located on the edge of the Trench, was pulling in nearby debris of moons and planets.

Without a sound, the golden ship, and the large Tear with Swarm reaching out from it, appeared right in the middle of the largest black hole. From the outside, the golden ship seemed calm and functional, but inside it was filled with alarms, smoke and a crew running around trying to put out fires and electric sparks.

"Cut the power to the table room!" Gus shouted, standing at the pilot room door, where Uzano and Nova tried to get back control of their vessel.

The golden ship was almost touching the Tear, both being pulled into the massive black hole with gravity so strong they had no hope of escaping.

"We are being pulled in with Swarm!" Nova shouted, tapping desperately on her black interface. "We need to jump again!"

"Not possible!" Gus shouted back, while engaging the air ventilation system to remove smoke from the table room. When most of the smoke had dissipated, he removed the cabling from the two large, depleted power sources, as well as from the smaller one, which was no longer glowing with a turquoise light, but was black instead. It had burned out. All three power sources had burned the table surface. Gus tried to remove the map crystals from the table, but they would not budge. The table had melted around them.

"Oh, no," said Gus, looking at Jon, who stood at the pilot room door. "We are in trouble."

"We will be pulled into the black hole in few minutes if we don't jump!" Nova shouted.

"We might be able to jump. I just have to change to a fresh power source. But there is a problem. The table controls are fried!" Gus shouted back. "Without setting new parameters, we might take a piece of Tear with us. We need more distance from it."

"Our thrusters are on full!" Uzano roared, after finally getting control of their steering. "It's no use, we cannot escape the black hole's gravitational pull!"

"I have an idea," said Jon, getting his thoughts together for a plan. "How many larger power sources do we have left?"

"Two," said Gus.

"Would our vessel stand a blast if we eject one and blow it up between us and the Tear?" asked Jon. "Could the shock wave be enough to push us away?"

"I believe so," Uzano replied, listening to the plan. "Our shielding absorbs energy, instead of deflecting it. We could use some of that energy also to boost our thrusters and get more distance."

"Great." Jon said. "Once we have enough distance from the Tear, we jump."

"It could work," said Gus, grinning. "With a teeny-weeny problem. The table interface is fried, and there is no time to fix it. I can connect the cabling from the dead power sources to a new, smaller, power source, but we would jump blind, with no idea where and when we would end up to."

"Still better than option A," Jon said and pointed to the black hole.

"Agree," Gus replied. "I will change for a new smaller source. Jon, pick up an unused large power source and take it to the airlock. Uzano, turn the vessel so that when the outer hatch opens, it will suck the power source out and send it towards Tear. Nova, be ready to blast that power source. I will call out when the table is ready. We don't have much time."

Everyone got ready and they performed their tasks like a well-oiled machine. The ship was ready, and Jon had returned to pilot room.

"Ready!" Gus shouted from the table room.

Uzano closed the interior airlock door and opened the outer one to space. The sudden change in air pressure sucked the large power source into space, sending it straight towards Swarm and Tear.

"Hold on to something!" Nova shouted and pressed a blinking yellow area on her interface.

Bright yellow beams shot out from the vessel. Each shot echoed inside the pilot room like someone blowing quick bursts of air into an empty glass bottle. With three direct hits, the power source ignited without a sound. A white blast wave expanded from the explosion, pushing Swarm and Tear towards the black hole, increasing the distance between the golden ship and the Tear. The ship absorbed energy from the blast, which Uzano guided back to the thrusters, giving them three hundred per cent power output. It worked for a minute until the thruster output began dropping back to normal. Nova was reading her interface, and when their ship had reached the safe distance from the Tear, she called Gus to make the jump.

"Now!" She shouted, just when the thrusters had used all the energy and the vessel was again being pulled back towards the black hole. Gus engaged the jump. A familiar crackling sound echoed in the vessel, and they were gone.

CHAPTER 14

UNITY

Jon took a deep breath. His diving regulator gave a dry hiss, just like when Darth Vader is breathing through his black helmet mouthpiece. Jon was deep underwater, diving. Instead of Vader's black helmet, he had a clear dive mask with a silicon nose cover sealing his face from the salty water. On every breath, air rushed into his lungs with pressure, taking much less effort to breathe than it did on the surface. It felt like the air pushed with force into his lungs. Jon glanced at his silvery stainless steel dive computer disguised as a large wristwatch which showed a dive duration of ten minutes so far, and the water temperature a pleasant 21 degrees Celsius. The large number in the centre of the display showed his depth, currently reading fifteen metres. Jon reached to his shoulder and grabbed the buoyancy controlling valve of his dive vest and let more air pass from the tank into the vest. The air made a hissing sound as it rushed in, squeezing his ribs and lower back slightly. His descent slowed, and he came to a full stop.

He hovered weightless in the water and it felt good. The dark blue sea loomed behind him and beneath his fins was two hundred metres of salty water before the pitch-black sea floor. In front of him, a beautiful and uneven wall full of coral and small fish extended to his left and right as far as he could see. Visibility was good, at least twenty metres in both directions before details disappeared into hazy blue. He looked up and saw three more divers through his bubbles, slowly descending and finally coming to a halt next to him. Holding thumb and index finger together, they all showed okay signs to each other. The first phase of the dive, descending, was now complete.

After a few minutes of slow swimming along the wall, the current picked up, and it slid all four divers along the wall of coral at walking speed. Jon took the comfortable position of sitting cross-legged, while holding the tips of his long fins with his fingers.

So, this is how being Yoda feels like, Jon thought, and kept floating next to the wall. Thirty minutes passed while the marine life changed from small orange and white clown fishes circling above anemones to morays and larger single fish.

Eventually, the current eased and stopped completely, leaving the divers to hover several metres deeper near the wall, which had now turned to bluish grey from the lack of sunlight. All four floated in the water, standing in an upright position, legs bent backwards from knees below. With the black abyss below them, Jon reacted to a weird sound reaching his ears. He turned to look at his fellow divers, who seemed to hear it as well. It was a sound of faint grunting, like a bug in a jungle, or a small bird during mating season.

From the looks on his fellow diver's faces, Jon knew he wasn't imagining. Everyone checked through their gear and electronics for malfunctions but found none. The voice grew louder. *Must be close now*, Jon thought, when something dark approached them from the vast blue background. Jon pointed it out for the other divers, who turned around with a single movement from their fins. They all saw it now. Something large was swimming at a distance, the water still too hazy to see what. Whatever it was, it was easily as big as a shark. The shape of the object became sharper the closer it got.

It was a dolphin. A beautiful big dolphin emerged from the blue and approached them at a fast pace with no effort. For a second it seemed like the dolphin was about to swim by, but suddenly it stopped within touching distance. The dolphin and the divers stared at each other. The round black eyes full of tranquillity stared at them one by one. It was a magnificent creature, silvery light grey colour, a light shade on the creature's underside, deepening to a dark colour on its back. It was the most beautiful thing Jon had ever seen. He felt an instant connection with the water and the dolphin.

Jon reached out with his hand. The dolphin turned to Jon and opened its mouth. A loud painful human like screaming came out from the dolphin's mouth. Jon pulled back his hand, confused. In horror, all the divers looked at the screaming dolphin, turning upside down, its belly now facing the surface. The dolphin twisted in agony and continued screaming while blood poured out of its mouth and eyes, mixing into the water like a thin dark veil. Then the dolphin's belly pulled outwards, like something was trying to get out, making the dolphin jerk sharply to all directions. The dolphin's thick skin gave way and out poured black branch-like organisms pulsing neon green light. It was Swarm.

Bubbles burst out from Jon's regulator when he yelled out in panic. He kicked backwards with his fins to avoid

Swarm, which slithered its branches under the other divers' masks, instantly sucking the life out of each of them, leaving behind skeletons wrapped in a vacuum by their own skin.

In panic Jon dropped his weights by unlocking the belt buckle on his waist, and then filled his dive vest to capacity with air, launching him upwards like a rocket. After ten metres rapid ascent, Swarm got hold of his dive tank. Jon spit out his regulator and unclipped three quick-release locks on his vest, releasing him from the vest and the tank. Both the vest and the tank continued its rapid ascent towards the surface, part of Swarm still attached to it. Letting air out bit by bit, Jon kept kicking and swimming up, hoping he would reach the surface before losing consciousness.

With a still a long way to go, the lack of air made him swallow the non-existent air inside his throat. He panicked. He kicked upwards with his fins and moved his hands until the burning sensation inside him became too strong to withstand. The surface was still too far. He would never make it. Eventually his reflexes forced him to inhale, pulling in the salty sea water first to his mouth. To his surprise, he inhaled air, not water. He didn't understand it. He could see the surface far above him, and Swarm circling him like a hunting animal circles its wounded prey.

Another burst of clean air filled his lungs. Then, instead of Swarm attacking, he felt a slap on his face. What is happening ...? he thought. Jon tried to make sense of it when another push of air filled his lungs and two more slaps landed on his face, this time accompanied by Gus's voice.

"Wake up!" Gus shouted as loud as he could and gave another slap on Jon's face. "Don't you leave us like this."

Jon's reality changed around him, bringing back the dolphin head in front of him, and giving him air mouth-to-mouth. Jon coughed hard and the dolphin's head morphed to a human face. It was Nova, face full of black smudge mixed with blood.

"So beautiful ..." Jon mumbled, disoriented.

"Yes!" Nova shouted and kissed Jon on his lips and cheeks.

"Welcome back, dude," said Gus, hovering right behind Nova. "We thought we lost you there for a second."

"Not a chance," Jon said coughing, while both Gus and Nova helped him to sit up against the wall. Alarms, smoke and electric sparks between the panels filled the ship's interior. "The Swarm? The black hole?"

"We made the jump," Nova answered first, "but the ship took heavy damage, and we have no clue where we are."

"*When* and where we are," Gus added. "Remember? Black Table interface got fried from bringing Swarm and the Tear near the black hole. We blew up one of the larger power sources to get some distance between us and the Tear."

"You did what?" Jon pretended surprised.

"It was your idea ..." Gus tried to explain, when Jon began laughing, but quickly reverted back to coughing.

"I know. I'm just messing with you,"

"I admire you, Jon Peterson," said Nova, looking at him, smiling. "Even amid our peril, you find happiness."

"Peril?" Jon looked back at her, smiling. "There is nothing to worry about," he said, pointing out to smoking ship. "We will cut the power from all but essential functions, then we put out the fire, turn off the alarms and assess the situation." He waved his hand like turning a page of a massive book. "We will be fine."

With those words, he passed out again.

◆————— ◆◆◆ —————◆

Later, Jon woke up on his bed in crew quarters. There were no alarms or smoke. Everything was dimly lit and quiet, except for the random rattle of metallic tools dropping to the floor and bouncing against each other. When trying to sit up, Jon gave out faint grunting sounds. He felt like a truck had hit him. Every muscle ached. Slowly, he forced himself to sit on the edge of his bed.

"Gus?" he called out. No response, other than rattling tools. "Nova? Uzano?" he called out again. Nothing. "Better not to be another Swarm dream," he mumbled and looked around the crew quarter walls for any signs of neon green infestations.

With a tremendous effort, he stood up and took few steps. He walked towards the door of their quarters and leaned against the door frame revealed with the *Star Trek* sound effect on his approach. In the table room, he noticed Nova's legs stretched out from under the control panels installed along the wall. Across the room, under another set of displays, stretched another pair of legs, Gus's. Without looking, both were reaching out for the tools lying on the floor near their legs.

"How about now?" Nova shouted, while working on cables halfway inside the wall.

"Yes! That's the one!" Gus shouted back from other side of the table room. "Hold it there!" he called and worked at his end, and the interface above Nova came back to life. "Yes!" both Gus and Nova shouted at the same time and wiggled themselves out, legs first.

"What's going on?" Jon asked from the door, making both Nova and Gus look at him with smiles. From the pilot room came a loud deep voice, "Jon, you are awake!"

Loud thumping sounds made the tools jump around when Uzano walked across the room and gave Jon a powerful hug. "We missed you, my friend."

"Missed you too ..." Jon managed to say while Uzano squeezed the air out of him. "How long have I been out?"

"Three days," said Uzano, and let him go. "You took significant damage to your head. We thought it best to let you sleep it out."

Jon put his hand on his forehead and felt a pile of bandages wrapped around his head. "How bad is it?" he asked worried and began unravelling the bandages. Once all were removed, he went over every inch of his head with his fingers. There was nothing, no scars, no stitches. "I don't understand," he said, confused.

"We thought it would look cool," said Gus. "That's how they make it look in movies if someone has a severe head injury," he said, while Nova grinned and held back a laugh.

"Hilarious," said Jon seriously, "but a good one!" he finished with a smile and squinted eyes, while pointing and waving his index finger at Gus.

"I told you he would get it," Gus said looking at Nova, as they both still sat on the floor surround by their scattered tools.

"So, what is going on?" Jon changed the subject.

"Well," Nova said, "after we cut the power off from all but essential functions, we could put out the fire and turn off the alarms. Then we assessed our situation and took necessary steps."

"Just like I said," said Jon, surprised. "So where are we at with everything?"

"Ship's navigation works, but so far Uzano can't make head or tail about our position," Gus said, while Uzano grunted hearing his status. "The Black Table is somewhat fried from the big jump with the Tear and Swarm. Just before our blind jump, the energy blast diverted to our shields and propulsion and blew every relay, causing spikes on our interfaces. And those are what we've been trying to fix for three days now. Actually, just before you woke up, we bypassed power for the table interfaces, making them operational again. And now that we know what to do, we are confident we can restore power to the rest of the ship."

"Guys, we did the impossible," Jon said with excitement. "We actually did it!" His voice raising hope and a feeling of victory for everyone on board. "I would like to suggest we name our ship," Jon lifted his hand to stop Gus from talking, "and no Gus, we are not naming it *Enterprise*."

Gus closed his half open mouth, ready to suggest exactly what Jon had predicted.

"I like this," said Nova. "We rarely name our transporters or buildings. It seems to be a regular thing on Earth?"

"Oh, yes," said Jon slowly and mystically. "Everything has a name on Earth. Sometimes we even organise competitions to find the best names."

"How about Excalibur?" Gus suggested from the floor where he still sat. "It's a legendary magical sword that kills evil and only yields for someone with a pure heart ..." Gus paused, facing a full silence. "Or not," he said looked around while tapping a screwdriver-type tool against the floor.

"We are not so good at this," said Nova, but was interrupted suddenly by a deep voice.

"Unity," said Uzano, looking at everyone intensively. "That is what we have here, unity. All the people and Azonians came together to make this ship possible. It also brought the four of us together. Unity."

"Unity ..." everyone said on their own, tasting the word and letting it melt before nodding in unison for approval.

"Unity," Gus said, raising his voice. "I like it." He got up.

"Me too." Nova stood up as well.

"*Unity* it is," Jon said, smiling at Uzano, who nodded.

The next days went fast with the crew having their hands full fixing broken conduits and changing broken parts for working ones. Gus stood next to Black Table. Once all cables were detached, he lifted one of the burned-out large power sources from the tool stand and placed it into an empty container on the floor. The power source was heavy and made a solid sound against the container walls when Gus let it go. The power source had black residue all over, leaving some of it on Gus's palms, which he wiped on his pants.

"One down, two to go," Gus declared and studied the melted Black Table surface. The table otherwise looked in good shape, except for the melted original interface.

"How bad is it?" Jon asked, looking at the black power source on the tool stand.

"Bad, but could be worse," Gus said, while removing the second large power source and placing it with a thump next to other one in the container. "The good news is that our plan worked," he said and lifted the smaller, tachyon powered energy source, and placed it next to larger ones. "The bad news is the table interface is destroyed beyond repair. Luckily, we had table functions also routed through my tablet to those interfaces on the wall." Gus pointed at displays integrated into the table room wall. "And a few days ago, we got them working. That means we have a working Black Table, just without the fancy 3D galaxy model." Gus closed the container with the three burned power sources and pushed it to the utility room. The utility room doors hissed *Star Trek* style when he entered and exited the room. It made Gus smile every time.

"Ship engines and all scanners are back online, also the weapon systems are operational again," said Uzano, joining the conversation. "I also have located a star system not so far from us."

"Life support and backup systems are also operational," said Nova. "But we are running out of supplies. Everything except for jello."

Jon winced, but said nothing.

"I also need some hardware parts to secure any future table operations." said Gus, while leaning against the tool stand next to Black Table.

"Please follow me." Uzano turned around and walked back into pilot room. He sat down on the seat designed for an Azonian's physiology while Nova took her place next to him across the aisle.

With the flip of a few switches, the entire wall in front of them came to life showing black space with a few random stars here and there. Uzano worked on his interface and an additional layer appeared in front of them, displaying information on the closest stars.

"That one," Uzano said and selected the largest star near them. In an instant, the star zoomed closer, displaying six planets orbiting a sun similar in size to Earth's.

"Based on sensory data, the fourth planet is supporting life. Our sensors can detect infrastructure and pre-atomic development."

"Perfect," said Jon and laid his hand on Uzano's shoulder. "Especially when it is our only option. How long till we get there?"

"Seven days," Nova read out the data from her interface.

"Seven days?" Both Jon and Gus shouted in surprise. "But it's right there." Gus pointed to the star system on their screen.

"In theory, any faster speed would kill us all if speeding up or stopping too quickly," Uzano said.

"How about those initial dampeners?" Jon asked.

"Inertia dampeners." Uzano corrected him. "They help somewhat but cannot perform miracles. That is why we built the Black Table network, allowing the universe to handle all the movement. We just hop on for the ride."

"Seven days it is," said Jon, feeling stupid from getting it wrong about the dampeners. "Unless we can use the table?"

"We cannot, not yet at least," Gus commented from the doorway. "The interface is working, but it is not detecting any other tables. We would need more data, which way and how fast the star systems are moving, and that would take more than seven days ..." Gus paused, looking concerned. "I'm afraid we jumped beyond the network."

"That would be the first time a table taking anyone that far," said Nova, while trying to collect more interstellar data. "Maybe in seven days we will have more sensory data to determine where we are."

"With Earth's, still simple telescope systems, they have estimated there to be over two hundred billion galaxies," Gus said, bringing out the worst scenarios he could think of.

"And that is with telescopes, without knowing all the facts. Let's hope we are still in our own galaxy, otherwise we may never find our way home."

"Before our trip to Portland, I read in the science new, that our universe is expanding," said Jon. "Can't we use that information to estimate star movements and then calculate where we are?"

"That might be true, that from Earth's perspective we have detected an expanding universe around us. Just like throwing a rock into water and observe the expanding waves," Gus explained, still feeling worried. "But what if there are more rocks thrown into water, billions of them, and we just cannot see them, yet? There would go the theory for an expanding universe. Science is facts based on current understanding. Let's work on what we have and go from there."

"Exactly," said Jon, trying to cheer up the mood. "Wherever we are, we will figure it out." He looked at Gus who took a deep breath, battling with all the things that could be wrong. "And whatever supplies we need, we'll find them." Gus seemed slightly more positive, already nodding to what Jon had to say. "And we will find our way home, all the way back to Azonia and all the way back to Earth."

"Yes, we will ..." Gus said looking out the transparent wall in front of them.

"Yes, we will!" Jon shouted and put out his fist.

"Yes, we will!" Gus shouted, smiling, and fist bumped with Jon.

CHAPTER 15

"JUMP"

Back on Azonia, Kentho, Julith and Bartho waited for Gus's and Jon's return. Two weeks after their departure, Muro came to visit their apartment unit. Muro was knocking on the door and Julith opened it, letting him in.

"I have wonderful news," said Muro, seeing all three together in front of him.

"They are back?" Kentho stepped forward, expecting to see Jon and Gus walk in any moment now.

"Oh, no. Not yet. There are reports coming in from all Black Table planets. Swarm is dead. It is no longer spreading or reacting on Black Tables," Muro explained. "Whatever they did, they succeeded. They disconnect the Swarm from its source."

"So, you have heard from them then?" Kentho asked, still hoping for actual wonderful news.

"Unfortunately, no," Muro replied. "There is no sign of their ship. I will let you know if we hear anything, anything at all." Muro turned around and walked out, leaving Kentho standing and watching the open door.

Months went by without a sign of the golden ship and its crew. After half a year, Bartho sat down with his family for a breakfast.

"I think we should go," said Bartho, his tray full of jello. "If they could come back, they would be here already. They have a Black Table with them after all."

Kentho could feel the lump in his throat but had already accepted the fact they were not coming back.

"Where would we go?" Julith asked.

"Gus said that the table on Earth might have information about our original home planet, Thatho," Bartho said, showing Jon's tablet to Kentho and Julith. "I think we should start there. Gus taught us how to use the crystals, the table interface, and this tablet. I think he did it exactly for this reason."

"I think that is exactly what we should do," Julith replied, poking her breakfast. "I'm becoming sick of this jello anyway."

"Is this our only memory left of them?" Kentho asked, taking the tablet off his father's hands. "Oh, look!" Kentho shouted and turned the tablet towards his parents. On the tablet's background image, Gus and Jon stood at Portland's Comic Con entrance, wearing their weird clothes and holding their arms over each other's shoulders.

"We will always have this," said Kentho happily and pressed icons on the tablet. "Here is some music Jon told me about. He recommended this one, Van Halen."

Kentho pressed the first song on the list and placed the tablet on the table, filling the Azonian dining hall with an impressive guitar solo.

"For Jon and Gus," Bartho said and held his hand in a fist over the table.

"For Jon and Gus," both Julith and Kentho replied smiling, joining Bartho on their group fist bump.

ACKNOWLEDGEMENTS

I have always wanted to write a book, to write something I would like to read. For over a decade, it was just a dream, until one day I just sat down and began typing. To my surprise, writing a book is easier than I thought, and so much more rewarding than I could have ever imagined. Getting a book polished, published and marketed is something else completely. I would have never thought the latter would be so taxing and costly. But here we are, and I could not have done it alone.

I have to start by thanking my awesome wife, Krisztina. From reading each early draft one after another and giving the constructive feedback I so much needed. She was as important to this book getting done as I was. Thank you, I love you.

Special thanks to Kim Smith, my editor, who not only polished the book to a professional level, but who also mentored me on the way. Thank you.

I'm eternally grateful to Anna-Kaisa for detailed input, and whom without I would not be here, writing. I am also grateful to my sister-in-law Riikka, and my brother Mika, for constructive feedback and suggestions for improvements. You were a crucial part of making the story as it is today.

Everyone on my beta reader team, Simo and Sami. Thank you for believing the book has potential. Also, thank you 100 Covers and Formatted Book for professional work done.

Finally, thanks to my dog Monk, who forced me into having breaks by sitting between me and my laptop. Woof!

Made in the USA
Coppell, TX
01 May 2021